Sycamore
Circle

BOOKS BY
SHELLEY SHEPARD GRAY
AVAILABLE FROM BLACKSTONE PUBLISHING

THE BRIDGEPORT SOCIAL CLUB SERIES

Take a Chance

All In

Hold On Tight

THE DANCE WITH ME SERIES

Shall We Dance?

Take the Lead

Save the Last Dance

THE RUMORS IN ROSS COUNTY SERIES

Edgewater Road

Sycamore Circle

SHELLEY SHEPARD GRAY

THE RUMORS IN ROSS COUNTY SERIES

Sycamore Circle

BLACK
STONE
PUBLISHING

Printed in the United States of America

First edition: 2023
ISBN 978-1-7999-2373-2
Fiction / Romance / General

Version 1

Blackstone Publishing
31 Mistletoe Rd.
Ashland, OR 97520

www.BlackstonePublishing.com

*For the many literacy volunteers who change lives,
one word at a time.*

"Peace I leave with you. My peace I give to you; not as the world gives, give I to you. Don't let your heart be troubled, neither let it be fearful."

John 14:27

"Once you choose hope, anything is possible."
Christopher Reeve

DEAR READER,

Several years ago I spent a weekend learning how to teach adults to read. It was sponsored by ProLiteracy, an organization I was familiar with thanks to my longtime association with Romance Writers of America. To be honest, I wasn't sure what the classes were going to teach me that I didn't already know. I taught elementary school for ten years and have a master's in Education.

It turned out that I didn't know much at all about teaching adults to read.

By the time I walked out of the building on Sunday night, I was completely humbled by the literacy volunteers who shared their stories, the guests who took the time to tell us about their journeys toward literacy, and the amazing dedication both the students and the volunteers needed in order to make the dream of reading a reality.

Eventually, I felt confident enough to put myself on the tutoring list . . . and then life happened. We moved six months later. Then Covid hit. Two years after that, we moved across county again.

All these years later, I still haven't gotten the chance to be a literacy tutor. However, I was so inspired that I knew I wanted to one day have a literacy volunteer heroine. When I began to map out *Sycamore Circle*, I knew I'd found the right book.

I hope you enjoy reading about Joy and Bo, Chloe, Finn, and the assorted other characters in the novel. The books in this series mean a lot to me. I've always wanted to write some novels about people who might not fit perfectly into what most of us imagine to be a romance novel. But, perhaps, that's why I enjoy working on them. I love to write about imperfect people who are more than what they seem to be at first glance.

Louisa May Alcott once wrote that we are all hopelessly flawed. I've always agreed with her about that.

Thank you for picking up the book and giving it a try.

With blessings,

Shelley Shepard Gray

CHAPTER 1

They'd been standing in line for five minutes and likely had another ten minutes to go before they could get out of there. Considering he hadn't wanted to go to Sacred Grounds in the first place, Bo was irritated. After a three-year stint in Madisonville, he didn't like to spend his time standing in line for much.

Waiting this long for a cup of overpriced coffee just seemed wrong.

"I can't believe you come here all the time, Mason," he muttered.

Mason shrugged. "This coffee is worth the wait. You're going to love it. I promise."

"Doubt it."

As usual, his longtime buddy paid him no mind. "Whatever. Look at your phone or something and chill."

Mason went back to doing exactly that, but Bo was in no

1

hurry to pull his phone out of his back pocket. If he did, he knew he'd see another four emails and twice as many texts from the guys who reported to him. He liked his job, but sometimes he needed a break.

Instead, he listened to the woman at the head of the line order some kind of complicated latte with almond milk and gritted his teeth. Why did everybody try to make simple things so difficult? Coffee was coffee. There was no need to add whatever kind of "milk" came out of an almond to it.

Mason sure had fancy tastes in his beverage choices, considering he'd come out of prison not too long ago.

At last, the almond milk gal had her drink and scone. They stepped forward in the line. Bo started to smile—until he heard the teenage girl at the front of the line announce she was ordering four drinks to go.

"Lord have mercy," he murmured. He meant it too. He absolutely was going to need some divine help in order to not pull Mason out of Sacred Grounds and drive to the nearest convenience store. There, he could get sixteen ounces of Maxwell House for two bucks, and even pick up a Slim Jim or two.

Mason looked up from his phone. "I'm telling you, it's worth it. Settle down." Lowering his voice, he added, "and try, for once, to look a little less like you're itching to wring somebody's neck. You're gonna make everyone around us nervous."

Realizing Mason probably had a point, Bo pulled his attitude down a notch. He wasn't a small man, and his sleeve of tattoos didn't always generate warm and cozy feelings either.

He knew that too. Shoot, it seemed like he spent half his life telling the men he was in charge of—fresh-out-of-prison guys in need of a hand—to remember that the regular population was real different than the one they'd been accustomed to in Madisonville.

It was obviously time to concentrate on something else. He looked around hoping to find something to capture his attention.

The coffee shop was a converted church in the middle of the square in their tiny downtown. Whoever had done the remodeling had kept the basic structure but had removed anything that might have religious connotations. He never would tell Mason this, but he remembered when the owners had bought the old place. They'd donated the sixty-year-old stained glass to a local church and replaced it with stained glass featuring a sun, a cup of coffee, and the shop's name.

Mason was obviously not the only fan of the café either. There were eight tables and six of them were filled. At least a dozen people stood in line, and three people worked behind the counter.

When they moved forward again, he heard the prettiest voice he ever heard. It was smooth, melodic, and kind. So kind.

Something inside of him stilled.

"Good job, Anthony," the woman said in a gentle way. It wasn't condescending or the slightest bit flirtatious. It was just plain *nice*. Nice in a way that clean laundry or breathing fresh air in the early morning was.

Her perfect, oh-so-nice voice caught his attention like nobody's business.

So much so, Samuel Beauman—called Bo by everyone who wanted to live—couldn't stop himself from turning his head to see who that voice belonged to.

It didn't take long to find her . . . and then, there she was, at a table next to the window across from a large middle-aged man. She was a pretty thing. So pretty, he almost wished he hadn't looked.

The man she was with—Anthony, Bo supposed—looked embarrassed and mumbled something under his breath.

3

She laughed. "Nope, I'm not going to let you go there. I'm proud of you."

The words, combined with the sound of her voice, so clear and melodic, rang out over the piped music playing on the speakers overhead. When the Anthony guy smiled at her, she laughed. Drawing him in even further.

It was almost a shame when it was his turn at the counter.

"What will you have?"

"Large coffee. Black."

The barista pointed to the bakery case. "Would you like something to go with it? Everything was baked this morning."

"Nope." Remembering Mason's warning about his resting expression, he smiled. "Thanks, though."

She smiled back. "Anytime."

He paid for his coffee. When he noticed Mason was talking on his phone, he stood off to the side, over by a table of napkins. And then he looked at the woman again.

She was pointing to something in a workbook.

Barely able to stop staring at her, Bo tried to figure out why she was affecting him the way she did. The woman wasn't flashy, she wasn't wearing much makeup, and her clothes were nondescript. Just jeans, a soft-looking sweater, and brown suede boots.

The women he dated tended to show a lot more skin, had more of an attitude, and were still in their twenties. This lady was likely older than him.

But maybe that was her appeal. There was something about her that made him want to linger a while, just to hear her speak. Needing something to do, he pulled off the plastic lid to his cup, grabbed a wooden swizzle stick, and stirred his coffee that didn't need to be stirred. All so he wouldn't look like he was doing what he *was* doing—loitering nearby.

The man mumbled something again, stumbled over a word, then corrected himself.

"That's right," she said. "Now you've got it. Look at you!"

He'd been thinking that very same thing. Look at you, lady. So sweet, so kind, so blessed with the kind of long brown hair that only God could give a person. It was thick, slightly wavy, and nearly reached her waist.

He'd never been one to stare at hair, but again, he couldn't seem to help himself. It was yet another thing about her that was beautiful.

As she and Anthony spoke softly to each other, a woman walked over to where he stood. Bo realized she wanted one of the stirring sticks too.

"Excuse me."

He stepped to the left.

"It sure is cold out," the woman said.

After an awkward pause, he realized she was speaking to him. He cleared his throat. "Yes, it is."

She smiled, her extremely red lipstick catching his attention. "And you don't even have a coat on." She stepped closer. Lifted her hand a couple of inches, like she was thinking about touching his arm. "Aren't you cold?"

She was flirting with him.

He bit back a sigh. He'd been blessed with what his Mama had called good genes. He had blond hair that he liked a little on the long side, light blue eyes, and good bone structure. One woman in a bar had once said he was a ringer for Brad Pitt in the nineties. He wasn't sure if that was the case or not.

What he was sure about was that his good looks weren't so much a source of pride with him as an inconvenience. Some people didn't take him seriously and some women couldn't seem to refrain from touching him. He really, *really* didn't like uninvited hands touching his skin.

The other guys in prison had commented on his looks, too—which was why he'd spent a good portion of his first month in the pen in solitary. The prison guards hadn't seen fit to step in when some of the lifers had wondered how he'd swung.

Realizing that he needed to say something, he tried to recall what she'd been talking about. Ah, yes. His coat. "I run hot."

She giggled. Tossed her head back, bringing with it a chunk of carefully highlighted blond hair. "I bet you do."

"Bo, you coming or what?" Mason called out from the door.

"In a minute." Turning to the woman, he nodded. "Excuse me, ma'am."

And just like that, all the heat slipped away. The frosty look the blond directed his way before sauntering out almost made him smile.

Glancing at the seated woman again, he realized that she was looking directly at him. The spark of amusement in her expression practically made his breath catch. When their eyes met, he knew he had no choice. He might not always believe in fate, but he sure believed in divine intervention. Given his past, Bo knew it was only because of God that he was standing on two feet instead of lying in a box six feet under.

He worked in mysterious ways, and Bo had long ago given up trying to understand the why's and the how's. All he knew was that there were times to pay attention.

This was one of those times.

As far as he was concerned, the big guy up in the clouds had put him in this place to meet this woman. He wasn't going to pass that up. After all, wasn't all of this taking place in a former church? There was something special going on and he intended to see it through.

Walking toward the door, where Mason was standing impatiently, Bo said, "I'm gonna need a few."

Mason's eyebrows rose a good inch. "To do what?"

"Not your concern." Thinking quickly, he said, "Adrian is working over at the house nearby. Go check on him then come back."

"Are you serious? All you've been doing since we arrived was complain about it taking so long."

"Give me an hour."

Mason didn't budge. "What am I supposed to tell Lincoln if he calls?"

Lincoln was their boss. The group—Lincoln and all of the men he employed—was made up entirely of ex-cons. Lincoln worked with the prison in Madisonville, a team of probation officers, and the local sheriff's department to help men who just got out to acclimate to the outside again. He got them jobs and tried to give them a support system so they wouldn't go right back in.

Bo was in charge of one of the systems—rehabbing old houses. Mason worked more on the business side, determining whether to keep the houses, sell them, or use them as rentals. "Don't say nothing to Lincoln," he replied. "Or, if you want, tell him that I'll explain myself later."

"Yeah, all right." Mason checked his phone. "I'll be back at noon."

"Thanks."

Noticing that Anthony was leaving but the woman was still seated, Bo knew it was time to make his move. It was now or never, and he really wasn't cool with never.

CHAPTER 2

Even though she had her calendar open in front of her and about a dozen things on her to-do list, all Joy seemed to be able to do was eye the guy standing against the wall. Directly in her line of vision.

One of his arms was entirely filled in with tattoos—various pictures, words, and lines all competing for space over a well-developed set of muscles. Worse, what wasn't on display was hinted at under a snug-fitting gray T-shirt.

It wasn't fair that a man could be that good-looking, Joy Howard decided. Especially since it seemed like he was unaware of how attractive he was.

Of course, maybe he was just used to what he saw in the mirror every morning and didn't think about it. She supposed that might be easy to fall into.

Unable to help herself, she'd been amused at the way he'd shut down the blond gal's attempt to start a conversation.

It was almost as if she had been an annoying fly and he didn't exactly want to squash her—just to get her out of his way.

That had been impressive.

What she wasn't sure about now was the way he was looking at her. His eyes kept darting her way and lingering for a few seconds at a time. Joy pretended not to notice, especially since she had no idea why his eyes would be on her, anyway.

"Do you have everything?" she asked as she watched Anthony stuff his materials in his backpack.

"I do. Just like always."

"You take care now."

"You too." Anthony's voice slowed. "Would you like me to walk you out, Joy?"

Ah. It seemed he'd noticed the stranger's stare too. "Thank you but I'm going to stay here a little while longer."

"Are you sure about that?"

"I'm sure." She smiled, just to prove that she was. "See you next week?"

"I'll be here. Like always, right?"

"Right." They'd first met years ago. Anthony had been essentially homeless. He'd hung out around the area, usually on one of the benches. Something about him had touched her heart. She'd started bringing him a cookie or snack whenever she left one of the restaurants in the area. Eventually he'd gotten a job at Sacred Grounds as the janitor, and they would exchange greetings whenever she came in. When she realized he couldn't read, he'd become her student.

"Well . . . thanks again."

"Of course." Joy smiled but made sure to stay where she was until he walked out the door. Once he was out of sight, she leaned back with a sigh. She enjoyed working with Anthony, but sometimes he was so anxious to please that everything between them seemed harder.

"Excuse me."

The guy she'd been trying not to notice was now standing next to her table. "Yes?"

"Can I, uh, buy you a cup of coffee?"

"Excuse me?"

He looked away, actually appearing like he was frustrated with himself. "I know. It's a bad line, but we are in a coffee shop." He shrugged. "What I'm attempting to do, and obviously not well, is get to know you."

"Me?" She chided herself for answering him with a question—because heaven forbid she actually give him a complete answer.

"Yeah." Looking even more uncomfortable, he shifted. "That is, um, if I'm not freaking you out. Or if your husband or boyfriend isn't gonna kick my butt for being near you."

She noticed there was a faint scar on his upper lip, which made her blush. Since when did she start staring at men's lips? As another second passed, her brain kicked in.

This guy was trying to figure out if she was available. Her! "You're not freaking me out." Not too much, anyway.

Still looking like he would rather be getting his fingernails pulled out, he added, "Do you?"

She blinked. "Do I what?"

"Have a husband or boyfriend?"

"I'm not married." Not anymore. "And, at the risk of sounding pretty pathetic, I don't have a boyfriend at the moment either."

Something warm entered his eyes. "That's not pathetic."

She shrugged. "It is what it is, right?" Thank goodness.

He looked a little more at ease though he still waited,

seeming to want to give her a moment or two to get used to him. "I didn't see a ring, so I guessed you weren't. And just for the record, I'm not married either."

"A lot of women don't wear rings. Just like a lot of men don't."

"I reckon that's true, but in my world, well, a man would want to make sure a woman like you had one."

It took her a second to realize that he'd given her a compliment. As in, in his world, she was the type of woman a man would want the world to know she was taken. It was a little caveman like. Even more surprising.

Did men even think like that anymore?

Tony sure hadn't.

He frowned. "Am I freaking you out again?"

"No. Um, maybe I *should* be, but no."

"Listen, you'll likely think this is a line, but I don't do this. I don't walk up to women in coffee shops and chat them up." His jaw worked as he obviously continued to weigh his words. "If you let me buy you a cup of coffee, I promise I'll leave as soon as you tell me to."

Joy scanned his face again. She thought about saying no but then decided that she'd been gun-shy for too long. Besides, she met all her students for the first time in places like this. She'd come to realize that most people were good. "I can't believe I'm saying this, but yes. You can buy me a cup of coffee."

His gaze warmed, making her heart start beating faster. "What may I get you?"

"A mocha latte?" Maybe she should've just asked for a plain cup of coffee, but the mochas at Sacred Grounds were divine.

"Yes, ma'am." He smiled. Looking over at the counter, he received another sign. Miraculously, no one was in line. "Coming right up."

He walked to the counter and placed her order along with another black coffee and four pastries.

Busying herself, Joy put her calendar in her purse and set her phone out on the table. Just in case her daughter, Chloe, needed her. And maybe in case this guy started creeping her out.

"Here you go," he said, handing her a mocha in a real ceramic coffee cup. "You're okay with drinking it here, right?"

"Yes. That's fine."

"Be right back." He retrieved his coffee and the plate of pastries. For good measure, he grabbed a handful of napkins. "I brought us something to eat too," he added, as he sat down in the chair next to her.

His nearness made her catch her breath. He smelled good. Like soap and man and something mint—maybe his shampoo?

"You okay, still?"

"Why are you asking?"

"You tensed. I know my word means nothing to you, but I promise, I didn't lie. I don't hang out trying to pick up women in former-church coffee shops."

"For some reason, I believe you." She shook her head, then continued as he kept studying her intently. "It's just that, um, well, I guess I thought you'd take the chair across from me." Where Anthony had been.

He moved to stand up. "Do you want me to sit there? Give you more space?"

She shook her head. "That's not necessary. But you really would have switched seats, wouldn't you?"

He shrugged. "I'm not into making you scared of me."

"I'm not scared." She gestured to the coffee and the pastries. "Just curious."

"About?"

She smiled. "Why you asked me to have coffee." Suddenly,

the obvious answer hit her hard. "Oh! Did you notice that I was tutoring Anthony? Do you need help reading?"

"I can read just fine." Looking embarrassed, he said, "I just realized that I never even told you my name. It's Bo. Bo Beauman." He closed his eyes like he was irritated with himself, then added, "I mean, it's Samuel Beauman, but everyone calls me Bo."

"I like Bo. You don't really look like a Samuel."

He smiled at her. "I've always thought the same thing." After a pause, he said, "What's yours?"

"My name?" She rolled her eyes. "Sorry, my name is Joy Howard. And I'm afraid that everyone calls me Joy."

The corners of his lips lifted. "Your parents named you Joy?"

"Yes. I was born in December." When he looked like he didn't get the connection, she said, "You know, Christmas? Joy? It's a bit much, I know."

"No, it's pretty perfect. That's what it is."

Lord. Have. Mercy. Doing her best to act like gorgeous, younger guys approached her all the time, she sputtered, "I always wished I had a better name. You know, maybe something more exotic or normal or . . . something." She covered her eyes with one hand. "And now I'm officially embarrassed. Sorry, I guess that's probably more than you wanted to know about me."

He didn't smile back. "At the risk of embarrassing myself, I have to say that knowing too much doesn't feel possible right now."

That was quite a line. It was too slick. No doubt, he pulled it out on any number of women, multiple times a week.

She sipped her coffee. Waited to feel awkward and uncomfortable.

But all she seemed to feel was flattered and intrigued.

It had been so long since she'd felt that way, she decided to stay a while longer. Just to hear what Bo said next.

CHAPTER 3

He needed to slow down. Seriously. He was making Joy uncomfortable, and Bo didn't blame her one bit. If their situations were reversed, he would've already told himself to take a hike. "So . . . you tutor?"

Her eyes lit up. "I do. Not always for money, though. I volunteer to help adults learn to read." Looking earnest, she added, "A lot of people don't realize it, but illiteracy still happens. People either quit school or even get out of school without knowing much more than the most basic of words. It's frightening."

"Frightening?"

"Well, yes." Looking like she was choosing her words with care, she said, "Illiteracy is frightening because it affects the rest of your life. If you can't read, you can't read road signs or directions or fill out an employment application. Illiteracy makes a person feel stuck."

"I guess it would."

Looking pleased that he understood, she nodded. "Over the years, I've helped quite a few people learn to read. And it's changed their lives. I love that."

He was loving the way her brown eyes shone. "I bet. What you're doing is a real good thing. Fantastic."

"Helping people like Anthony is one of the best parts of my week, for sure." She smiled happily.

"What else do you do?"

"A couple of things, but my main job is taking care of my daughter."

"You have kids."

"I do. A sixteen-year-old girl."

"You have a sixteen-year-old?" Once again he wondered how old she was. He couldn't care less, but it would give him something else to know about her.

"I do. Her name is Chloe."

"What about her dad?"

She looked him in the eye. "I'm divorced," she blurted, as if she thought he'd be scandalized to hear it.

He was simply pleased she was single. Now he just had to figure out how out of the picture her fool of an ex-husband was. "When did that happen? Did you get divorced years ago or more recently?"

"We got divorced four years ago. I don't know if that counts as the past or recently."

"How does it feel to you?"

A hint of a smile played on the corners of her mouth. "Sometimes like four years ago and sometimes like four weeks. It all depends on the day of the week."

"Do y'all get along?" Worried he was sounding like an interrogator, he added, "You don't have to answer. I'm just curious."

"Have you been married before?"

"No." Jenny came to mind. She'd been his girlfriend before he'd gotten arrested. They'd been close—maybe even in love. But had he been even close to marrying her? Nope. And after he was sentenced to three years, it became real obvious that she hadn't been anywhere close to marrying him either.

"Oh, well then you might not see the humor in your question. I think it's pretty hard to get along with an ex. It's the nature of a broken relationship, don't you think?" Before he could answer, she added, "It was in my case."

"I'm sorry about that."

"He loves our daughter and spends time with her, so I can't complain." She exhaled. "What about you?"

"I'm not near as good as you. I don't tutor or anything and I've never been married. I don't have any kids either." It was time to tell her the truth about himself. Unfortunately, he wasn't sure where to start.

"What do you do for a living?"

"I do a couple of things, but mainly, I work for a guy I know. His name is Lincoln, and he works with a number of organizations who help ex-cons transition into civilian life."

"You help ex-cons."

Glad that she looked interested and not scared, he added. "Yeah. Lincoln takes a couple of guys under his wing every year. He helps them find a place to live and get a job. But more than that, he gives them a hand getting back into the world, so they won't feel alone."

"What do you do?"

"Well, sometimes I help with a couple of construction projects that Lincoln has around town, but mainly I work with men fresh out of Madisonville. I meet with them a couple of times a week, make sure they don't skip their meetings with their parole officers and such. The guys call me if they start slipping into their old ways or need a pep talk or an extra hand. I guess you could say I'm a babysitter in a lot of ways."

"Wow. That's so good, Bo."

"Like I said, I'm not teaching someone to read, but I'd like to think I'm making a difference."

"No, you don't understand. You've taken me by surprise. When I first noticed you, all I saw was a good-looking guy who was a few years younger than myself. Then, when you started talking to me, I was pleasantly surprised. Now that I know you spend your days helping men from a population most people don't even want to think about? Well, it's . . . more than I expected."

She was looking at him like he was something special. Bile formed in his throat. It was going to hurt like hell when she realized just how *unspecial* he was.

"Joy, I'm not all that good. You see . . . "

She leaned a little closer. Close enough that he could smell the faint scent of perfume on her skin. "How did you get into that line of work? Do you know someone who's spent time in jail or something?"

"You could say that." Mentally preparing himself for her to back away fast, he looked her directly in the eye. "I got into this line of work because I've been through the process myself. I was in prison."

Her eyes widened.

And, just as he expected, she moved back to her original spot. He could practically feel her guard go up. Her open expression definitely turned a little more circumspect. "I see." She swallowed. "Um, what did you do? That is if you don't mind me asking."

"The short version is that I got in a fight with my cousin's buddy. He was messing with her. The fight went south and he got hurt pretty bad. Almost died. The judge and jury ruled that it was felony assault. I was sentenced to three years and served two."

"You must have hurt him really bad to be sentenced for so long."

And that, in a nutshell, was why they would likely never have a future. She thought what he'd done was real bad. He didn't disagree—but he had learned that men could do many things that were a whole lot worse.

"Joy, I've been out for six years. I have a job, a house, and I pay my taxes. I've done some things I'm not proud of, but I don't go around hurting people, and I sure don't hurt women. Ever."

"Okay . . ." She didn't look all that sure, though.

"Look, I didn't want to lie to you. I can give you my record and you can read up on me if that makes you feel better." He swallowed. "If you were ever inclined to do something like that."

Boy, he was messing this up. Shoot, he probably already had. "Joy, I'm sorry. I asked you for coffee and next thing you know I'm telling you all about my prison record."

She swallowed.

He lowered his voice. "Look, if you don't want to see me again, I'll abide by that. If our paths cross in the future, I promise to leave you alone. That said, I'm a grown man. I'm responsible, and I'm decent. I'd also like to know you better. If you'd let me call you, I'd like that."

"And then?"

"It's up to you. I meant what I said, Joy. You have the advantage here. I can't be anything but what I am, and I'm well aware that what I am might not be anything that you want."

Mason sauntered in and walked to his side. "Excuse me, ma'am," he said before turning to him. "Bo, we gotta go. Lincoln called."

"All right." He glanced back at Joy.

She was staring at Mason with wide eyes, making Bo realize that any chance he had of ever seeing her again was out the window.

But still, he tried. "Joy. This here is Mason. He works with Lincoln as well. Mason, this is Joy."

Mason nodded politely. "Good to meet you."

"Hi."

Something shifted inside of him. He'd been such an idiot. Women like her, nice women with daughters and altruistic jobs, didn't give men like him the time of day. It was time to leave her in peace.

Feeling weary, he got to his feet. "Wait for me at the door, Mace."

Mason's expression tightened. "We've got to go."

"I know. Just give me another second."

The minute Mason walked out of earshot, Bo leaned down slightly. Joy was still sitting. She also looked more than a little shaken by everything that he'd just thrown in her lap. "Joy, thank you. I appreciate you letting me sit with you for a spell. You take care now."

He'd taken less than a step when she called out to him. "Bo, wait."

He turned. "Yes?"

"Give me your hand." When he held it out, she pulled the cap off the pen she was holding and wrote her number on his hand. "That's my phone number." She smiled.

Feeling like a goof, he smiled back as he closed his fist, like he was worried the numbers she'd written there were going to go off and leave him. "Thank you for this." He stood there another moment, wondering if he should say something else. But he couldn't think of a thing that would come close to summing up how he felt.

So he headed to the door. "Let's go," he said to Mason.

Mason got in the driver's seat and pulled out. When they were out of sight, he grinned. "Come on now, fess up. Did she really just write her number on your hand like you two were in middle school?"

"No comment."

"Come on. Really?"

"Really." When Mason looked like he was tempted to argue, Bo added, "Did Lincoln really buzz or were you just bored?"

"He buzzed." Looking irritated, he said, "You know that kid who started working for Seth? That punk named Red or what have you?"

"What about him?" The guy actually went by Blaze, but whatever.

"Well, he got himself arrested last night."

He mentally groaned. "Doing what? Have you heard?"

"Sounds like he was harassing someone, then mouthed off to the cops when they showed up."

"I knew that guy couldn't keep his mouth shut."

"You were right. From what I've heard, he's saying all kinds of stuff too. No doubt hoping something sticks so he can catch a break."

That wasn't likely. "And let me guess. He named all of us as his new best friends."

"Bingo." Stopping at the light, Mason added, "Seth is ready to go beat him up. I tell you what, for a guy who was raised to ride around in buggies, Seth's got a temper."

"I reckon that's why he isn't Amish no more."

"You have a point. Anyway, Seth being pissed off ain't the worst of it. Lincoln is going to be ticked."

"Yeah, he is. He wasn't too happy about Blaze in the first place. The guy is going to be lucky if Lincoln doesn't start calling in favors just to make the rest of his life miserable."

While Mason drove, Bo pulled out his phone and entered Joy's number. He sure didn't want to risk smudging one of the digits and therefore not being able to call.

Of course, Mason noticed. But instead of looking amused, he merely looked curious. "Hey, Bo, no offense, but what was it about her? I mean, you didn't know her before you went to Madisonville, did you?"

"I'd never seen her before in my life."

Mason darted another look at him but kept his mouth shut. He knew he was treading on thin ice.

"I'm not really sure," Bo answered at last. "I guess it was the way she was speaking to the guy she was tutoring."

"Like how?" He raised a hand. "And I'm not being a jerk. I'm really interested."

Figuring he needed to understand what was happening himself, he said, "She has this sweet voice that was patient. No, I mean, that's how her whole demeanor is. But under that? There's a rod of steel and a vulnerability. It was like she was all about helping this guy she was tutoring but expected nothing in return.

"Like she's gotten used to expecting nothing in return from most people in her life. It got to me."

"That was it?"

Still trying to make sense of it himself, he shrugged. "Maybe. All I can tell you for sure is that one minute I was just standing there and the next I knew I had to get to know her."

"Bam, huh?"

"I don't know. All I can say is that I might have made a mistake but I had to try."

Mason looked confused but didn't speak of it again.

Bo was glad, because he really had no idea what was going on with him. But at the moment, he didn't even want to try to figure it out.

CHAPTER 4

One day a week, Tony picked up Chloe from school. Even though she was sixteen, their daughter was in no rush to get her driver's license.

Joy made no attempt to hide her relief about that. She couldn't afford a second car and had no desire to pay for the extra insurance. Tony was on the same page, though for different reasons. He had always said that as long as Chloe still needed him to drive her around, he would have a pretty good chance of spending time with her. Once she had wheels of her own, he was afraid she'd become even more independent and the gap that had formed between them would widen.

Chloe always rolled her eyes and protested whenever her dad said things like that. It was sweet, but she also never went so far as to declare that she would always need him. Their daughter was growing up.

On that one afternoon a week, Tony picked her up from school, took her out to eat, drove her to dance practice, picked her up again, and tried to help her with whatever she needed his help with—then she either spent the night or he brought her back to Joy's around eight.

Though their divorce paperwork stated that Tony would do this on Wednesdays, the two of them had agreed to be flexible with whatever evening worked best for him. He traveled a lot, so it was easiest to work around his plane flights instead of him being sure he was always available on a Wednesday evening.

Joy's lawyer had cautioned her about being so flexible, saying that Tony could easily take advantage of that. But, so far, he hadn't. The fact of the matter was that Tony might not love her anymore, but he adored their girl. In the four years since they'd divorced, he'd only backed out a handful of times. In addition, in every instance, he'd asked to make up the time he missed that weekend or the following week.

Their system worked for them.

It hadn't been an easy adjustment for Joy. The first time Tony picked Chloe up from school, Joy had been a nervous wreck. She had been afraid he'd forget to pick Chloe up, or would forget to feed her, or wouldn't remember to take her to her dance class or to collect her things at the studio—Chloe didn't always remember to grab her leotard and tights after she changed. Or maybe even that he would simply ignore Chloe, which would have devastated the teen.

But their daughter had returned home with both her dance costume and a smile on her face. In addition, her assignments had been done and neatly returned to her backpack. When Chloe had shared that she'd not only eaten dinner, but she thought that her dad made better spaghetti than her mom, Joy had barely been able to keep a straight face.

That all had made Joy cry, of course, because that had been

the state she was in. Only later had she forced herself to remember that Tony had never been a bad or uncaring father. He just had stopped loving his wife.

Tony had left her after admitting that he'd had an affair with one of his coworkers. The woman had been pretty, successful, and had traveled with him often. He said she'd been hard for him to resist. Though he supposedly broke things off with her after their brief affair, Tony had admitted that the experience had shown him that he'd wanted more than what Joy could give him.

It had taken quite a bit of counseling for Joy to realize that she also wanted a lot more than what Tony gave her.

• • •

It was just after seven o'clock when Joy's phone rang. Seeing that it was an unfamiliar number, her pulse raced. Was it Bo calling?

Her nerves jangled as she picked up. "Hello?"

"Joy?"

"Tony?"

"Yeah, sorry. My phone died and Chloe's is in the car. I'm using a clerk's phone here at the mall."

Huh? That wasn't part of their normal routine. "What are you doing at the mall? Is Chloe there?"

"Yeah. That's what I called about. I took her to dance class as usual, but when I picked her up she was pretty upset."

"What happened?"

"I don't know." Sounding frustrated, he continued. "I'm pretty sure it had something to do with the substitute dance teacher not liking her posture or . . . something." He lowered his voice. "I can't really get it out of her. You know how Chloe gets when she's pissed off. She shuts down and hardly talks."

"Oh, gosh. Yeah, I know it well. Miss Diamanté is on a

cruise this week. The substitute is pretty old school."

"She is definitely old."

Joy couldn't help but chuckle. "Usually I'd tell you that isn't very nice, but you're right."

"Right?" He paused. "Anyway, Chloe looked like she needed a little pick-me-up."

"So you took her to the mall? Tony."

"Don't freak out. I'm not going to get her anything too crazy. Just something to make her smile. I'll have her home by nine."

Tony might irritate her, but Joy couldn't deny that his doting on Chloe was sweet. He was being a dad. "All right. Fine."

"Great. See you in a while."

"Thanks for letting me know what you're doing."

"Anytime."

Glancing at the clock, she realized she now had another two hours before Chloe was going to get home. She decided to heat up a frozen pizza and get some painting done. She had been commissioned by a new client from Columbus.

She changed into her yoga pants, old T-shirt, and tennis shoes, then walked to her spare room. It used to be Tony's office but now was where the computer was kept, Chloe did her schoolwork, and where she painted. When she was pregnant she'd painted a mural on Chloe's bedroom wall. She'd taken a picture of it to show one of the nurses at the pediatrician, which led to the doctor asking if she'd paint the examining rooms.

Soon, some of the patients' parents asked if she'd paint smaller paintings of the whimsical animals. Now, thanks to word of mouth, she had a good little business. She'd never get rich off her paintings, but they did allow her to take care of her family—and to regularly add to her savings.

Two hours later, she'd eaten three pieces of pizza and was

just about finished with a scene featuring a lion wearing a crown when the phone rang. Seeing it was an unfamiliar number again, she picked up with a frown. "Tony?"

"Ah, no. This is Bo."

"Bo? Oh my gosh. Hi." Of course, the second the words were out of her mouth, she wished she could take them back. What grown woman said things like that?

He chuckled. "Joy, you sure are a constant source of surprises. Did I call at a bad time?"

"Not at all," she said quickly. Appalled by her almost breathless-sounding voice, she took a breath. "I mean, I'm surprised to hear from you."

"Really? Because you wrote your number on my hand. Or, were you expecting someone else?"

"No."

"Any chance you want to tell me who Tony is?"

Though she felt like he was being a little pushy, she forced herself to imagine how she'd feel if he answered the phone saying another woman's name. "Tony is my ex-husband. He called earlier from an unfamiliar number. When I didn't recognize your number, I thought he might be borrowing another phone."

"Ah. Is everything okay?"

"Yes." She sat down. "Well, I think it is. Chloe got upset at her dance class today, so Tony was taking her to the mall for some retail therapy. Hopefully when she comes home tonight, she won't have half the mall with her."

He chuckled. "You think that's a possibility?"

"Have you ever been around a sixteen-year-old girl?"

"Not lately."

She chuckled. "Well, for future reference, yes, it is a possibility. Chloe can shop for anything, anytime, anywhere. And her dad? Well, she's got him wrapped around her little finger."

"Whew. You have your hands full."

She chuckled softly again. "To be honest, I don't. Not really. Tony takes Chloe once a week and every other weekend. Having an evening just for myself always sounds good, but half the time I'm usually wondering what to do with myself."

"You don't usually go out on the town?"

Hearing the teasing in his voice, she smiled. "Nope. Most of the time, I just hang out at home. I heated up some cardboard pizza and now I'm working on a painting. And . . . now you know exactly how boring my life really is."

"It doesn't sound boring at all."

He sounded like he meant it. Feeling a little better about herself, Joy said, "What about you? Did everything go okay at your meeting or whatever it was?"

"Yeah. It turns out that this guy had already been pushing the boundaries, so we sent him on his way."

"What does that mean?"

"It means that some guys get out of Madisonville but don't act like they want to stay out. If a person doesn't want to change, then they won't. And when that happens, I'm usually the person who has to remind them that the real world isn't exactly full of folks who want to give ex-cons second and third chances."

"I guess you have to be tough with them."

"Yeah."

"Ah." Joy wasn't sure what to say to that. She wanted to sound supportive but not pretend she had any experience with what he was talking about.

After a second passed, Bo made a noise that sounded like something between a groan and a sigh. "Hey, you know, maybe this was a mistake."

"What is?"

"Calling you." He paused, then added, "No, trying to talk to you like we had something to say to each other. You're a high-class girl. A sweet thing. You've spent your day helping people learn to read and worrying about little girls' ballet classes. Here I am, talking about dealing with felons."

He wasn't wrong. Everything he'd been describing was outside anything she'd ever imagined or thought about. She wasn't scared or sorry it happened. "You know what? I don't regret giving you my phone number." She was telling the truth.

"You sound real sure about that."

"Yes. All night I've been wondering why I gave it to you in the first place. You might not chat with women in coffee shops, and I don't give my phone number to men I hardly know."

"Good."

She smiled. "Good?"

"Girl, if you went around writing your phone number on men's palms around town, I wouldn't be happy. That's not safe."

She rolled her eyes. "Did any of your friends notice?"

"That I had a phone number written on my palm? Mason, the guy I was with, did. And likely some of the other guys too."

"Oh no."

"Don't worry about it. No one is going to call you but me . . . and I couldn't care less what they say to me about it."

She wasn't going to lie to herself. Everything he was saying felt sweet. She kicked her feet out and smiled. "I have a feeling that talking to you is never going to be boring."

"I hope not, but I don't know."

Curious as to what he meant, she chuckled, but then she heard a car in her drive. Peeking out the window, she saw Tony was there. "I'm sorry, I've got to go. Tony's here with Chloe."

"If I call you again later this week, will you pick up?"

She couldn't resist smiling. "I will."

"Then put my name by this number, yeah? It hurts a man's pride to get the nerve to call up a pretty girl, just to hear her say another man's name."

"I won't do it again."

"Mom, we're back!"

"Oops, I've got to go. Sorry, Bo."

"It's not a problem. Bye, Joy."

Hanging up, she hurried to the door. "Chloe!" she said, giving her a hug.

"Hey, Mom. Guess what? Daddy took me shopping."

Noticing the three shopping bags next to the door, she laughed. "So I see." Looking at Tony, she raised an eyebrow. "Did you two have a good time?"

"We sure did. Right, Chloe?"

"Yep." Her eyes were dancing.

"Maybe too good of a time?"

"Don't get mad. I didn't plan on going into three stores."

She shook her head, but just laughed as she met Tony's sheepish smile. "You are a wimp."

"Can't help it. Tears were involved." Bending down, he kissed Chloe's brow. "See you on Friday night, sweetheart."

"Bye, Dad. Thanks again for all my stuff."

"Anything for you." He winked then walked out.

Joy watched him walk away. Even a year ago, she used to feel a pinch every time Tony left. There had been a part of her that always secretly wished that he was going to suddenly want to get back together with her.

Now, she was delighted to realize that she didn't want to be anything more to him than a co-parent and a good friend.

No matter what.

And at the moment, all she felt was grateful that he'd been the one to deal with Chloe's tears and not her.

She turned to her daughter. "Let's sit down and you can show me what you got."

She fell into the chair and tossed her bags on the table. "Mom, I can't believe Dad took me to PacSun and then to Pink Tulip too."

Joy pointed to another shopping bag. "Looks like you two hit Macy's as well."

Chloe's pretty eyes widened. "I didn't make Dad go. He said he wanted to see the purse I was telling him all about."

"I bet he did. Well, pull it out and show me."

She didn't move. "Are you mad at me?"

"No, honey. Not at all."

Though she was a little annoyed about Tony's spoiling, Joy was actually relieved that she wasn't going to have to buy Chloe that purse when her birthday arrived.

She spent the next hour hearing all about school, ballet class, their burgers and shakes, and the shopping trip. When she finally looked at her phone again right before she went to bed, there was a text from the same number.

Good night. I'll call again soon.

Her smile faded when she saw a second text from a different unknown number. But this one sent chills down her spine.

You better watch out.

CHAPTER 5

Chloe was sick and tired of every single guy in her school. They were selfish, loud, and seemed to always act like they were all that. Since she'd gone to school with most of them since kindergarten, she knew better.

Every time she'd told her mother how she felt, her mom had just smiled. She seemed to think that the boys probably weren't all that bad—it was more that Chloe was tired of them. Ten years of dealing with anyone could take a toll.

Chloe admitted that that might be true, but it didn't change the fact that some of the guys were just plain insufferable. Especially Kennedy Park.

He was fairly good-looking and fit—he wrestled in the winter and played lacrosse in the spring. But he acted like he was God's gift to women all year long.

Ever since the last bell rang, he'd been walking next to her like their clothes were stuck together and she'd had enough.

"Kennedy, I know you heard me the first time. Thanks for the offer, but I don't need you to give me a ride."

"Come on, Chloe, why are you being like this?"

"I'm not being like anything. I just don't need a ride. That's all."

"But you're on my way home."

Though she figured her house wasn't a big secret, it still bothered her that he knew exactly where she lived. Sharing a look with Baylee—who'd stayed nearby like a best friend should—Chloe shook her head again. "Thanks, but I'm not going home. I've got dance class."

He frowned. "I thought you had that last night."

"I did. I go to ballet four times a week."

"What's so special about ballet anyway?"

She had no idea what he meant. Why did any of them do all sorts of sports and volunteering and music stuff? College applications? Because it was better than doing nothing? Because they liked it? She settled for being sarcastic. "Toe shoes?"

Kennedy rolled his eyes. "Whatev. You should be cheering. That's what all the cute girls do. Right, Bay?"

Baylee, who was already on the varsity cheer squad, grinned. "Sorry, but nope. Chloe never could figure out how to do a back handspring."

When some guys called his name, Kennedy turned to see who it was. "I've gotta go." He walked toward the other boys before either of them could say a word.

"He's so annoying," Chloe said.

Baylee nodded. "He is, but he's cute."

"Not that cute."

Baylee dug in her purse and pulled out a giant key ring. "Are you sure you don't want a ride from me? I don't mind."

"Thanks, but I'm good. It's only a couple of blocks away.

I'm going to walk over to Lane's, grab something to eat, and do homework before class. My Mom's picking me up after."

"You need to get your license, Chloe. Then you won't have to rely on your parents to take you wherever you need to go. Or walk."

Chloe knew her girlfriend wasn't trying to be clueless, but it obviously hadn't occurred to Baylee that a driver's license didn't automatically mean she'd get a car. "I'll get my license soon."

Baylee gave her a long look that said she'd believe it when it happened. Chloe pretended not to notice.

The truth was that her dad was kind of a jerk about money. He'd buy her clothes and maybe help her with a car, but there was no way he'd ever help her mom pay for insurance or gas or even driver's ed classes. No way could Mom afford all that. Chloe would've been happy to work to buy her own car or at least work enough to pay for insurance and gas, but she danced too much to have a job.

She waited a few minutes—long enough for most of the parking lots to empty—then started toward Lane's. She was glad the weather was decent and not too hot—and that she had babysat the Casey kids last weekend. At least she could afford to get something to eat.

As she stepped inside, she heard her cell chime. She'd just looked down at her phone when she felt two hands grip her shoulders. "Whoa there."

Stunned, she looked up.

An Amish boy with light brown hair, a dark tan, and really blue eyes stared at her. After the slightest hesitation, he dropped his hands. "Sorry," he murmured. "We were about to run into each other."

"No . . . ah, it's okay. You're right. Um, I'm sorry. I should've watched where I was going."

He looked like he was going to say something else, then seemed to think the better of it. He turned and headed to the back.

"You need a table, hon?" Mary asked.

"Yeah. Thanks."

"Not a problem. Go take one of those booths over there." Just as Chloe was about to grab the first one, Mary added, "That boy you almost ran down is my nephew Finn. He's only been here two weeks but he's a good kid. It just might take him a moment to acclimate."

After looking to make sure he wasn't in earshot, Chloe asked, "You have an Amish nephew? He is Amish, right?"

Mary chuckled. "Oh, he's Amish all right. And yes, I do."

"How old is he?"

"Seventeen." Mary winked. "He's kin, but I've always thought he was easy on the eyes. Don't you agree?"

Chloe nodded. The truth was, she found Mary's nephew a whole lot more than "easy on the eyes." He was pretty much in the "gorgeous" category. Just under six feet, his shoulders and arms and chest were already filled out, and he had a flawless jawline under a fine layer of scruff. Baylee would have called him *hot*.

Mary made a shooing motion with her hands. "You go take a seat. And hon, try not to give Finn too hard of a time. I promise, he's trying real hard."

"I'll do my best," she teased. She was curious about why an Amish boy had decided to work at Lane's, but figured it wasn't any of her business.

Taking a seat in the booth, she scanned the menu.

Finn walked over right away. "Do ya know what you'd like?"

Chloe put down the menu and looked up at him. "I'll take a vanilla malt, please."

He wrote it down. "What else?"

"That's it."

"You came in here for just a malt?" He frowned.

"Yep." When he was still standing there, like he was trying to get his head around it, she cleared her throat. "Is that a problem?"

"*Nee.* I mean, no. I'll go get it."

"Thanks."

"It ain't a problem," he muttered. When he walked away, it looked like he was thinking about something hard.

He really was awkward. She kind of loved that.

Her phone dinged, signaling an incoming text.

> Where are you?

It was her mother. She texted back.

> At Lane's.

> Did you get a ride?

> Nope. I walked. I'm getting a malt and doing homework.

> Are you okay?

Her mother worried way too much.

> I'm fine. Don't worry. See you at seven.

Something was going on with her mom. She sounded more uptight and nervous than normal. She wondered if it had something to do with her dad, but she kind of doubted it. Her parents got along for the most part.

"Here's your malt." When she looked up, he put down both the malt and the metal cup that held the extra amount on the table.

She smiled. "Thanks."

"You want anything else?"

"Nope."

"Okay." Fumbling a bit, Finn wrote the final amount, tore off the receipt from the pad of paper then set it on the table. "Here."

"Thanks."

He gazed at her a long moment before walking back to Mary.

When his back was to her and he couldn't see her stare, Chloe studied Finn some more. Noticing that he was just as well-built from the back, she also realized that he was wearing jeans, which was a surprise to see on an Amish boy.

She wondered how he could get away with that. Did his church district not care about his clothes? Or was he in the middle of his *rumspringa*, and so his family was more lax? Thinking about it some more, she wondered, was he completely out and just hadn't gone completely "English"? She'd seen a couple of Amish teenagers like that around.

After another minute passed, she took a sip of the malt, thought about how good it was, then opened her backpack and took out her French books and folder. She had forty-five minutes before she had to go to dance. If she got busy, she could be done with the assignment before she left the diner. That meant that she'd only have to do a couple of equations in math when she got home.

She could be done by seven and have some time to relax. That would be awesome.

Pushing the rest of her thoughts from her mind, she pulled out a pen and got to work conjugating verbs. She pretty much hated French, but she hated putting stuff off even more.

CHAPTER 6

Finn was pretty sure he was going to lose his job if he didn't stop staring at that girl. He wouldn't blame Aunt Mary for firing him either. Staring at customers was creepy. He knew better. But he couldn't seem to help himself. She was so pretty—and she also seemed sweet but kind of aloof at the same time. He knew plenty of Amish girls, but they either acted helpless or like they could run the whole community. This girl—with her pretty, long brown hair and light brown eyes—was different.

Different in a good way.

"Finn, go take that couple's order," Aunt Mary said.

"All right." He looked around the diner, trying to remember who'd been there a while. When he saw the older couple looking around like they were hoping someone would come over, his stomach sank. "I'm sorry," he told his aunt again.

"Don't get in a tailspin. They just got here."

He hurried over, took their orders, and then brought the

ticket back to Lane, just like Mary had shown him on his first day on the job.

"Thanks, Finn," the cook said as he scanned over the ticket. "You did a good job with this."

"Danke." Finn smiled at Lane before he headed back to the front of the dining room.

Unable to stop himself, he glanced over at the booth. The girl was still there. She was scowling at the textbook she was working on. Her entire shake was empty.

He was surprised that she had already drunk the whole thing. The girl wasn't very big, and the malt was. She'd even managed to drink the extra bit that didn't fit in the glass. Finn had thought there was no way she'd be able to finish it. He was wrong.

Walking over, he picked up the empty glass and silver container. "Want anything else?"

She glanced up at him. "Yeah. A way to conjugate French verbs without losing my mind. Any way you can help me with that?"

"Sorry, no."

"That's what I was afraid of." She frowned. "I really hate French." She was glaring at the book like she found it personally offensive.

"How come you're taking it then?"

"Because I have to take a language and I mistakenly thought that it would be a lot easier than Spanish or Latin. It isn't."

"Why did you think it would've been easier than the others?"

"Because I know some French dance terms." She shook her head. "I should've known better."

"I'd help you if I could." Even though he knew he should leave, he couldn't help but say something more. "If you were taking German, I might have been able to, but I don't know any French."

"You know German?"

He lifted a shoulder. "Well, *Deutsch* is pretty close to it."

"I guess it is." She leaned back against the red vinyl and gazed up at him. "How come you're working here?"

"I need some money."

"Finn?" Lane called out.

"Sorry, I've gotta go," he told the girl. He hustled back over to Lane.

"Order's up, kid."

"Thanks."

Lane lowered his voice. "Watch the flirting with the girls too. Mary's not going to like that."

He felt his neck heat up. "Okay." He wasn't flirting, but he guessed it had looked like it. Especially since he hadn't been able to do much besides stare at that girl since they'd run into each other.

Carefully bringing the older couple their orders, he set the plates on the table in front of them.

"We'd like more water."

"Sure. I'll be right back."

As soon as he reached for the pitcher, Mary shook her head. "I'll take care of them. You go tell Chloe that it's almost four."

"Who?"

"Chloe. Hurry, now. Otherwise she's going to be late," Aunt Mary said before heading over to the couple with a plastic pitcher of water.

Feeling kind of stupid, Finn walked over to the girl. "Are you Chloe?"

"Yep."

He stuffed his hands in his pockets. "My aunt said to tell you that it's almost four. I'm guessin' that means something to you?"

Her eyes got big. "Oh no! Thanks." She started stuffing

everything in her backpack, pausing only long enough to pull a ten-dollar bill out of her wallet. "Here."

"I'll go get you some change."

"Keep it."

"It's too much of a tip."

"It's fine. Seriously."

He didn't know what to say. "Thanks."

Chloe shrugged like his tip didn't matter one way or the other. "Wish me luck. I've got to hurry and get changed or Miss Diamanté is going to kill me."

"Who's she?"

"My dance teacher. I take ballet lessons next door."

"Ah. Well, good luck getting changed." Feeling his cheeks heat, he told himself to stop being such an idiot.

She giggled then smiled. "Thanks. See ya."

"Yeah. See ya." Unable to help himself, he watched her go, thinking all the while that he'd never seen a girl as willowy as her.

Aunt Mary walked to stand beside him. "She's a pretty thing, isn't she?"

She was, but he wasn't going to say that out loud. "She says she takes dance classes next door."

"She sure does. I talked to her *mamm* about it once. Chloe does a lot of ballet. Her mother thinks she's gonna get a scholarship to college for it. If she keeps her grades up, of course."

"I didn't know you could go to college for dancing."

"Me, neither, but I reckon it's not that surprising. People get their higher education for all sorts of reasons these days." Giving him a sideways glance, she added, "Even Amish kids."

"Yeah, right."

"I mean it, Finn. Are you still thinking about jumping the fence?"

He nodded. "I don't think I can stay home much longer."

It was an understatement. His father was constantly angry with him, and his mother seemed perpetually overwhelmed and disappointed. He supposed he couldn't blame them—he was the middle kid of five, but had always seemed like an odd duck. He'd given up attempting to fit in and be the person they wanted him to be. He'd sure tried . . . and failed.

His aunt pursed her lips. "I sure am sorry, Finn."

"Me too."

"Will they still speak to you if you jump?"

There was no way they'd ever talk to him if he didn't join the church. "*Nee*. You know that, Aunt Mary."

"I had kind of hoped that maybe Ruth would've softened a bit."

"*Mamm* hasn't softened and *Daed* probably never will." Finn smiled so his words would maybe not seem so pathetic.

Aunt Mary didn't smile back, revealing that his act wasn't fooling her for a minute.

The truth was that they demanded he stay within the church and, in their efforts to make it happen, they'd taken to intimidation. Their threats included immediate expulsion if he elected to not get baptized and telling him he'd have to start paying them rent until he *did* join the church. "Things are getting real bad."

"Finn, you can live with me, but that might be hard on both of us. You keep your eye out for other places and I will too."

"Danke."

The door chimed, bringing in a pair of hard-looking men. When Mary saw them, she hustled over to their sides. "Hey, Bo. Hey, Seth, how are you doing?"

"Good. You?"

"Can't complain." As she seated them, Finn watched Seth settle into the booth. If he wasn't mistaken, Seth had been Amish about ten years ago. He'd heard the man had even served time in prison.

When Seth met his gaze, Finn felt his cheeks heat as he turned away. He was going to need to find a way to talk to Seth. Just to hear his story.

That would be better than focusing on Chloe. She was completely out of his league.

CHAPTER 7

When Lincoln had moved next door with his new wife and made his former home into the official headquarters of T-DOT, which stood for "Tomorrow Depends on Today," he had given Bo one of the back rooms to use as an office and meeting space. The big house on Edgewater Road was made of white wood and had a large front porch. It was a little run-down but solid and perfect for its purpose.

Bo had done what he could with his meeting room. It had a small kitchenette, a grouping of comfortable chairs, a desk, a couple of cabinets, and even a flat-screen television hooked up on the wall.

It had quickly become a comfortable place where the guys didn't mind meeting with him. He'd sit with recent parolees, discussing- everything from their parole officers to jobs to families to more complex ideas, like the adjustment to being able to make their own decisions again. It was amazing how accustomed a person could get to being told what to do, what to eat, and practically how to think after living in Madisonville. Bo often commiserated with them about things like how overwhelming a trip to the grocery store could feel after living behind bars.

Even though all these things were good things, there were moments when Bo would sit in one of his comfortable chairs, sipping a canned iced tea, and wish he was literally anywhere else.

This was one of those moments.

The kid sitting across from him was crying. Looking at the guy and knowing his troubled history, Bo figured he deserved a few tears. He'd learned from experience that every so often, even the strongest man needed to give into his emotions.

He'd never faulted that. Not even when he'd been in the pen and showing emotion was seen as weakness and was practically an invitation to get beaten up or abused by anyone stronger.

That said, Grafton was starting to become annoying.

As Bo had never been long on patience on the best of days, he figured the kid was only getting another five minutes before he cut him off.

Allowing Grafton to fixate on his misery wasn't going to help him get through the next four months, and it was Bo's job to make sure that he did just that. He took it personally when one of his guys gave up on going straight and ended up back in prison before the guards even had a chance to forget his name.

"I don't know what I'm going to do next," the twenty-something said around a wet sniffle. "Molly was into me."

It was moments like this when Bo really missed the time when Lincoln was constantly nearby. Bo was okay with guys crying and whining from time to time, and he was even okay when they lost their temper and freaked out. All those things were normal when one was acclimating back to the "real world."

But as much as his obvious compassion might help, Lincoln's presence had inspired a good amount of fear in the men.

Few of the guys had ever wallowed in their misery for long when Lincoln was in hearing distance.

After handing Grafton a box of tissues, Bo turned one of the wooden chairs near the table around so he could straddle it. While Grafton blew his nose, Bo rested his forearms on the top of the chair and watched. He mentally counted to ten.

Grafton sniffed.

Bo gritted his teeth. Counted to twenty.

Finally, finally, the kid leaned back and sighed.

It was time for some hard truths. "Grafton, you need to get it together."

The guy's dark-brown eyes filled with hurt. "I'm trying, but it's unbelievable, you know? All she ever used to write in her letters was that she couldn't wait for me to get out. Her letters were so sweet too. And hot." Grafton met Bo's eyes. "Molly's letters were sexy as all get out. You know?"

It was hard to keep his distaste from showing but he tried. "Uh-huh."

Grafton waved his hands. "When I first got out and saw her, I couldn't believe it. She looked so great—and happy to see me! She kissed me. I thought she was mine." He swallowed. "Now, just a couple of weeks later, she's gone. She promised to be there for me, but she isn't." Looking at Bo intently, Grafton added, "I don't know what that means."

It meant that Molly was a liar or that Grafton had turned out to be more than she wanted to deal with on a constant basis. Bo figured either option made sense, but given the way Grafton was carrying on, he would have put money on the latter.

"I hear what you're saying," Bo murmured, just like one of the counselors back in Madisonville had been fond of saying.

The truth was that Grafton's story wasn't unusual. It happened all the time. Some women really liked having a lovelorn pen pal. They wrote lots of guys and led them on with empty promises.

But writing a guy who was safely behind bars was a whole lot different than dating a bitter ex-con without a whole lot of job prospects. They dropped the men like hot potatoes.

And honestly, who could blame them?

Grafton inhaled, then released it with a messy, wet sigh. "I can't believe she blew me off like that, man. How come she wrote to me for three years and even started visiting me once a month— but now doesn't want to give me the time of day?"

"I don't know."

"That's all you can say?"

If the kid only knew everything Bo was thinking! "Nope. Buddy, you've got to get over her and think about your future."

Dark eyes clouded. "Molly *was* my future."

"Yeah, well, she's not now."

"You're heartless."

"Maybe. Or maybe I'm trying to help you, yeah? Grafton, you've got to get on with your life and stop wishing for things that aren't going to happen."

Finally something Bo said seemed to sink in. Grafton blinked. "Do you really think Molly ain't going to change her mind?"

"Yep. She's not going to change her mind." Hating the hurt that was shining in the guy's eyes, Bo continued, telling himself that little kids didn't get to hear good stuff all the time either. "Molly doesn't want you, Grafton. She doesn't want an ex-con boyfriend. No matter what she might have written to you or hinted when she visited once a month."

Grafton picked up the can of pop that had been sitting on the coffee table and gulped down half of it. "I don't know what to do."

"That's fine, because it's my job to tell you what to do. You need to stay working, stay out of trouble, and keep in with your parole officer. Otherwise you're going to slip up and be right back on the top bunk in Cell Block C." Giving him a hard look, Bo added, "You don't want to be back in Cell Block C, Grafton."

Grafton slowly nodded. "You're right."

Bo felt like shouting *hallelujah*. He settled for moving things along. "Who else have you talked to? Your family?"

"My sister. That's it."

"How did it go?"

He shrugged. "She took my call. So there's that."

Thinking of how his own brother thought he was scum, Bo nodded. "It's hard, ain't it?"

"Yeah. Did your Ma ever want to see you again?"

"Yep, but she's down in Kentucky. We only see each other two or three times a year."

"Is that enough?"

Bo shrugged. "It is what it is."

Grafton pursed his lips. "We done?"

"Yep." Standing up, Bo clapped Grafton on the back. "Listen, I want you to think of something to do every time you start pining for Molly. Work or work out. Watch a movie, read a book . . . something, you know?"

"In other words, keep busy."

He nodded. "It sounds stupid, but it helps."

"I'll try." Just as he was about to open Bo's door, Grafton turned around. "Hey, any luck with that woman?"

"What woman?"

"The woman who wrote her number on your hand. Did she give you the time of day?"

It seemed Grafton wasn't the only one who'd been naive. Bo

really hadn't thought that Joy's number on his hand would've caused anyone's notice. "I'm not talking about her with you."

"Fine." He held up his hands. "I won't ask about her again."

After Grafton went on his way, Bo looked for Mason. He found him in the kitchen, talking with Elizabeth next to the stove. She came in to cook three times a week. At first, Bo had been leery of having a woman working as a cook in the house, but Elizabeth had shown him real fast that he had nothing to worry about. Elizabeth didn't put up with anyone's nonsense, and she made sure the guys knew it.

Both Mason and Elizabeth looked his way when Bo entered.

"Hey, Bo," Elizabeth said. "You staying for supper? I'm making chicken casseroles tonight."

"Thanks, but no."

"Did Grafton ever calm down?" Mason asked. "We could hear him carrying on through the pantry wall."

"He did, more or less."

"What happened? His girl dump him?" Elizabeth asked.

"As a matter of fact, yes. How did you know?"

She opened up two cans of soup and poured them into a bowl. "I figured it was a matter of time. The kid wears his heart on his sleeve. That don't ever end well, you know what I'm saying?"

"I'm afraid I do. Sounds like you do too."

Elizabeth shrugged as she stirred in some cornbread stuffing mix. "My father always said that you can't live forty years without experiencing hardship. I always thought there was something to be said for that."

Bo raised his eyebrows but didn't comment. He turned to Mason. "I'm fixing to head out. You good?"

"Yep. Adrian's here. Charlie said he'd stop over around eight. Plus, we've only got four guys staying here right now. I'll close things down tight round midnight."

"Do you know if Lincoln is coming by?"

"He was here early this morning. I'm not sure about the weekend."

"'Kay. I'm out of here then. See you on Sunday."

"Yep."

"See you, Bo."

"Thanks, Elizabeth." He gave her a little salute, checked in in with a couple of the guys hanging out in the main living area, then headed out to his car.

He had two vehicles. One was a five-year-old Ram truck. His other was an eleven-year-old BMW in black. The car was sweet and just run-down enough that it didn't draw a lot of attention. Whenever he drove it, he felt a little like the man his momma always wanted him to be.

Bo's mom had worked two jobs, hoping that Bo would be the first in the family to go to college. He hadn't been able to do that for her, but he had graduated high school. Now she worked as a receptionist in a dentist's office. She had a really great smile and the folks there liked her enough to make sure she kept it that way.

She'd been the type to dream about becoming someone a little bit fancier. Not a lot. Just, say, the type to maybe get on a plane from time to time and stay at the Marriott instead of taking road trips and getting a room at the Motel 6.

One day he was going to make something like that happen for her. Something to make up for all the pain he'd caused.

Bo's house was twenty minutes from Lincoln's and was in a small neighborhood made up of midcentury ranches on one-acre lots. His house looked like all the rest on the outside. Red brick, tan siding. One chimney, lots of trees.

Inside, though, it was gorgeous. Bamboo flooring, white woodwork, leather furniture, stainless steel appliances and countertops. Original movie posters from old B-movies decorated the walls in sleek frames.

The work he did as a catalog model for Renegade had paid for most of it. It filled him with great satisfaction.

Even better, only a couple of guys had ever seen it. He kept to himself most of the time. Watched shows on Netflix. Read. Listened to music.

He'd fixed it up for himself. But now he realized that it was a nice enough place to have a woman like Joy over. If they ever got that far.

Thinking that he maybe wasn't all that different from his mother with her hopes and dreams, Bo realized that he was pinning some of his hopes on Joy. If she answered the phone again when he called, that was a step forward.

He'd worry about real dates and visits to his house another time. He'd learned not to expect too much.

CHAPTER 8

It was raining. Given that it was Saturday, and that she and Chloe had made plans to have lunch at a cute café before walking around the square in Chillicothe, Joy was bummed. Her teenager hardly ever had a whole Saturday free.

Even though they weren't going out to eat and window shop, Joy decided the day wasn't a total loss. Chloe had decided to stay home instead of hanging out with Baylee or one of her other friends. She was grateful for that.

They were also making the best of a rainy day. Chloe was binge-watching old seasons of *Stranger Things* on the couch and painting her nails.

Since Joy was nursing a small cold, she was using the rain as an excuse to stay in her pajamas and make a big pot of soup.

If she felt up to it, she could also finish the two last paintings for her customer in Columbus, but she had a little bit of time before the gal was going to be expecting them.

"Mom, your phone's buzzing."

"I'll get it." Now all she had to do was figure out where it was. "Is it in the living room?"

"It's in my hand. You left it on the couch. Hey, who's Bo?"

Bo was texting? Doing her best to ignore the little burst of happiness that brought, Joy hurried over to the couch and practically snatched it out of her daughter's hands. "You aren't looking at my phone, are you?"

"Well, yeah, but I'm not reading your texts or anything. Who's Bo?"

She looked at the screen. Bo had just sent a second text.

"Mom, you didn't answer me. Who's Bo? Is he one of your reading guys or something?"

Pulling her eyes away from her phone's screen, she glanced at her daughter. Chloe's attention was back on the television. It would be so easy to say that Bo was one of her tutoring clients. Then she wouldn't have to worry about Chloe asking any more questions. But she couldn't do it.

For some reason, it felt wrong to lie about Bo. "No. Bo is . . . he's a friend."

Her daughter looked back in her direction with interest. "What kind of friend?"

"He's a friend who's a man." She instantly felt stupid.

Chloe pressed pause on the remote. "What are you talking about? Wait—is he like a *boy*friend?" Her voice rose an octave. "Mom, are you dating him?"

"No, I am not. He's just someone I met at Sacred Grounds."

Chloe narrowed her eyes. "How long ago?"

She tried to act like she didn't know exactly. "Maybe a week? Don't read anything into this, Chloe."

"What's he like?"

Handsome. Southern. Sexy. "I don't know. Nice?" Feeling

even more awkward—and like a liar—Joy picked up her phone and punched in the security code. To her surprise, she had a third text from Bo and another from an unknown number.

Her thumb hovered over the screen as she debated which number to tap first. Was the other text from a telemarketer? Or, was the creepy person who'd texted her the other night texting again?

Or was it just another client?

Chloe was still studying her intently. "Mom, you're acting weird. What's going on?"

"Nothing, dear." Pasting what she hoped was a very reassuring smile on her face, she added, "It's nothing for you to be worried about."

Chloe sat up straighter. "Why would I be worried about you texting a friend?"

Boy, she was making a mess of things. "You wouldn't. Of course you wouldn't. Don't worry about it, all right?"

"Fine." Chloe slumped back down on the couch and picked back up the remote.

Joy knew, however, that Chloe was anything but relaxed. She was likely stewing on this new information and trying to figure out how she felt about it. Her daughter was a thinker.

Glad for the reprieve, Joy sat down in her favorite comfy chair in the corner of the living room. After telling herself to stop acting so . . . so juvenile, she tapped Bo's name.

Morning. How's your day going?

The second message was more to the point.

> Any chance I could see you in
> person this weekend? I could
> meet you somewhere. Even buy
> you another mocha latte?

The third text made her smile.

> So, I wrote you about an hour
> ago. You okay? Or do you want
> me to leave you alone?

Pleased he remembered the drink he'd bought her, she sat down. Her fingers hovered over the screen as she debated about what to write back. Boy, it was moments like this when she wished she was a lot older, or Amish or something. Anything where texting immediate answers wasn't expected.

> So far, my day's all right. Since it's
> pouring down rain, Chloe and I
> are still in pajamas hanging out.
> I'd forgotten about my phone.

His reply was immediate.

> It's raining here too. So, coffee?

Part of her wanted to . . . but the majority definitely didn't want him to see her with a red nose. Or to have to explain to Chloe what she was doing.

Thanks, but I don't think it's going to work out. Chloe and I are staying in. I must have picked up a cold or something too. So that's another reason you don't want to see me.

Another? What was the first?

Well, I guess that's more about why I don't want to go out. Chloe's here. She's fine on her own, of course, but I rarely get a chance to just hang out with her.

That was all true, but Joy knew it was also painting what they were actually doing a little too flowery. She and her daughter were not baking cookies and having heart-to-hearts. For the last couple of hours, they hadn't even been in the same room together.

I could stop by and bring y'all coffees. What do you say?

Was she ready for him to meet Chloe—or to answer more questions that would come from her daughter the second he left? *Absolutely not.*

Her finger hovered over the screen. At last she typed,

I'm sorry, but it feels a little
too soon. Besides, I'm sure
you've got better things to do.

Not really. But I get it. You got
someone taking care of you?

For a cold? No.

Joy noticed that even though Chloe had gone back to her show she was now glancing at her curiously.

I mean for everything.

Joy bit back a sigh. That text was swoonworthy. When was the last time she'd felt like someone had her back?

That was easy. Before Tony had decided that he didn't want to be married to her anymore.

She pushed the suspicious text she'd received the other night to one side. At last, she responded:

Thanks, but I'm good

All right . . . but if you get worse,
let me know. At the very least I
can drop something off, yeah?

Thank you

Nothing to thank me for. You
haven't let me do anything.
Not yet.

Resolutely pretending that she wasn't flattered—and yes,
suddenly tempted to ask him over—she carefully texted the safe
reply.

Thanks for offering.

When he didn't text right back, she clicked on the other
text from the unknown number.

I still miss you.

She could practically feel all the blood leave her face as she
stared at the screen.

Still? Who was texting her? She couldn't think of who it
could possibly be. It wasn't like Tony missed her. Plus she already
knew he wasn't that kind of creepy texter.

She frowned, glanced back at Chloe, debated whether or
not she should delete the text, finally deciding to keep it. Just
in case she needed to show it to someone. After staring at the
screen again, she set it down.

"Hey, Mom?"

Taking a breath, she tried to sound carefree and not freaked
out. "Yes?"

"Are you still texting that guy? Bo?"

"No." She tried to shake off the twinge of uneasiness she was currently feeling. "I'm done. Why?"

"I don't know. Hey, are you two going to start dating?"

"I'm not sure."

"Are you ever gonna start dating, Mom?"

As much as she wanted to shrug and not answer, Joy decided that it would be better to be honest. She smiled. "Maybe. I've been thinking it's probably time to give dating a try. One day soon." Since Tony had found someone—well, several some-ones—to date over the last three years.

"Is Bo like Dad?"

The comparison was almost laughable. "No."

Chloe sat up taller. "Really? How come?"

"Well, Bo is younger than Dad."

"Is he younger than you?"

"Yes. Likely by several years." Feeling her cheeks heat, she continued on. "He's also, um, a little rough around the edges."

Her daughter's eyebrows went up. "Really?"

"Really. He, um, is nice though." She jumped to her feet. "There's nothing for you to wonder about, anyway. Like I said, I'm just getting to know Bo."

Chloe stared at her for a long minute, then seemed to come to a decision. "Want to watch *Stranger Things* with me?"

"Yeah, that sounds great. Let me stir our soup then I'll come sit with you."

"'Kay."

After adding barley and stirring the soup a few times, she sat back down on the couch. Chloe's eyes were at half-mast. She'd be sound asleep in minutes.

Sitting next to her, Joy rearranged the blanket around her daughter's middle and tried to relax.

But all she could seem to think about was what she might have said yes to, if it wasn't pouring down rain, if she didn't have a cold, and if she didn't have a daughter to look after.

Or if things were different.

She was wondering what things would be like if she was someone else.

CHAPTER 9

Joy had shot him down, and Bo wasn't sure how he felt about it. It wasn't like he thought he was *all that*, but it wasn't an exaggeration to say that he was usually the one being pursued. He couldn't remember the last time a woman had politely said that she didn't want to see him.

Come to think of it, he was kind of into the refusal. It wasn't because he liked playing games—not that he thought she was doing that—it was because he liked her being so honest. He also liked that she was protective of her girl. Joy hadn't been shy about letting him know that he was going to prove himself a whole lot more before she'd risk getting her daughter involved.

When their text conversation had ended, he realized that he was going to need to be real patient if he wanted a chance with Joy—and that he was going to have to bring his A game too. She was not the kind of woman to accept a date on the fly or put up with him being anything but respectful and kind.

It had been noted.

But that still left him wondering what to do with the rest of his Saturday. Well, besides head over to the house and check on the guys.

His sister Carrie's phone call was a welcome distraction. Almost.

After they exchanged greetings and pleasantries, Carrie blurted, "Sam, I can't believe you're sitting at home all alone. If you're doing nothing, you should have been doing nothing with us. You know how much we miss you."

Carrie would never know how much comments like that meant to him. He'd experienced some pretty dark days in the middle of his incarceration when he'd been sure he'd lost his whole family. Their love had gotten him through it. Well, their love, Lincoln, and the Bible study he'd started going to. "I miss y'all too, but I can't."

"Uh-huh."

He never could pull one over on her. Not easily, anyway. "Carrie, you know I wish I could."

"You're just five hours away."

"A ten-hour drive, round trip, is not insignificant, girl."

"Oh, hush. Hey, want me to call Janie? Maybe we could come up and see you." Sounding even more excited, she added, "We could go to that diner you like so much, and then spend the night. It would be like old times."

Bo rolled his eyes. They'd never had a whole lot of fun times hanging out together on Saturday nights. He'd gone out as much as he could get away with. "Sorry honey, but no." The last time his two sisters had come to town they'd drawn attention from some unsavory types, and he'd come real close to beating up four guys. His sisters were too cute and too friendly and attracted men like nobody's business.

"You know Brian won't mind."

"Well, he should. Ross County is a long drive from y'all. Besides, all you two ever want to do is hang out with me and my friends—the majority of who are ex-cons."

"First of all, Brian treats me like a grown-up." She laughed softly. "Secondly, everyone knows that you are twice as protective as he is. Or a Doberman."

"Sorry, sugar, but I'm not heading down to Kentucky today and you and Janie can't be coming up this weekend."

"Why not? Do you have a date or something?"

"No, I do not."

"Are you working?" She lowered her voice. "Are you taking off your clothes for that catalog again?"

Unable to help himself, he laughed. "No. I told you they only ask me to model for them twice a year." He kept his being the face of Renegade Clothing on the down-low. Hardly anyone knew that two times a year he went to a warehouse in Chillicothe, hung out with the team from Renegade, and got his picture taken wearing—or almost wearing—their sports and outdoor wear. He'd been horrified the first time he'd modeled and was asked to just wear a pair of pants and "hold" one of their T-shirts, but he got over it soon enough. The money was insane, and he gave a good portion of it to their mother.

He wouldn't have even told her or his sisters about the gig if they hadn't been so sure he'd started doing something illegal.

"I swear, I think some of Renegade's clients buy those clothes just to keep that catalog coming their way. Janie and I are sure that there are folks pinning those pictures of you on their walls."

Just the thought of that made him feel squidgy. "I hope not."

"Come on." She lowered her voice. "I don't know how you got that six-pack, but it's impressive."

His cheeks were heating, and not much could embarrass

him. "Geeze, Carrie. Please don't mention my stomach ever again."

"Fine. I'll shut up about it."

"It's about time."

"I'm not going to ask you anything else about women, either. I've learned my lesson there."

"Good." He smiled. "Now tell me about Momma."

"She's good. Janie and Eric went to see her on Wednesday. She cooked them up some chicken-fried steak."

"Dang." He'd do crunches for two hours if it meant eating an entire plate of his mother's signature dish.

"I know. Momma's steak is amazing. Eric even texted me a picture of it." She paused. "I guess he didn't text it to you too?"

"You guessed right." His mother might love him no matter what and his sisters might have forgiven him, but it was likely that his brother never would.

Her voice turned tentative. "Do you think Eric's ever going to warm up to you?"

"No."

"Really?"

"His brother went to prison, Carrie. He's ashamed of me, and I can't say I blame him." Bo meant that sincerely. Eric had gone to the University of Kentucky on a half dozen scholarships. He graduated with a degree in business and now worked for a big company in Cincinnati. He was married, went to church, and lived in a house in the suburbs. There was nothing about Eric Beauman that wasn't steady and good.

Well, nothing beyond the fact that he was content to pretend that his brother didn't exist.

"Last time I saw Eric, I told him that he was being judgmental and mean."

"I wish you wouldn't have."

"How could I not? You served your time, Bo. And now you're doing all kinds of stuff that's good." Her voice lowered. "Our stick-in-the-mud baby brother needs to move on."

"I appreciate it, Carrie, but I've made peace with his decision. He's a good man and looks after his wife and Momma. That's all that matters."

"You matter too."

Carrie was going to get him choked up if she wasn't careful. "Enough now. Okay?"

She sighed. "All right. Well, other than trying to finagle an invite to come see you . . . I just thought I'd call to see how you were doing."

"I appreciate the call. I'll come down and see you soon. Promise."

"You better."

"Tell Brian hey."

"Will do. Don't forget to call Momma, now."

"I called her first thing this morning. You know I don't forget that." He owed his mother a lot. She sacrificed so much for them after their dad died back when he was in middle school. Times were tough and she'd been sad to only be able to give them chicken or beef once or twice a week.

He'd repaid her by being a juvenile thug and getting sentenced to prison.

"You're a good person, Sam."

As always, her praise made him feel sick to his stomach. Yeah, he'd been set up and forced to take the blame for a crime he hadn't committed. But he'd done plenty of other things that he should've served time for.

He swallowed hard. "Love you, Carrie. You stay safe now."

After they hung up, thoughts of his family stayed with him. They'd never had a lot of money, but they'd never gone without anything they'd had to have. He didn't remember ever being hungry or wearing clothes that didn't fit or that embarrassed him.

His brother Eric might have different memories—being the younger brother, he'd had to wear plenty of Bo's hand-me-downs.

So why had Bo been the one with such a chip on his shoulder?

He'd been right in the middle of the road when he was a teenager. Good-looking enough to not worry about girls, but never the best-looking guy. Same with school and sports. He'd made Bs and Cs and made it onto the teams, but he had never been the star player. Janie always said that he'd coasted through life back then, and he reckoned that was a good description.

If he'd had so much going for him, why had he taken such a wrong turn? Why had he started drinking too much, smoking weed when he knew it would get him kicked off teams, doing stupid stuff when he knew if he got caught his mother would have to help him pay for it?

Why had he never cared?

Hating the direction his thoughts had turned, Bo stood up and decided to work out. He had a set of weights in his basement, and sit-ups and push-ups didn't need anything except for him to get off the couch. He'd learned that in prison.

He'd just completed his first set of fifty sit-ups when his phone buzzed. He picked it up gratefully.

"Lincoln."

"Hey." His boss's familiar, gruff voice sounded a little off. "You busy?"

"Nope. What do you need?"

"Babysitting."

"Hunt?" he asked hopefully. Hunt was Lincoln and Jennifer's adorable one-year-old baby. The kid had just started walking and talking and loved to do both—and to watch cartoons. He'd watch the little guy any day of the week.

"Sorry, but it's Chance. He needs a hand on Monday morning. I was going to drive him around and check in with him, but Jennifer's got a doctor's appointment, so I have to stay with Hunt."

"She okay?" Jennifer was as sweet as Lincoln was gruff. They'd all fallen in love with her the moment she'd shyly offered them cinnamon rolls warm from her oven in exchange for their help shoveling her drive.

There was also the time when she'd been attacked and harassed—all while her no-good father was lurking around. Bo still had nightmares about the phone call he'd received saying that Jennifer was about to be loaded onto an ambulance.

Bo didn't know a single guy who wouldn't drop everything to help her, even if it was just to fill her car with gas. She was truly adored.

"Yeah." Lincoln paused. "Jen doesn't want everyone to know yet, but she's pregnant again."

Bo grinned. "Hey, that's great. Congrats."

"Thanks." Lincoln's voice filled with warmth. "We're real happy. The doctors said it was doubtful she'd get pregnant again on account of some female problems, so I'd been thinking Hunt was going to be our one and only."

"And now she's got another on the way. That's a lot to be thankful for."

"Yeah." Lincoln's voice turned soft. "It's a miracle, that's what it is. But she's feeling like crap. Got morning sickness twenty-four seven. She'll likely be on the couch all weekend—which is why Chance is gonna need you on Monday."

"Where's he living?"

"At the house. I know Mason would run him around but you know what it's like when he leaves."

If Mason was gone for five hours, all hell would break loose around T-DOT. "I'll do it. That's no problem."

"Thanks, man. I don't think it will be more than four hours, tops. If you take him to lunch, keep the receipt, yeah?"

"Will do. You got anything in mind for him?" Sometimes these one-on-one times with fresh ex-cons were actually an excuse to give them a kick in the pants.

"Nah. Chance is good. He's shy. I swear, sometimes I have no clue how he survived in Madisonville."

"No worries. Tell your girl to hang in there."

"Stop by one day soon. You know she and Hunt miss you."

"I miss them too. I'll stop by as soon as you let me know she's feeling better."

●●●

On Monday morning, Bo headed over to the main house early, spent a couple of hours making phone calls and filling out paperwork, then got mentally ready to cart Chance around. Babysitting grown men wasn't his favorite activity, but at least he wasn't sitting alone with his thoughts. He'd ended up spending the rest of Saturday and most of Sunday sitting home by himself.

He found Chance hanging out in the main room. A couple of guys were playing Xbox. The kid looked bored though. When he saw Bo, he stood up. Obviously Lincoln had passed the word that Bo would be taking him around.

"Thanks," he said when they got in Bo's truck. "I can't wait until I get my own wheels."

"One thing at a time, right? So, where do you need to go?"

"Walmart and the library."

"You need to go to the library?"

Chance looked away. "Yeah."

"What, you out of reading material or something?" he joked.

"Yeah, no. Sorry for the trouble, but I'm supposed to meet

someone there." Still not meeting his gaze, he added, "I'll likely be there an hour or so."

Feeling like he was being taken down a road he had no intention of going, Bo paused before shifting the vehicle into reverse. "Who are you meeting?"

"It's a woman."

Now he was simply getting irritated. "I'm not driving you around for hookups, buddy."

"What?" His voice rose. "It ain't like that at all."

"What is it like?"

"It's . . . well, she's a tutor. A reading tutor. This is the first time I'm meeting her."

Everything was starting to make sense. Taking care to keep his voice soft, he said, "You can't read, Chance?"

"I can read some. Not much. Enough to get by." The kid was looking anywhere but at Bo. "When I told Lincoln about how I didn't read too good, he said I ought to look at getting some help, on account of me needing to stay busy anyway."

Telling himself that there was likely a whole lot of reading tutors in the area, Bo nodded. "Tell me where to go. Which one is it?"

Chance named the street and Bo calculated his route, turning at the next light. "You all right with taking me there? Boss said it wasn't too far."

"I'm fine, and he was right. It's close."

The kid looked even more uncomfortable. "Thanks for doing this. I know this probably ain't how you want to spend your day, but if you hadn't been able to take me, I would've had to cancel."

"I wasn't doing too much. Besides, this is important. I'm guessing that that phone call to get a tutor wasn't easy."

For the first time, a hint of a smile appeared on his face.

"Oh, man. I was sweating like a pig when I called and then told her what I needed help with. I don't think I was even that nervous when I got arrested."

Bo chuckled. "The first time you do something, it's always hard. That was real good that you called." He pulled into the library parking lot.

"Thanks. Ah, I'm not sure how long I'll be."

"I'll come in. And don't worry, I won't sit and watch. I'll go read a magazine or something."

"All right."

Bo followed Chance in, letting him take the lead. The kid looked scared to death, staring around the big room.

But then Bo saw Joy. "I think that's her," he said.

Joy recognized him. Her eyes widened as she got to her feet. "Bo?"

"Joy. I can't believe it." His insides seemed to slide back into place as her expression warmed. Suddenly, he was even prouder to know her—and a little proud to be doing something small to help a man learn to read too.

"Why are you here?"

"I'm doing a little bit of chauffer service today." Remembering that Chance was standing next to him and growing more confused by the second, Bo added, "Any chance you're waiting here for a new student?"

"I am." She held out a hand. "Are you Chance Tatum?"

The kid looked a little shell-shocked. Bo couldn't blame him. Joy looked as pretty as a picture in skinny jeans, a gray sweater, and a pearl necklace. Her long brown hair was once again flowing down her back.

"Yeah."

"I'm Joy Howard. It's nice to meet you."

After darting a look at Bo, Chance shook Joy's hand. "Hey."

She looked him in the eye while they shook. "If you're ready, we can get started." She smiled.

"Yeah. Sure." Chance took a step, then turned back to Bo. "How do you know each other?" His voice was filled with suspicion.

"We only met the other day. I promise I had no idea this was who you were meeting. This is a real coincidence."

"Oh."

"Are you sticking around, Bo?" Joy asked.

"Yeah. I'm his ride. But don't worry, I'll stay out of the way." He pointed to a comfortable-looking spot over by a fireplace that had long since been filled in with plaster. "I'm going to hang over there."

"Sounds good." She lowered her voice, saying something to Chance that almost made him smile. Then the two of them went to the table she'd been sitting at.

Feeling left out though he knew he had no call to be, Bo pulled a pair of books off of the new-release section and sat down. Unable to help himself, he looked over their way again, but there was nothing to see. Both Joy and Chance had their backs turned toward him.

He sat and watched them for a moment. Noticed the way she didn't fuss with her necklace or hair or clothes much. She sat still whenever Chance talked, like the guy had something important to say.

He was glad for Chance to have a tutor like Joy. He was such an awkward kid, so shy and wary. Joy would no doubt help him gain some confidence and give him some tools to read better.

So Bo was real glad Joy was speaking to her student in that soft, kind way of hers. He just couldn't help but feel a little bit jealous that she wasn't talking to him instead.

And that, Bo reckoned, was why his brother was perfectly justified in thinking that his older brother wasn't worth much.

CHAPTER 10

Chance Tatum looked like he could've been a banker in another life. He had a studious, serious look to his eyes and still carried the last vestiges of baby fat in his cheeks. He was just under six feet and was wearing a pair of jeans that had a hole in one knee, a snug T-shirt that had been washed a hundred times, and designer tennis shoes.

Joy imagined a lot of young girls probably gave him a second look—and a lot of those girls' mothers likely would as well, but for a different reason. No doubt they would zero in on the scar on Chance's lip and the wary shadow in his eyes. This was a guy who had been through a lot. Maybe even a guy who wasn't done with whatever darkness he had seen.

That wary shadow was in full force and currently directed at her. "Did you tutor Bo too? Is that how you know him?"

"Oh, no. Bo and I just happen to be friends."

"Friends?"

"Mm-hmm. We met in a coffee shop not too long ago."

Chance looked at her with a furrowed brow. Did he think she'd said something goofy? Maybe she had. She smiled slightly, hoping to show that she wasn't concerned by his questions, but also that she wasn't going to just sit there and give him information. Figuring that this discussion was doing as well as anything to break the ice between them, she couldn't resist teasing him a bit. "Chance, tell me the truth. Do you think it's strange that Bo and I met in a coffee shop or that he started talking to me at all?"

The boy looked taken aback, then grinned. "Truth?"

"Of course."

"Maybe both. No disrespect, ma'am, but Bo isn't really the kind of guy to hang out and sip coffee. Most guys I know try their best to give him space. And you . . . well, you just look like you wouldn't have a lot in common with an ex-con. Besides teaching him to read, I mean."

She chuckled. "I think you're right. There's no reason anyone would think that the two of us would meet over coffee. But I guess that's what friends are for."

"What do you mean?"

"The world is made up of all sorts of people. I always thought it would be a shame not to meet half of them on account of thinking that you wouldn't have anything in common with them, right?"

Chance shrugged. "I couldn't say."

"It doesn't matter anyway. What matters to me is that you reached out to get help with your reading. That's what's great."

"Not really." He lowered his voice. "I can't hardly read much."

"I'm sorry, but that's why I'm here, right?"

Looking even more ill at ease, he shrugged.

Boy, she hated that a young man like him would have to

carry around such a burden. "Did any of your teachers ever mention what they thought was wrong?"

"What do you mean?"

"Did they think you had dyslexia, maybe? Or another reading disability?"

"No. But I didn't go to that kind of school."

She was confused. "What kind of school did you go to?"

"The kind of school that had a whole lot of kids in every classroom and old, worn-out textbooks." He shrugged. "Maybe the teachers were worn-out too." Still looking pensive, he added, "What I'm trying to say is that all anyone seemed to care about was that you were sitting in your seat. It didn't matter if I understood what was going on, as long as I was quiet, yeah?"

Joy hated to hear his story but had long ago made peace with the fact that there were a number of reasons people never learned to read—one of which was that no one at the school took the time to even notice if they could.

"All right. Well, I have a workbook for us to use." She pulled it out of her bag and slid it across the table toward him. "We'll use this every time we meet."

He looked at it like it was going to bite him. "Yes, ma'am."

He still hadn't touched the workbook. She gestured to the workbook and the other books she had on the table. "Do you have any questions before we get started?"

"Yeah." Chance seemed to brace himself, then blurted, "Do you ever have anyone who never ends up reading? You know, who just can't do it?"

She looked him in the eye. "No."

"You telling me the truth?"

"I am. I wouldn't lie about that. Some students might take a little longer than others, but everyone learns. Especially since I don't give up." She smiled.

"Huh."

"Chance, I promise I'm a really good teacher. You're also worth me doing everything I can to help you learn to read. Now, are you ready to get started?"

"Yeah."

She smiled. "Open up the book." When Chance did as she asked, Joy pointed to the first word on the page. "This word is *can*. That *c* is a hard *c*." She made the sound. "Most times you see that *a-n* combination, it's going to sound like *an*." She lowered her voice. "You say it now."

Chance narrowed his eyes. "Can."

"That's good. Now look at these words: man, ban, pan, fan, ran." She broke apart the words and said the sounds, asking him to do the same.

Almost an hour later, she closed the workbook and leaned back in her chair. "Chance, we made really good progress today. I'm proud of you."

He smiled before seeming to remember himself. "All I did was read just a couple of words that most first graders can figure out."

"Who cares? It doesn't matter what other people can do. All that matters is what *you* can read."

His lips twitched. "Does thinking like that really work for you?"

"If you mean does it help to not always weigh myself against the rest of the population? It absolutely does." Seeing that he was serious, Joy lowered her voice. "Years ago, I used to put myself down all the time. It was a struggle, you know? I gave myself so much grief because I wasn't better."

"Really?"

"Oh, yes. Anyway, once I gave up trying to be something I'm never going to be, my life got easier. I learned to accept my good points and deal with my bad." She leaned toward him. "Now, I'm not saying you have any bad parts, just that it's easier to focus on going forward instead of wishing for change in those parts of you that can't be changed."

He raised his eyebrows. "Maybe you've got a point."

She leaned back and folded her hands on top of the booklet they'd just read. "I like to think so. And I just want you to learn to read. Don't you?"

"Yes, ma'am."

"Good. Now you go over those words a couple of times before I see you on Saturday, all right?"

"All right. Thank you. I appreciate you giving up so much of your time, especially since you're not getting paid or anything."

She smiled. "I promise, these tutoring sessions are the best part of my week." Realizing that Bo had just joined them, she hoped she didn't sound as nervous as she felt. "It was good to meet you."

"Same." When Chance glanced at Bo, his expression was guarded once again. "You ready?"

"Almost. Hey, give me a sec to speak with Joy."

"Want me to go outside?"

He nodded. "I'll be out in a couple." The minute Chance was out of sight, Bo's grin seemed to fill up the room. "Joy, that was incredible."

"What was?"

"The way you handled that kid. He was a nervous wreck coming over here. You soothed his nerves and got him reading. You did it all in such an effortless way too."

"You're giving me too much credit. Chance is going to be fine. He only needs to start believing in himself."

"Really? You think a shot of self-confidence is all he needs?"

"No, I think he needs people to drive him to meet me. He needs reasons to practice reading, and he's got to want to read as much as I want him to. But he's off to a good start."

"What do you think about the two of us meeting for coffee or something soon? Can we do that?"

She wanted to see him again, but what if it was a mistake? What if he decided that she was too old for him? Or that they had nothing in common?

What was she going to do if she finally let down her guard just to get disappointed when he eventually lost interest in her? "I don't have a lot of extra time," she hedged.

"Is that code for *no thank you*?"

Realizing that he'd seen right through her lame excuse, she laughed. "It's more like I'm a busy woman."

He studied her for a moment. "If you want to think about it for a spell, I'll back off. Or . . . if you want to, say, maybe meet me for breakfast, I'll try not to make you regret it."

"You are persistent."

"I am, but I'm not a bully. It's your call."

Joy bit her bottom lip. The thing of it was—she didn't want to say no. She wanted to see him again. "I can do breakfast. Chloe leaves for school early. But we'd have to eat early too—like around seven or eight." She half expected him to balk. Maybe she was counting on him saying no?

"I'll pick you up tomorrow at seven."

Thinking about her schedule, she shook her head. "I can't do tomorrow, but I can do the next morning."

"You sure? You're not going to go and cancel on me, are you?"

"Of course not." Though, wasn't that what she'd been doing? Giving herself a grace period in case she changed her mind? "Where would you like to meet?"

He lowered his voice. "Will you let me pick you up? I'll take you wherever you want to go for breakfast and then take you back home. Please?"

"Oh, all right." She supposed him having her address would be okay.

His eyes lit up and a smile cracked across his face. "Thank you. Text me your address."

He turned and walked out before she had a chance to change her mind. Maybe that was for the best? She didn't know.

She wasn't sure why she had agreed to letting him pick her up so easily. But maybe it didn't matter. What did matter to her was that she was finally moving forward. At last, she was ready to put Tony and his dissatisfaction with their marriage behind her.

She was ready to trust again.

CHAPTER 11

The best part of Finn's day always followed the worst part: telling his father that he was leaving. Dreading the confrontation that was about to take place, he walked to the barn feeling like he was pulling a lead weight behind him.

His father was where he always was in the early afternoons: standing in front of his workbench and oiling and cleaning their horses' bridles, lines, and other assorted tack. His father loved keeping both the tack and the horses in perfect condition. Everything about the inside of the big old red barn soothed him—it was pretty much the only time their father ever looked content or at ease.

Usually, he looked permanently let down and irritated by life.

Finn made sure to make his footsteps land heavy when he entered. The noise would startle his father enough to get his head back to reality. If it happened quickly, *Daed* would recover before he came face-to-face with him.

They all knew to do this, even his little brother Caleb. Their mother had quietly demonstrated to all her children dozens of ways to make life with their father almost bearable.

For some reason, Finn's *daed* couldn't handle being startled. Not at all.

This time it took his father almost a full minute to notice Finn's heavy steps on the concrete floor. He jerked, dropping the bit he was cleaning onto the barn floor. It clattered as it bounced, then slid a few inches.

Only after he picked it up and set it on the bench did he face Finn. "*Jah?*" As always, his father looked surprised—and a little angry—to see him.

"I'm leaving for work."

"All right. Are you still at that diner where Mary's at?"

"I am. I'm waiting tables at Lane's." They went through this every day.

"I don't understand why you're working there. You're needed here." He frowned. "You have chores. Did you forget?"

"I didn't. They're done."

"Don't expect your mother to leave a meal waiting for you. Leaving here is your choice."

"I understand." Well, he understood that his father wouldn't allow his mother to leave out a meal for him.

"Where's your mother?"

"*Mamm* is inside. Rachel and Lucy are helping her do laundry. Caleb and Eddie are still at school."

"Fine." His father studied him a moment longer before returning to the items on the counter. Grumbling under his breath, he picked up a rag and dipped it in lemon oil.

Finn turned away and headed out of the barn, then quickened his pace when he reached the drive, and then finally the main road. Only then, when their farm was fading into the distance, did he slow his pace and relax his shoulders. He was free.

From this minute until nine or ten at night, he was free of that pressure, and it was the best feeling in the world—even better than when he used to leave home to attend the Amish school (on account of him never being a very good student). He was good at sums and math but never reading. The teacher, a woman who likely meant well, but had no better idea about how to help him than his father, would constantly have him stay after school to try to redo all the work he messed up.

Now, though, he could read enough to get by and do almost any basic equation in his head. It was more than enough to do well at his job.

And he *was* doing well. He'd been there several times now and felt more confident with every shift he worked. His aunt Mary was encouraging too. She had even teased him, saying she was pretty sure that they were busier during his shifts. Her teasing embarrassed him, but it didn't really matter. The only person he cared about seeing during those shifts was Chloe.

Every time she came in, she took a booth, ordered a vanilla malt, and chatted with him when he brought it over. All in all, their conversations weren't much and didn't last very long.

But it didn't matter to him what they said. All that mattered was that she was like nothing he'd ever seen, and he lived for her smiles.

Half an hour later, when he walked into the diner, he scanned the area, didn't see Chloe, and breathed a sigh of relief. He hadn't missed her.

"Hey, Finn," Aunt Mary said from the back counter, where she was filling saltshakers.

"Hiya, Mary." He walked over to her with a smile. "Would you like me to do that for ya?"

"*Nee.* I'd rather hear about you." She lowered her voice. "Did leaving go okay today?"

He raised a shoulder. "Well enough."

"I don't know what we should do about your father. More than one person has shared that he seems to be fading more and more into his own world."

Though it still felt strange to confide in someone about his home life, Finn's aunt was helping him learn that talking about it helped. He was no longer carrying quite as much of the burden. "It seems like that to me too. *Mamm* is okay with it, though." In some ways, his mother seemed to be relieved about his father's confusion. She was able to take care of the house and the bills without him interfering.

Mary set the large container of salt on the counter. "Do you worry about your siblings, Finn?"

"*Nee.* He is gentle with them."

"Just not with you."

"Aunt Mary, you know that ain't nothing new." Finn wasn't sure why his father didn't like him, but he'd long given up trying to figure it out. Knowing the reason wouldn't change his circumstances.

"I know." Mary darted a look toward one of the booths, seemed to make up her mind, and then stepped closer to him. "Finn, there's a pair of men here. They're good men. One of them is Seth Troyer. Do you know him? He jumped the fence a while back."

"I know who Seth is." Everyone knew he hadn't so much as jumped as gotten kicked out of his house. Not long after, he'd gone to prison. Now he was English but had a lot of friends in the community. He was always helping out one family or another.

"Well, I want you to go talk with Seth and the other man."

"Why?"

"I talked to them the other day about you. They work with a lot of men who've just gotten out of prison."

He inhaled sharply.

She held up her hand. "I know, I know, that ain't you. But . . . you are a man in need, and they might be able to help you make some connections for when you do decide to jump the fence."

He glanced over at them again and started when he caught a pair of blue eyes staring directly back at him.

"You ready?"

"You mean, right now?"

"There's no time like the present, Finn. Ain't it so?" Before he could answer, she tilted her head. "Come on. I'll take you over."

He followed, feeling a combination of nervousness and hope. Both men looked up at him when he and Mary stood at the end of the booth.

"Seth, Bo, this here is Finn, the boy I've been telling you about."

Finn stuffed his hands in his pockets so he wouldn't do something stupid like wave to them. "Hey."

Bo lifted his chin. Seth, on the other hand, motioned for him to join them. "Good to meet you, Finn. Mary's been telling us a lot about you."

The men were sitting across from each other. Though there didn't look like a ton of room on either side, he sat next to Seth. "Mary told me about you, as well."

"What have you heard?" Bo asked.

His mouth went dry. Why had he said anything? "I don't know."

"You don't know, or you don't remember?"

Mary, who'd been walking by, rapped her knuckles on the table. "Bo, settle down and be nice to Finn. He's not one of your ex-cons." Turning to Finn, she winked. "Don't be nervous, and don't take any more than fifteen minutes, hon. I'm gonna need your help if anyone else comes in."

"All right."

When she walked away, both of the men were staring at him. Feeling like they were sizing him up and finding him wanting, he didn't say anything. Just continued to sit there.

"I'm guessin' Mary told you that I jumped the fence a while back," Seth said.

"She did, but I already knew that."

"Are you thinking about it? Seriously?" He lowered his voice. "Or, are you just wondering about what it would be like? Either way is all right." Seth's tone was gentle but held a note of steel in it too. It told Finn loud and clear that he wanted Finn to be honest.

"I'm seriously thinking about leaving."

"Why?" Bo asked. When Finn hesitated, Bo added, "If you do something like this, everyone's going to be asking you, right?"

It was hard to believe, but he'd never had to actually cite why he wanted to jump the fence. Until this moment, it had always felt like it was a secret wish that never had any hope of actually coming true. "I'm tired of pretending to be someone I'm not," he blurted before he lost his nerve.

Looking satisfied, Bo leaned back. Then, to Finn's surprise, he nodded. "That makes a lot of sense."

"It does?" His neck heated as he realized that he was likely squeaking.

"Have you told your folks?" Seth asked.

"I've kind of told *mei mamm*, but not really."

"They'll be mad, I reckon."

"*Jah*. My mother will be upset, but my *daed* will be mad. It don't matter. He's mad at me all the time anyway."

Both men eyed him intently. "What does that mean?" Bo asked. His tone was much softer. Almost gentle.

Feeling emotionally naked, Finn weighed the pros and cons of being too honest, but then figured he had nothing to lose. "It means *mei daed* and I don't have much to say to each other. It means he don't like much about me and isn't afraid to show it." He swallowed. "Now that I'm older, I don't care to live under his thumb for much longer."

Bo frowned. "Is he hurting you, boy?"

There was a new edge to Bo's voice. It took Finn off guard until he realized that Bo's anger wasn't directed at him, but rather *for* him. That difference made the way Bo called him *boy* almost easier to take. "It's nothing I can't handle." I was nothing like it used to be—before Finn got big enough to fight back.

Seth and Bo exchanged looks again before Seth spoke. "Finn, have you been baptized yet?"

"*Nee.*"

"Okay, so you won't be shunned."

Finn shrugged. He didn't want to be shunned because he didn't want to be forbidden to see his younger brothers and sisters. However, if he left, his *daed* would likely forbid them to talk to him anyway.

That was going to be hard. He worried about missing his siblings. He hoped the little ones wouldn't hate him for it.

But he wasn't worried about the Lord being upset with him. He'd started talking to God on his own years ago. Though it wasn't something that he was comfortable sharing, he was pretty sure the Lord was still going to have his back whether he was Amish or not.

Seth continued. "You got a job here, which is a good start. Where are you looking to live? Or do you even want to stay nearby?"

"I think I'd like to, just to be near my little brothers and sisters, but I haven't thought that far."

"Well, you might want to, from time to time." Smiling encouragingly, Seth added, "What was your favorite subject in school?"

"In school? Well, I didn't have one." Figuring he had nothing to lose, he added, "I wasn't a very good student."

"Well, what do you like to do? Work here?"

It seemed like Bo thought working at his aunt and uncle's diner wasn't something to be proud of. "There's nothing wrong with working here."

"I didn't say there was, kid," Bo said softly.

Just as Finn clenched his fists, Seth murmured, "Calm down, Finn. We're not judging you and we certainly don't want to scare you, okay?"

Bo sipped his water. "All we're doing is trying to make sure you do some thinking before you take off from home."

Seth nodded. "Bo's right. We help guys try to do better all the time. Now, don't worry. I'll help you find someplace when you're ready."

"How will I know when I'm ready?" The question came out before he could stop it. He clenched his jaw, thinking he must sound so foolish to these men.

"I canna tell you that, Finn," Seth said. "But I reckon that one day you'll just know. That's how it was with me."

"Finn, I need ya," Mary called out.

He moved to stand up. "I've got to go."

"Hold on a sec," Seth said. Pulling out a card, he wrote a couple of things on the back. He turned it over and tapped the top name with his finger. "That's me. Seth. That's my phone." Pointing to the next name, he added, "That's Bo and his cell. Call if you need anything."

"Thanks." He took the card and stuffed it in the back pocket of his jeans.

"Finn, I don't give my number out lightly. You know what that means?"

"*Nee*. I mean, no."

"It means, if you need me, call. If you get hurt or something goes wrong, you call me." Seth's voice hardened. "Do you understand?"

"Yes. I mean, I think so."

Bo clapped him on the shoulder. "What Seth's trying to say is that you ain't alone, bud. We've got your back and we're not going to forget about you."

"If you want to call me to talk about anything, I'll listen. If you call and say you need me, I'll be there," Seth said. "Either of us will be."

"Danke." Finn felt choked. "I gotta go."

Bo grinned. "Yeah, you do. See ya, kid."

He scooted out of the booth, turned around, and came face-to-face with Chloe. She was sipping her vanilla malt and watching him.

He wondered how much she'd overheard. Unable to help himself, he stared right back.

CHAPTER 12

Chloe knew it was probably rude, but she couldn't help watching Finn. He looked like he was in the middle of the most intense conversation with the two men in the next booth. At first, she thought he was in trouble or something, but after a few seconds, it became obvious that the men were simply talking to him about something important.

Looking at the men more closely, Chloe decided that they looked kind of tough, but they were both good-looking. Okay, one of them might even be called hot, even though he was kind of old.

One thing she was sure about was that they weren't Amish. She wondered how they knew Finn.

Mary interrupted her thoughts. "You need anything else, sweetie?"

Pulling herself away from thoughts of Finn, she smiled up at the woman. "No, I'm good."

"You going to your dance class again today?"

"Yep. I've got to be there in about fifteen minutes."

"I like how you've been coming over here for a spell before class." Her eyes twinkled. "You're becoming a regular."

"It's a good place to get some homework done before I go dance." And, of course, to catch a glimpse of Finn. Realizing that she'd been sitting there for a while, she blurted, "Hey, do you want this booth for other customers? I can move."

"Nope. We're not too busy, so you take your time in this spot. I'll send Finn over in a sec to see if you need something before you go."

She couldn't have stopped her blush if she'd prayed with all her might. "Thanks." After Mary moved away, Chloe pulled back out her literature book and opened it to *Our Town* and the worksheet her English teacher had given her for guided reading. She didn't really mind the play. In fact, she liked it a lot. Well, she would've liked it if she hadn't been forced to read it—as it was, she just wanted to get it read and get the worksheet finished so she could not think about it anymore.

Flipping through the second act, she kept reading the text, then checking the worksheet. When she ran out of malt, she started chewing on the end of her straw.

"Do you want some water? Or maybe another malt?"

She froze and looked up at Finn. "No."

"You sure about that?"

She knew he was teasing. "Boy, you're sure getting full of yourself. It's night and day from when you started here."

He almost smiled. "I don't know about that, but I will fetch you another glass of water if you want it."

She glanced at the clock again. She had five more minutes. If she said no, he wouldn't come back. "Sure. Thanks."

"I'll be right back."

Happy that his back was turned, Chloe watched Finn stride

over to the counter, pull out a plastic cup, and fill it with ice. He paused to say something to the men he'd been talking with and nodded. Then, looking intent, he pulled out a plastic lid and a paper-covered straw from a cup and carried both the straw and the glass to her.

"Here you go."

"Thanks." She tore off the paper cover and popped it in the water. "Can you sit with me for a few minutes?"

He shook his head. "I can't. I already was talking to some people."

"I noticed you sitting over there," she commented. So cool, as if she hadn't been staring at him practically the whole time. "Are they friends of yours?"

He looked surprised. "*Nee.* I mean, no. They're not." Looking even more flustered, he added, "I mean, they're friends of a friend. I think."

She chuckled. "Sorry, but you're not making much sense."

"I know." He shrugged. "It's kind of complicated. It ain't nothing you need to worry about."

For some reason she felt a little stung. She knew they didn't know each other real well, but it felt like he was purposely keeping a secret from her. "Oh."

"Sorry. It's nothing personal."

She took another sip from her water before pushing it away. "I know. Don't worry about it. I mean it's not like we're friends or anything. Not really."

Looking frustrated, he pursed his lips. Then, after a second or two, he pointed to her open book. "Looks like you're reading a play."

"I am. It's *Our Town.* Have you read it?"

He smiled like he thought she was joking. "No."

"Is it because you don't like plays or because you haven't gotten the chance to read this one?"

"It's because I'm Amish, so we finish up school in eighth grade. And it's also because even if I had gone to school as long as you, I likely wouldn't have been able to read it too good."

She was embarrassed. "Oh." She stood up and started shoving her books in her backpack. "Look, I'm sorry. I should've just ignored everything that's none of my business. I was just curious. That's all."

"It's just—"

She stopped him there. "It's no big deal. And, ah, Finn?"

"Yeah?" His expression was still guarded.

"What I said about not being friends, I didn't really mean it. I think of you as a friend."

His lips twitched. "Me too."

"Finn, I need you," Mary said.

"Sorry, I've got to go." He turned and walked away like he couldn't get away from her fast enough. And maybe he couldn't. Maybe she just really messed things up between them because she was asking him about something he obviously wasn't proud about.

Watching him out of the corner of her eye, she saw that Mary was talking to him in a stern voice. He nodded, then started bussing two tables. When it was obvious that he was going to avoid catching her eyes for a while, Chloe tossed another ten-dollar bill on the table and rushed out of there. She had to figure out why she was the way she was around Finn. She either needed to stop being so curious about him or find a new place to do homework before dance.

• • •

Three hours later, she climbed into her mom's car with a moan. Miss Diamanté had seemed determined to kill them one pirouette at a time. "Hi."

"Hey." Her mother leaned over and kissed Chloe's brow. "How was dance today?"

"So hard. You should've seen us all, Mom. Gretchen and I were out of breath by the end of the first hour."

"I'm sorry, hon."

Chloe pulled off her flip-flops and wiggled her left foot. "My feet hurt so bad. Plus, I think I have two new blisters on my big toe."

"How come? Do you need new toe shoes?"

"It's about that time, I guess, but I don't think that was it. We just danced a lot." Closing her eyes, she murmured, "So many pirouettes and stupid leaps."

"Do you need more lambswool?"

"No, Mom."

Her mother frowned. "I promise, we can go get you some new shoes if you need them. I sold a couple of extra paintings this month."

Good toe shoes were expensive. Since she danced so much, she needed a new pair every couple of months. She'd need them even more frequently if she got one of the leads in this year's ballet. Then there were all the lessons, the leotards, the time her mom spent picking her up . . .

It wasn't anything new, but Chloe felt guilty about everything her dance life entailed. Especially since she knew her dad didn't understand why she had to have so much *stuff* just to dance. Glad that they were in a dark car, she said quietly, "Mom, maybe I should tell Miss Diamanté that I want to take a step back."

Her mom was trying to turn left at a light. "I don't know what that means."

"You know. Maybe not push myself so hard," she said as her mom turned and started down the long stretch of road that led to their subdivision. "Not always do the three-hour class. Maybe only go to three classes instead of four every week."

Her mother looked shocked. "Where is this coming from? Are you worried about the cost?"

Chloe was actually starting to realize that she'd been taking the cost of her classes for granted. Thinking about Finn cleaning tables at the diner made the feeling even more pronounced. "I'm not even sure why I'm dancing so much anyway. I mean, it's not like I'm going to go join the Joffrey Ballet or anything."

"You love to dance. You're good at it—oh, you're amazing at it. You have a gift, honey, and you need to use your talents."

"But—"

"Who's to say you won't use all this ballet when you get to college or even after? Maybe you'll want to be in one of those community theaters, or you could teach ballet."

"What? So I can teach more girls to dance nonstop for nothing?" The minute she said the words, Chloe winced. "Sorry. I didn't mean to sound like that."

Her mother's hands tightened on the steering wheel. "Maybe we need to shelve this discussion for another day."

"Fine."

When her mother stopped at a stoplight, she said, "Did you finish your homework?"

"Yep. I finished it at the diner." Thinking about Finn again, she said, "Hey Mom? I met this Amish boy there. He's been working at Lane's."

"An Amish boy is working there? That's unusual."

"His aunt and uncle run the diner."

"Oh, that makes sense, then." Her mother glanced at her. "Have you two been chatting?"

"Yeah. He's really nice. Shy, though."

Her mother smiled softly. "Maybe he's just not used to being in the English workplace. Even if it's his aunt's and uncle's, talking to English people all day long could be strange."

"Maybe, but he kind of seems to like it."

"Well, that's good. It's nice you're being nice to him."

"It's not hard to do. But, ah, Mom . . . I think I offended him when I asked him about school."

"You're a smart girl, dear. Maybe he's seen some of your assignments and is intimidated. Or not."

"I think I overheard a conversation with some men. I could've been wrong but I think he's thinking about leaving his house because his dad isn't nice to him."

Her mother frowned. "I hope that's not the case, but you're old enough to know that not everyone has a great relationship with their parents."

"I hope he's going to be okay."

Pulling into their garage, she smiled. "It sounds like you two are becoming friends. That's nice."

"So . . . you don't think it's strange that I've become friends with Finn?"

"No, Chloe. I'd rather you be friends with all sorts of people than not. If he's nice and you like him, that's all that matters." Her mother shrugged. "That's just my opinion." Her mother smiled. "Now, go take a hot bath and let me see your feet when you get out. I'll help you bandage them."

"Thanks, Mom."

"That's what I'm here for. We've got each other, right?"

"Right."

It was just her and her mom. And she and her dad too. It wasn't bad anymore. They'd finally all settled in, and it was

93

almost normal, especially since her dad had broken things off with the woman he'd been dating, Sandy.

Grabbing her backpack, she slowly followed her mother into the house. Thinking about Finn. Thinking about how she'd told him that she'd thought they were becoming friends.

And how he hadn't told her if he felt the same way.

CHAPTER 13

Bo was babysitting Chance again.

The previous afternoon, Lincoln had planted himself in Bo's office, gone through a couple of other items of business, and then looked Bo directly in the eye and asked that Bo give a little more attention to the kid.

Bo told Lincoln that he would. It wasn't like he'd had much of a choice, but he probably would've done it even if Lincoln hadn't asked. Chance was kind of a lost soul and needed someone to keep an eye on him.

But that didn't mean Bo was all that thrilled about having a new shadow. Especially when Chance was asking about things that were none of his business.

"What's going on between you and Joy?" Chance asked the next evening. "If you don't mind me asking."

They'd spent most of the afternoon over at one of the houses they were remodeling. Seth and his crew were putting up sheetrock, and he and Chance had helped them out for far longer than he'd planned on.

Now it was dark out and they were almost back to T-DOT on Edgewater Road. Bo was tired and he'd absolutely had enough of interacting with the guys for one day.

Realizing that Chance was still staring at him, waiting for an answer, Bo clenched the steering wheel a little tighter. He was annoyed. It was none of Chase's business.

The fact was that he *did* mind Chase asking about Joy. Just because he'd been willing to drive the kid around didn't mean that he was eager to start discussing his personal life with him.

"Why are you asking?"

Chance's eyes widened. "No reason. I just was asking. I mean, you two seemed close."

"She's my friend."

"Gotcha."

Even though the discussion was essentially over, Bo felt the need to clarify things a little bit further. "Joy is a single mom with an ex who doesn't seem to be all that involved. She deserves to have someone to look out for her, so I figured that it might as well be me. Understand?" He was annoyed that he had to say anything at all. Bo liked to keep his private life separate from work, but it didn't always work out that way.

"Yep."

Bo pursed his lips. It was obvious the kid wasn't going to say anything more, but Bo couldn't help continuing. "Look, all I'm saying is that I've taken a personal interest in Joy Howard. Don't you forget to treat her with respect, yeah?"

"I'm not a kid, right? I don't need you to teach me how to respect people. And she's teaching me to read. I'm not going to go mess that up, right? That's the last thing I want to do."

"Just wanted you to be aware," Bo said as he parked.

"I heard you loud and clear." Chance exited, nodded to a couple of guys on the front porch, then headed inside.

Watching him saunter on his way like he had something to prove made Bo clench his jaw. Why did every person he came in contact with recently want to make him want to lose control? He really needed to get a handle on himself, and the sooner the better.

While he would've liked nothing more than to back out of the parking lot and head home, Bo didn't have that luxury. He had other guys to talk to, and he needed to give Mason and Seth a break. Tomorrow afternoon he was supposed to stop by Renegade for a fitting for an upcoming photo shoot. Then the next morning, he was finally going to see Joy for breakfast then sit in a bunch of meetings about the guys who were about to transition out of T-DOT.

Already exhausted by things he hadn't even done, he got out of his truck and headed toward the house. After shooting the breeze to the guys on the porch, he walked inside and found Mason sitting at a table in the living room. Usually everyone played poker there, but at the moment, the guy was staring at a stack of papers.

He looked up in relief when Bo approached. "Hey."

"What's that?"

"Some of these invoices aren't making sense. I'm trying to figure out if it's me or if we've got a problem."

"Want me to take a look?"

"Thanks, but not yet. Adrian is going to help me go through them."

They'd learned that Adrian was some kind of math genius. Knowing he would likely be able to figure things out in half the time, Bo left it at that and went to the back room, where he needed to look through more of his own paperwork. Glad to only be surrounded by papers, he tuned everything out, determined to get through as much as he could in the next hour.

Just as he stacked the papers to one side, he heard a bunch of shouting, followed by a crash.

He rushed out to see none other than Chance and Grafton trying to kill each other in the middle of the living room. Five or six guys were standing around rooting for one or the other like the space was an abandoned parking lot.

He walked over to Mason. Mason was leaning against the wall and simply watching, just like the fight was on TV instead of directly in front of them.

Bo raised his eyebrows. "What the heck?"

"Yeah, I know what you're thinking, but these guys have been chewing on each other for days now. I figure we might as well get it over with."

"In the middle of the living room?"

Mason shrugged. "They know the drill. They break it, they've got to fix or replace it."

"Lincoln's going to hold them to that."

"I am too." When Grafton's fist connected with Chance's jaw, Mason winced. "That had to hurt."

"Mason. We've gotta get involved."

"You can if you want, but I'm tired of treating them like they don't have a clue."

Watching Chance pull Grafton down to the floor, Bo whistled low. "They kind of don't."

"What brought this on, anyway? I was with Chance all afternoon. We hung sheetrock with Seth on the new house on Adams. He seemed fine."

"Yeah. I'm sure he did. He only falls apart when he doesn't have a babysitter." Mason sighed. "Chance isn't all that good with time on his hands."

"And Grafton?"

Mason rolled his eyes. "Grafton's just an idiot."

When the coffee table cracked, Bo stuck two fingers in his mouth and whistled, drawing the attention of everyone in the room. "The party's over. Everybody, go someplace else. Grafton, Chance, come on over here." When both looked ready to protest, Bo interrupted. "Now."

Five minutes later, Mason and Bo were sitting on one side of the poker table and Grafton and Chance were sitting on the other. It was hard to say which of the four of them wanted to be there least. Mason looked fed up. Grafton and Chance were ticked off and out of breath.

And Bo? Well, he was more confused than anything. "Do I even want to know what set you two off?"

"Ask him," Chance said. "I just got here."

Dutifully Bo turned to Grafton. "Well?"

Grafton shrugged. "It weren't nothing. We were just messing around."

"Don't play that game with me," Bo said. "I'm not a guard in the prison yard. My job is to make sure you don't go back to prison, which means you've got to get your act together. What happened?"

"Chance was asking me about Molly. I know he asked just to mess with me too."

"I wasn't doing anything." Chance turned to Bo. "I was just thinking about you and Joy and started thinking that it's got to be hard to find a girl who sticks around. I mean, other than Lincoln and his wife. Her name's Jennifer, right?"

"Don't you start thinking about Lincoln and Jennifer," Mason warned.

"And while you're at it, stop thinking about Joy too," Bo added.

Chance's cheeks flushed. "Fine. I won't ask anyone about anything."

Bo glanced at Grafton. He was still breathing hard, and his hands were clenched. "Calm down, Grafton."

"Whatever."

Mason sighed. "Here's the deal. Real life on the outside ain't like life inside. If someone nudges you in the middle of the grocery store, it's probably nothing more than they weren't watching where they were going. If someone asks you about a girl or whatever, it doesn't automatically mean that they want to start a fight. You guys need to get some perspective."

"Can we be done?" Grafton bit out.

Bo exchanged a look with Mason. It seemed like their little discussion wasn't over yet. "Chance, go clean up the living room. I'll send Grafton out to help in a minute."

Chance gave Grafton a wary look then headed over to the coffee table. When Bo saw he was occupied, he lowered his voice. "Grafton, you've got to get a handle on things. You've been out three months and you haven't found your bearings yet."

"I can't help it. I miss Molly." Meeting Mason's eyes, he added, "I'm not cut out for this."

"You'll find another girl," Mason said.

"I'm not talking about that. I'm talking about this." He waved a hand. "I don't want to keep meeting with you and working and dealing with all your rules. Putting up with kids like Chance."

"If you drop out, we can't let you back in."

"I don't want to come back."

"I also won't be able to run interference between you and your parole officer," Bo warned. "You'll be on your own."

"I don't need your help." Before Bo could respond, he added, "Every guy who gets out doesn't come over here. They do just fine." Grafton crossed his arms over his chest. "Who ran interference between you and your parole officer?"

"No one."

"See? If you can do it, I can too."

"Are you sure about this?" Mason asked.

"Yeah. I'm sure."

There was a new hint of anxiousness in Grafton's eyes, but Bo didn't try to convince him to stay. Besides, the guy was firmly under Mason's watch, and it was obvious that Mason had had enough of his antics.

Mason stared hard at Grafton, then finally seemed to come to a conclusion. "All right, then. Let me grab a form for you to sign."

Grafton frowned. "That's it?"

"Yeah. When I talked to you in Madisonville, I said this program was a voluntary thing. I didn't lie. No one's forcing you to stay." Mason walked to a cabinet, unlocked the door, and pulled out a form. "Here you go. As soon as you sign it, you're done."

Finally, *finally* the consequences of walking away from T-DOT seemed to sink in. "I, ah think I'm going to wait on this for a minute. Maybe I just need a week off or something. You know, like a break."

Bo had heard all kinds of excuses for why guys didn't want to stick around and "needing a break" was at the top of the list. The problem was most of the guys' definitions for "a break" involved the kind of stuff that got them in the pen in the first place.

He shook his head. "Breaks aren't how T-DOT works, Grafton. You're either in the program or you aren't. T-DOT stands for 'Tomorrow Depends on Today,' right? You can't want to toe the line only sometimes. You've got to be committed."

"So I've got to decide now?"

"You're the one who brought this up, not us," Mason said. "It's getting late. Either help pick up this room and settle down or sign the release, get your stuff, and get on out of here."

"Where's Lincoln? Maybe he'll—"

Bo had had enough. Grafton wasn't a kid. He marched over and leaned his face close to Grafton's. "You've already pushed me as far as I want to be pushed tonight," he said, his voice low and menacing. "You piss me off some more, you're going to regret it."

Grafton's eyes widened before his ego kicked in. He twisted, obviously wanting to fight Bo.

Bo's temper flared at that—which just went to show Bo that he might try to be a good man, but he still had a long way to go before he was gonna be a son his mother could be proud of. He stepped to one side, grabbed Grafton's arm, and pulled it behind his back. "You seem to forget that I learned a few things in prison too. Now, either grow up and settle down or get your stuff and leave." He released him and stepped back, an expression of stern warning plastered on his face.

Grafton took a deep breath. For a moment, it looked like he was about to say something, but then he changed his mind. He walked over, picked up two chairs, then strode up the stairs.

"That guy is going to drive me to drink," Mason muttered.

A couple more men had appeared, and all of them watched Grafton head to his room on the second floor.

"Is he staying or going?" Charlie asked.

"I reckon he's staying. At least for now."

Charlie stared up at the empty stairs for a long moment. When he faced Bo, it was obvious that he'd come to terms with something. "If he doesn't calm down about that girl, I doubt Grafton's going to make it much longer. He's too emotional. In two months, he's either going to be dead or back behind bars."

Bo hoped that wasn't the case, but he knew it was out of

his hands. He wasn't the guy's mother, and he wasn't God. "I'm out of here. I'll be back around noon tomorrow."

Once he was alone, he hung his head. He'd lost his temper with that idiot. It hadn't been his best moment, not by a long shot. Feeling a twisted combination of disappointment with the way things had gone and relief that he could finally go home, he walked out to his truck.

Days like this made Bo wish he'd tried harder to go home to Kentucky.

CHAPTER 14

It was five minutes to seven and Joy was calling herself ten kinds of a fool. She'd known better than to give Bo her address. He might be sweet and seem normal, but it wasn't like she knew him all that well. He could be a master of manipulation too. After all, he'd been in prison. That was not an insignificant thing.

And now he knew where she lived.

Pacing her living room, she tried to pull herself together. She was overreacting. And it wasn't like she lived in a mansion. It was just a three-bedroom ranch in the middle of a quiet cul-de-sac. Even her street's name—Sycamore Circle—wasn't anything special. Pretty generic and run-of-the-mill.

She didn't have much worth stealing, anyway.

From the moment she'd gotten up she'd been going over a handful of scenarios in her head. Sometimes she would let Bo inside. In other ones, he didn't show up at all. Then there was everything else in between.

So, she'd cleaned the entryway and kitchen, just in case he did come inside.

Her doorbell rang.

Taking a deep breath, Joy peeked through the window on the top of her door, saw Bo's familiar face, and pulled open the door.

His gorgeous eyes fastened on hers a mere second before he smiled. "Morning."

"Hi."

"You get your girl off to school okay?"

"Yes. Her bus leaves early, but she's a morning person. I'm glad I never have to fight with her much about getting out of bed."

He grinned. "My momma would've enjoyed a day in your shoes. She'd wake me up and then have to wake me up again ten minutes later."

"I'm glad Chloe doesn't put me through that. She's wonderful about getting up. Her only problem is that she leaves her stuff everywhere. I'm constantly tripping over various pairs of shoes."

"I'm one of four. So my momma had her hands full. It's a blessing that the others were easier to raise than I was."

Noticing that one of her neighbors was walking by very slowly, and obviously taking in the fact that Joy was chatting with someone new right on her front door stoop, she stepped backward. "Would you like to come in for a second?" She could practically feel her conscience flip out. Hadn't she just been telling herself that Bo could be a dangerous criminal?

"Sure." He glanced out at the street before closing the door. When he faced her again, his expression looked a little less open. "You worried about someone seeing me here, Joy?"

There was a slight edge to his voice. She realized he thought she was embarrassed to be seen with him. "I'm trying to hold off the gossip about me having a man here."

"No one's used to you dating?"

"No." She paused, wondering how to phrase the situation without making herself sound pathetic. "When Tony left four years ago, everyone was pretty shocked about our breakup. The gossip mill got busy, and everyone speculated about why he didn't want to stay married to me. None of the ideas were very flattering."

"Wait, your neighbors blamed you?"

Even more embarrassed, she shrugged. "It's the normal route people go, right? I mean, if a man leaves a marriage, there had to be something he was missing."

"Yeah, they do that . . . if they're idiots. Joy, I'm telling you right now, whatever made your ex decide to lose his mind and leave you, it sure wasn't your fault. You . . . you are real special. He was lucky to have you."

His praise embarrassed her. "After you get to know me more, you might change your mind." She made sure he knew she was joking, but there was a part of her that was serious too. Tony's betrayal ran deep.

"I know you're kidding, but I'm not. You're worth sticking around for, Joy. I know it."

Her whole body was turning to mush. It had been so long since she'd had a defender, she didn't know how to handle it. "Let me get my purse and, um, a jacket. I'll be right back."

She hurried down the hall to her bedroom and pulled on a tan suede jacket. She admired her outfit in the mirror—fitted jeans, a loose white oxford shirt, the tan suede jacket, and some soft suede loafers. No doubt she looked like exactly who she was—a suburban mom who kept herself in reasonably good shape. She had put on two thin necklaces and three bangles. It made her feel a little more fancy, a little less like she was ready for the carpool lane.

When she returned to the entryway, Bo was standing near the front door texting something on his phone.

Why had she assumed that he'd want to wander all over her house, exploring for new pieces of her?

"I'm ready."

He stuffed his phone in a jeans pocket. "Me too."

He opened the front door and stood by as she carefully locked it, then stayed by her side until they got to the driveway. "Bo, you've got a BMW?"

"It's an old one, but it's held up good."

"It's pretty."

"It is." He opened the passenger door for her.

"I'm surprised you don't have a truck."

"I've got one of those too. It's almost as old as this Beamer."

After he was buckled in and pulling out, she said, "I guess you really like cars."

"Not really. Like I told you, I drive a lot of ex-cons around. I'm not going to take them out in this." He paused. "And I reckon I'm not real eager to have you in that truck. You deserve better than that, yeah?"

She shrugged. "I don't mind trucks. I am hungry, though. Are you?"

"Always. Now, did you decide where you want to eat?"

"I don't have anywhere special in mind. Do you?"

"Well, I thought if you didn't have a preference, I'd take you over to the diner on Claybourne Boulevard. Katherine's, I think it's called. Have you been there?"

"Once. I liked it. That sounds good."

"All right, then." He shifted and continued to drive.

She watched him, liking how easily he handled the manual transmission. She also liked how easy he drove, even when they came upon a little bit of traffic. Tony was a good driver but also an intense one. He was always commenting on someone else's driving ability or complaining about traffic.

At a stop light, Bo glanced her way. "You went quiet on me. Everything good?"

"Yes. I . . . well, I guess I was just thinking about how the traffic doesn't seem to bother you."

"It's just cars, right? No big deal." When the light turned, he shifted back into first, then second. "What about you? Do you get tired of fighting traffic?"

"We're out in the country so there's not that much. But no. It's part of my job. I meet all my students at a mutually agreed upon place. Some are closer than others."

"But they're all public, safe places, right?"

She nodded. "They're not all places like Sacred Grounds, but most are safe. It's the nature of the job though. I mean, no one is going to get together with a tutor if they mean to do her harm."

His jaw worked. "Do you have someone looking out for you? You know, making sure that whoever you're meeting with is safe?"

"Everyone fills out a form. It's good."

"What about your schedule? Someone know where you are?"

"Bo, you're starting to scare me. Stop." She laughed.

"I don't want to do that. I guess it's my nature to worry. I know what guys can be like."

"Well, so far it's all good."

He pulled into the Katherine's parking lot. It was more than half filled. "There's a big crowd for so early, don't you think?" she said, looking around the lot.

"It's a popular place." He parked and turned off the ignition. "I'll come around for you."

She unbuckled and watched as he came around, opened her door, and reached for her hand. "Thanks."

He nodded but didn't release her hand. Instead, he shifted his hand so their fingers were linked. Not firm enough that she couldn't pull her hand away.

But she didn't.

It had been so long since she'd held a man's hand. Even when she was still married to Tony it had been a while since he'd done anything like take her hand or hold it while they were walking.

"Two, Katie," he said when they entered.

"Hi, Bo." The hostess looked over Joy from head to toe, seeming to linger on their linked hands. "How about in the booth near the back?"

He turned to her. "Are you good with that, Joy?"

"Yes. Of course."

After allowing her to walk in front of him, Bo stood until she got settled before getting into the booth across from her. After the waitress brought them two cups of coffee, Joy smiled at him again. "You're the most mannerly guy I've ever gone out with."

"Tony didn't look out for you?"

"No, he did. But not like that." Thinking about how she'd put up with so many things from her ex, she murmured, "Now I'm kind of wondering if I never thought it was possible."

"That's a shame."

It was a shame. She opened the menu. "I can't decide what to eat. I was going to get an omelet, but everyone's waffles look so good."

He flashed a smile. "I was thinking the same thing."

After they ordered, her phone beeped. "Let me check this. Sometimes the school—"

She shivered when she saw the text.

I see you with him. You
can't hide.

"What was that?"

"Nothing."

When he simply stared at her, silently conveying that he
didn't believe that, she explained. "Somebody started sending
me weird texts from an anonymous number."

"That's what that was?" When she nodded, he glared at the
phone. "What did it say?"

Her inclination was to push it aside, but she was freaked
out and couldn't hide it. So she ran a finger across the screen,
punched in her security code, and then clicked back on the
message.

When he read the words, his expression turned even darker.
"You've been getting a lot of these?"

She nodded. "About one a day."

"Girl. Did you call the police?"

"Of course not. What could they do?"

He looked at her like she was sixteen-year-old Chloe. "They
could try to trace the number so you wouldn't have to wonder
who it was. Or they could take your worries seriously, give you
advice, and maybe even give you some peace of mind. They
could even start driving by your house from time to time."

His list made so much sense, she was embarrassed that she
hadn't stopped by the police station. To save face—at least with
herself—she said, "You and I both know that even if they do all
that, nothing is likely to come of it. It's just some creepy guy."

"One creepy guy texting you is one too many, Joy."

She sighed but she didn't argue. Especially since she was pretty sure he was right. "The truth is that I've been kind of hoping that they'd stop on their own."

"Hope ain't a game plan, sweetheart."

Meeting his gaze and seeing both his concern and the seriousness that was shining in his eyes, she nodded. "I have a feeling you're right."

The reality was that someone was watching her, and he wasn't going to go away on his own.

CHAPTER 15

Bo was pretty sure that driving Joy directly back to her house after all that was the wrong thing to do. Their breakfast hadn't exactly ended on a good note, and there was a tension between them that hadn't been there before.

He suspected there was a good chance that he wasn't going to see Joy Howard again once he'd dropped her off. And he really wanted to see her again.

Joy opened the car door the moment he'd put his car in Park. "Thank you for breakfast," she said as she got out. She treated him to a fake smile too. The kind women gave to security guards and annoying salespeople. Like she was glad for his place in her world, but she didn't want them to connect on a regular basis.

On another morning, his pride might have gotten a little pinched. That minute though, he was veering somewhere between frustrated and annoyed.

"Hold up, Joy," he barked.

When she stilled, he scrambled out of his vehicle. "Do you think I'm just gonna sit her and wave goodbye to you like I'm in the carpool lane?"

She pursed her lips. "No. I mean . . . Bo, it's not necessary that you walk me to the door. We're not on a date."

Bo frowned. "It was a date to me. We made plans, I picked you up, we drove to the diner, had a meal, and now I'm dropping you off. It wasn't a date to you?"

"No, you're right. It was." She opened her purse and pulled out her keys. "But, um, I still need to go."

"I get that you're anxious to get inside, but would you please give me a minute?"

Her expression fell. "Yeah. I'm sorry. I . . . I don't know what's wrong with me."

Unable to help himself, he brushed back a piece of her hair that had settled against her cheek. "Is it me or the texting that's got you so spun up?"

"Maybe both?" She ran her teeth over her bottom lip. "I kind of feel like I'm in over my head—but I'm not even sure what, exactly, I'm stuck in."

He smiled. "As hard as you are on a man's pride . . . I reckon I feel the same way."

She pushed her hair behind her ear and sighed softly. "Yeah, right."

As much as he wanted to touch her, he remained still. "Joy, in case you didn't notice, I really like you. I'm trying to go slow and not scare you off, but being so patient isn't in my nature. All this is new for me too. Give me a chance, okay?"

Her brown eyes warmed on his. "I want to."

"Good. And I'm happy to help you deal with the texts and the police. All you have to do is ask."

"I can go there by myself, Bo. I can take care of myself."

He was disappointed she wasn't taking him up on his offer, but he supposed he shouldn't have expected anything different. "Let me know what happens, okay?"

Looking more at peace, she nodded. "Okay."

"All right. I'll let you go." Before she could move away, he pressed his lips to her forehead. Allowed himself to breathe in her sweet perfume for a split second before giving her space. "Have a good day."

"You too."

He grinned as he turned away. As first dates went, it wasn't exactly all that good, but it had turned out better than he'd feared it might for a while. He'd take it.

Instead of going home, he drove over to Lincoln's. He needed some relationship advice, and he didn't want to ask either of his sisters. He hoped both Lincoln and his wife Jennifer were available, because if they weren't, he was going to lose his mind.

He knew exactly what Joy meant when she'd admitted to feeling in over her head. He felt the same way. He had no clue how to date a woman like her. All of his former girlfriends had either just wanted a good time or to be taken care of.

On the other hand, Joy was as far from being a good-time girl as a woman could get. She could also take care of herself just fine. She didn't really seem to appreciate it when he acted like she could use his help or advice.

He had to figure out how to be the man he was without scaring her or driving her away.

"Too bad you didn't think about that earlier, Sam," he muttered to himself. "If you hadn't gotten all in her grill, she might not have been so freaked out."

After she'd shown him the text, it had been more than obvious that Joy was uncomfortable with not only showing it to him but also his anger about it. He reminded himself that he was trying to develop a relationship with her. The last thing he'd wanted to do was bring her another source of discomfort.

But he'd still had the urge to ask her a hundred questions and spend the rest of the day trying to figure out which one of her clients was giving her grief—it had to be one of her clients. Right?

He was relieved to see both Jennifer's and Lincoln's vehicles in their driveway when he arrived at their house. He parked behind Jennifer's Toyota, checked his phone, and then got out.

Lincoln opened the door before Bo had time to knock. "I saw you pull up," he said. "What's going on?"

"I need some advice."

Lincoln frowned. "Don't we have a meeting at the house later?"

"Yeah, but this is personal. That okay? I wanted to get Jennifer's perspective too. Is she available?"

"She should be. She's putting Hunt down for his morning nap. Have a seat."

Bo sat down, listening to Lincoln's deep voice softly speak to his wife. Sometimes when he heard or saw his boss talk to her it caught him by surprise. The John Lincoln Bennett he'd known before Jennifer hadn't taken much flak from anyone and had been unafraid to make sure everyone knew it.

He wondered if it was love that had changed Lincoln or merely the passage of time. Bo had always been more mellow than Lincoln, but he'd never had the aura around him that his friend seemed to have now. Lincoln was content. Bo was starting to wonder if he was content—or maybe he wasn't capable of it. He didn't know.

"Hi, Bo," Jennifer called out as she came downstairs. "I heard you missed talking to me."

He loved seeing her confident smile. She was so different than the woman he'd first met several years before.

He stood up to greet her. "Are you trying to get me in trouble, girly?" he teased.

She reached out and gave him a hug. "Not necessarily. But I've missed you too. If I had known you were coming, I would've made you some cinnamon rolls."

He smiled. She'd served him and Mason a warm plate of rolls the first time he'd shoveled her driveway. "I would've enjoyed that, but well, I came over here for some advice."

She sat down. "I'm happy to give you free advice too." Looking at the coffee table, she frowned. "Did John not offer you anything to drink? Do you want some coffee or a glass of water?"

"A glass of water sounds good. But I'll get it."

"You sit. John's on his way down. He'll want a glass too."

Yet again, he seated himself, waiting while Lincoln crooned—or whatever he was doing—over his progeny upstairs and Jennifer got him a drink.

He wondered how his life with Joy would be if they ever became a couple. Would she be the type to fuss like this over company? He didn't know if he cared if she was or not—it was just another thing he realized he didn't know about Joy.

"So what's going on?" Lincoln asked after Jennifer brought over some glasses of water and the three of them were sitting together.

"I met a woman."

Jennifer smiled tentatively. "Oh?"

Lincoln laughed. "She's being kind, Bo. What she's really wanting to know is if this woman is any better than Tami." He cocked an eyebrow. "Is she?"

"Yes." He didn't hold back from rolling his eyes. He and Tami had had more of a "friends with benefits" thing for a very short time. He'd never intended Jennifer and her to ever meet. "I didn't date her long."

"I didn't know if you dated her at all," Lincoln laughed. "I thought she was your late-night hookup."

"Tami and me were in complete agreement about our . . . uh, plans." He cleared his throat. "However, to answer your question, Jennifer, yes. Joy is very different."

"Her name is Joy?"

"Yeah. It's pretty, right? Plus, she has a daughter named Chloe."

"She has a baby girl?"

"Not exactly. Chloe's sixteen. Joy's divorced."

"So she's older," Jennifer murmured. "How old is she?"

"Thirty-six. Why?"

"No reason. I'm just asking."

"She a nice lady. She lives over on Sycamore Circle. You know that area? All the streets are named after trees and such? It's like Mayberry over there."

Lincoln propped a foot over the opposite knee. "Now what's going on? Does she not trust you or something because of your background?"

"She knows I'm an ex-con. That ain't it." He rolled his shoulders. "I feel bad for her. I feel like her, uh, ex-husband wasn't too attentive." Maybe if he felt more secure with him and Joy, he would feel like sharing that her ex-husband broke up with her because he wanted to move on to better pastures. That felt like too much to share just yet.

Jennifer's expression softened as she looked at her husband. "If he wasn't attentive, maybe it's good they're not together anymore."

"I don't know. So anyway, I've got that going for me. She's older, has a kid, has an ex, and is a literacy tutor. And some kind of artist too. She paints."

"You have just as much going on. It sounds like the two of you are a good match too."

"She's worried and I don't want to rush her." That was where question one was embedded, he reckoned.

"Then don't rush her," Lincoln murmured. "If she's the one, and you've waited all this time to find her, then let her set the timeline."

"There's just a problem."

"What is that?" Jennifer asked.

"She's getting hang ups and creepy text messages."

Lincoln frowned. "From who? The ex-husband?"

"No. From unknown numbers." He waved a hand. "And they could be from anyone. Plus, she drives all around God's green earth, meeting strangers in odd places."

"Because of her tutoring job?"

"Yeah." Hating the idea of her being out in the world alone, he scowled. "She needs a keeper—or at least someone keeping tabs on her. I mean, someone needs to know when and where she's meeting clients, right?"

Lincoln's lips twitched. "Are you volunteering for that position?"

"It doesn't matter if I am or I'm not. Because if I start doing what I think I should—which is put a stop to all of her gallivanting around . . . I'm going to lose her and I don't even have her yet."

Lincoln leaned back. "Whoa. You've got yourself twisted up into knots there, Bo."

"I've come to that same conclusion." He cleared his throat. "Jennifer, what do you think? I need a woman's perspective."

"Does she know how you feel?"

"About what?"

"About all of it. Does she know that you really like her, Bo?"

"She should. I'm afraid I've been obvious."

"Well, then . . . does she know that you're worried about her? And that your advice and such comes from that concern?"

"I couldn't say."

Her expression softened again. "What did you say when she told you about the messages?"

"I told her to call the police. At least then they'd have a record of her complaints." Feeling like he might as well admit everything, he added, "Actually, I told her that I'd be happy to take her to the station. Which, by the way, isn't exactly my favorite place to visit."

"Did she like that idea?"

"She did not. Not even a little bit."

Lincoln frowned. "I'm not sure what Jennifer thinks, but I think you're going to have to learn to back off. Just as you said, Joy isn't going to be pleased with you telling her what to do. Even if you're sure you're in the right."

"So I'm stuck."

Jennifer smiled at her husband before turning back to him. "Your problems remind me a lot of some of the things Lincoln and I went through. Giving up independence is hard. So is leaning on other people. I used to worry that if I leaned too hard on someone I might fall."

"I wouldn't let her fall."

"Oh, Bo. You know that and I know that." Looking a little sad, she added, "Joy might even want to think that. But to lean on you, she has to trust you, and trust is something you have to earn over time." She folded her arms across her middle. "Bo, why do you like her? No, better yet, how did you first know that you liked her?"

He answered immediately. "Her voice. The way she was tutoring this guy and making him feel like he was worth something."

"I could be wrong, but I think if you'd seen her in a fancier spot, surrounded by people making sure she was safe and not tutoring . . . you might not have given her a second glance. Right?"

"You might be."

"Well, if I am . . . and the very things that make her vulnerable are the things you admire—don't you think it's time you gave that some credence? It sounds to me that she's been doing all right on her own. Maybe she doesn't need you being her watchdog."

"So . . . step back." It wasn't what he wanted to do, but maybe he could equate it to taking cough medicine or something. It wasn't exactly pleasant, but the end result made it worthwhile.

Jennifer reached for Lincoln's hand. "Maybe it's more like step out of her way but linger close by. I have a feeling she's going to like having you near."

"Be close but not too close. Got it." He didn't, really, though. As much as he wanted to walk that tightrope like a pro, he figured it was more likely that he'd fall flat on his face. After all, hadn't he already messed things up too much in his life for that? Jenny had dropped him, his brother had written him off, and he certainly caused his sisters and momma their fair share of tears.

Lincoln chuckled. "If you're able to do all that, this woman is gonna lead you on a merry dance, buddy."

"I can't wait to meet Joy," Jennifer said. "If you're willing to work so hard to make things work then she must be special."

"She is. You'd like her. You both would." He picked up his glass of water and drained it. He hoped he and Joy would one day get to that point.

One day soon.

CHAPTER 16

After delivering two paintings, giving one tutoring session, and taking a trip to the grocery store, Joy couldn't wait to get home and relax before she had to run Chloe to her dance class. She'd splurged at the bookstore recently and had a growing TBR pile.

She pulled onto her street already mentally sorting through her stack of books . . . then was brought up short by the Buick in the driveway.

Her mom had come for a visit.

Pulling in behind the car, she wondered where her mother was, then realized that she'd let herself in.

Joy really hated when she did that.

After maneuvering around the vehicle, she pulled into the garage then finally gathered her things.

The sound of the vacuum running greeted her when she walked into the house. "Mom? Mom, are you in here?"

"Hi, honey," she called down. Just as if Joy should've

expected her to be there. "I'm vacuuming the upstairs hallway. I'll be right down."

Joy pulled off her jacket and shoes then wandered into the kitchen, looking for clues to tell her how long her mother had been inside. Since the kitchen was clean, at least an hour.

As always, her irritation warred with her gratitude for the help. It was hard being a single mom, especially since she had neither a set schedule nor a "usual" week. Lots of things never got done and there were times when the house absolutely looked like it. So, her mother was a lifesaver in that regard.

But did she appreciate these pop-up visits? No. No, she did not.

Her mother came downstairs just about the time Joy got the last of the frozen food put away. "Hey, honey," she said.

"Hi, Mom." Like always, her mother was wearing jeans, tennis shoes, and one of her many national park sweatshirts. She said she'd given up dressy clothes when she turned fifty and Joy was pretty sure she had kept up that promise to herself. She looked comfortable and fit.

And . . . maybe a little bit guilty too?

Was it wrong that Joy felt a little glad about that?

Her mom stuffed her hands in her jeans' pockets. "Joy, I know you don't like me showing up out of the blue, but I promise I didn't come over here to spy on you or get in your way."

"I don't think you're spying, but you are being inconsiderate. You can't just come over and let yourself in whenever you feel like it."

"Oh, I wasn't doing that today. I just happened to be in the neighborhood when I decided to stop by to see if you wanted to grab a late lunch. When you didn't answer, I decided to write you a note—and drop off a cute little card and gift certificate I got for Chloe." She paused. "And then I noticed your kitchen counters."

"So you decided to clean them? And do the dishes? And vacuum?"

"One thing led to another." She frowned. "I know you don't want me fussing with your things. I didn't go near your bedroom or laundry."

She felt her cheeks heat. The first time her mother had done this, Joy had come home and discovered her mother pulling her lingerie out of the dryer. Joy had been so horrified, she'd given her mom a mouthful—and her mother had never forgotten it.

"I appreciate the help. I can't keep up with everything the way I'd like, and that's obvious. But that doesn't mean it's okay for you to wander around without me here."

"Do you want me to leave now?"

"So close to Chloe coming home? Of course not. Come on. Want a Coke?"

"Sure. I want a soda—and I want to hear all about what you've been doing."

Grabbing two cans of soda, Joy sat down on the couch. "I've been working and running Chloe around." There was no way she was going to mention anything about her breakfast with Bo—or about the weird texts. "What about you? Are you planning anything fun? Have you seen Alice or Rand lately?"

"As a matter of fact, Dad and I are working on our next trip."

"Which national park are you gonna go see?" Her parents had picked up a National Park Passport booklet and were now happily in the process of getting as many stamps as they possibly could.

Her mother's brown eyes—the exact same shade as Joy's— lit up. "We're debating between going to see some missions in San Antonio, Crater Lake, or the Everglades."

"Talk about three different places."

"I know! Dad says that it's time we stepped outside our comfort zone."

"What do you want to do?"

"I'm leaning toward San Antonio. If we go there, we can go on the river walk and eat Tex-Mex."

"That's hard to beat."

"And no, I haven't seen either your brother or your sister lately. Alice is busy selling houses, you know. She's gotten so successful. I'm sure you're as proud of her as Dad and I are."

"I am." Joy was proud of Alice too. She just wished that Alice's good marriage, happy children, and successful job didn't sometimes make her feel like her life was a little bit wanting. Pushing off that negative thought, she smiled. "And Rand? How's he?"

"And . . . Rand is in love." Her mother sounded like she'd just eaten a bunch of lemon juice.

"Mom, what's wrong with that?"

"We met her. She's not who we would've expected him to date."

"What happened to stepping outside your comfort zone? Maybe she's really nice."

"She's not." She lowered her voice. "Your father and I are worried that your brother's going through some midlife crisis."

It was all Joy could do not to roll her eyes. "What's the woman's name?"

"Candy."

She did her best not to grin. "That's cute."

"It's not that cute." She sighed. "I don't know, dear. I'm trying to be open-minded but sometimes I guess I'm more comfortable when things are as I expected."

Her mother's comment stung. Though they'd come around, their first reactions to her divorce hadn't been exactly supportive. "Expectations don't always end up how you want them to be."

"I know. I think you have a point too. I mean, Tony certainly ended up being a putz, didn't he?"

"You could say that." Joy usually described him far more colorfully.

"On the bright side, he hasn't turned out to be a terrible *ex*-husband." She sipped her Coke.

Joy knew her mother wasn't wrong. "Tony and I have settled into a good routine. That's true."

Her mother reached out a hand. "You know what? Maybe he's changed. Maybe you and he—"

She wasn't even going to let her mother finish that thought. "No. No, Mom."

"Mom?"

She jumped to her feet. "Hey, Chloe. Look who's here."

"Hi, Grandma." Tossing her backpack on the floor, she trotted over to her grandmother's side and gave her a kiss. "I didn't know you were coming over today."

Sharing a wry look with Joy, she murmured, "Your mother didn't either."

"Grandma, you know you aren't supposed to do that."

"I already got my lecture. You don't need to give me another one." She brightened. "Guess what? I came over to give you something."

"You did? What?"

"I put it in your room. Want to come see?"

"Of course."

As they started up the stairs, Chloe called down. "Hey Mom, don't forget that I have ballet today."

"I haven't forgotten. After you look at your present get changed and I'll get you something to eat." Seconds later, she heard the telltale squeal of a happy gift card recipient. "Grandma! Oh my gosh! Thank you!"

Joy shook her head. Well, it didn't look like her mother had listened to her protests about spoiling Chloe either.

When her phone rang, she glanced at it, then seeing it was Bo, answered. "Hi."

"Hey. You busy?"

"Kind of. I'm about to take my daughter to ballet class."

"Ah."

"Why?"

"No reason."

She wondered if that was the truth—or if he was trying to see if she'd spent the day at the police station. Which she had not. "What are you up to?"

"Nothing too much. Just work stuff. I've got a guy about to be released from here and I've been talking him through some things."

Pushing off her worries, she focused on him. "You really do a good job."

"Sometimes, I don't know. Not like you. Chance couldn't say enough good things about you, by the way."

"He's sweet. I'm seeing him again tomorrow."

"Where?"

"At the library again."

"Ah. Good to know. So, did you stop by the police station?"

"No, I didn't."

She could practically see him trying to weigh his words. "All right."

Ironically, she now felt guilty. "I had a lot of things to do, but I did hear what you said. I'll go by there later this week."

"I hope so." He lowered his voice. "I'm not trying to boss you around, honey. It's just important, yeah? You want to keep safe."

"Joy?" Her mother was standing just two feet away.

Joy jumped. "Um, I'm sorry, but I've got to go."

"I'll text you later, girl."

She got little chill bumps every time he said that. "I hope so. Bye."

"Bye."

What was it about that guy? Without even trying he could lift her spirits and make her feel warm all over.

"Was that Bo?" Chloe asked.

Oh . . . oh, crap. "Um, yes, it was."

As expected, her mother pounced on that tidbit. "Who is Bo?"

Chloe smiled. "Grandma, Mom met a man named Bo and he's been texting her." She waggled her eyebrows.

"You didn't tell me you were dating, Joy."

"I'm not. I'm just, ah, testing the waters."

"What's he like? And is he French?"

French? Where did her mother get that? "Uh no. Why?"

"Beau—or is it short for Beauregard?"

She giggled. "It's short for Beauman. His last name. His real name is Sam but everyone calls him Bo."

"I like Bo better," Chloe said.

"I think I do too. But we should, since he likes it better."

Her mother turned to Chloe. "Do you like this Bo, Chloe?"

"I haven't met him." She winked at her. "I don't think Mom's ready to share him yet."

Oh, for heaven's sake. "It's not that. It's . . . well, I don't know."

"It's good you're being smart and cautious, Joy." Lowering her voice, she added, "He could be like Candy."

"Who's Candy?" Chloe asked.

"Uncle Rand is dating a new woman."

"I guess you don't like her, Grandma?"

"Let's just say she's not my favorite person."

"How come?"

"She's a little rough around the edges, dear."

Thinking that Bo could very well be like Rand's Candy, but also that that wasn't a bad thing, Joy said, "I went to the store and got your favorites, honey. Grab a banana and a protein bar. We've gotta go." Looking at her mom, she added, "You can walk out with us, Mom."

"Fine."

Chloe giggled. "That's what you get for showing up uninvited, Gram. My mom really doesn't like surprises."

"I'm figuring that out, dear," her mother said as the three of them headed out the door.

Joy shook her head but realized she did feel better about most everything. Nothing was perfect but today was going pretty well. And her floors were vacuumed, too. That was a plus.

CHAPTER 17

It was the day that would never end. First, she'd driven almost to Cincinnati to deliver a painting—only to find out that the customer had no intention of paying her upon delivery. When she'd refused to let him pay her in a couple of weeks, he'd gotten angry.

Next thing she knew, he was calling her names. She'd been trembling when she got into her car. It had taken her almost the entire trip home to calm down.

Then, one of her newer tutoring clients hadn't shown up. Though Joy did volunteer work for literacy, she also had a handful of students who paid her for her services. She wasn't sure what had happened to Regina, but Joy was annoyed. It was the second time Regina had booked an appointment then not shown up. It not only messed up Joy's day, but it also hurt her financially. Her weekly budget counted on that money.

Now, as she stood on the driveway with Tony while Chloe

ran back inside for something out of her room, Joy was wishing she was anywhere else.

She was also wishing she hadn't promised herself four years ago to do everything she could to keep a decent relationship with her ex-husband. Tony's sudden interest in her dating life was sure making that hard, though. "Tony, you know I don't want to discuss my personal life."

"Your personal life is my concern. I still care about you." He lowered his voice. "All I'm trying to say is that I'm surprised that you're dating someone."

Everything about that comment rubbed her wrong. After the day she had, she didn't want to let him off the hook. "And why is that?"

He looked uncomfortable. "You know what I mean, hon. You've always put Chloe's needs first. Now you aren't?"

"Me dating has nothing to do with Chloe and it sure isn't interfering with her life."

"She said she doesn't know much about him."

"She probably said that because she doesn't know much."

"Why are you keeping him a secret? Joy, how much do you really know about him, anyway?"

He was driving her crazy. "That isn't any of your business."

"I just don't want to see you hurt."

That was sure rich—considering that he hadn't had any problem breaking her heart several years ago! "Don't worry about me."

"Someone needs to. You run yourself ragged."

She wouldn't have to if she wasn't a single mom and if his lawyer hadn't fought her for every dime he paid in child support and alimony. She would also have more time if he ever volunteered to be more than a one-night-a-week parent.

But all of that had been discussed ad nauseam.

"Tony, I'll see if I can help Chloe find whatever she is looking for and get her out here. Have a good evening."

For a second, she'd been sure he was going to argue but he only nodded instead. "You too, Joy."

Shoving away the wave of irritation she was feeling from the conversation, Joy hurried back into the house. "Chloe! Get a move on."

Chloe poked her head out of her room. "I still can't find my black shrug."

"You're going to have to do without it then."

"Mom, you know I can't do that," she said as she pulled handfuls of leotards and tights out of a drawer. "I came home on the bus instead of running to the diner just to find the stupid thing."

"And your dad came over here just to take you. He's waiting."

"He's going to have to wait another second." Chloe threw open her closet door, got on her hands and knees, and began pulling through a pile of clothes in the back corner. "Miss Diamante said we had to have our shrugs for today's practice."

Looking at the pile of clothes, Joy shuddered. How did one tiny teenaged girl make such a mess? She glanced at her watch. "If you don't get a move on, you're going to be without a shrug *and* show up late for practice."

"You don't understand how important this is."

"I'm afraid I do but it doesn't mean I can help you. I asked you last night to make sure you had everything so I could launder anything that was missing. You said you were good."

"But—"

"Chloe, I'm not going to argue with you. Go on now."

"Hold on. Oh! I found it!" Holding it in a hand, Chloe flew past her, tore down the stairs, and out the door. It stayed open behind her.

"Pick your battles," Joy muttered to herself as she slowly descended the stairs. She stood in the doorway and waved as Tony pulled out and drove down the street.

Chloe might be a mess and Tony might be driving Joy crazy, but at least the two of them were joining forces to give her a break. Boy did she need one.

Relieved to finally have a few minutes to herself, Joy walked down the driveway and retrieved the mail. She flipped through the stack of flyers and catalogs, looking for bills—but then stopped when she noticed she received a letter.

It didn't have a return address.

Curious, she tore open the envelope and unfolded the letter. And then froze.

Two sentences were boldly printed in block letters across the paper.

YOU ARE STILL MINE. I'M NEVER GOING TO LET YOU GO.

Chills ran up her arms as she clenched the paper. Her hand tightened. She was tempted to throw it away, but the words were too frightening.

So was the realization that whoever had sent this now not only knew her phone number but the address of her house.

Bo had been right. She should've already gone to the police station. She needed to get some help.

No, what she really needed was to start letting more people in, instead of always acting like she was fine. She wasn't fine.

Glancing at the paper again, Joy realized that Bo might grumble that she should've already gone to the police, but he'd be at her side as soon as he could.

If he could get away.

Besides, doing nothing no longer felt like an option.

CHAPTER 18

After everything that had happened—all the stress of the missing shrug, and then her father not-so-subtly interrogating Chloe about her mom's dating life—they arrived to discover that Miss Diamanté had canceled class. The story from one of the other dancers was that their teacher had gotten some kind of flu, had determined to power through and teach anyway, and then gotten really sick just a few minutes before class time.

Since Chloe had shown up late, she'd missed all the commotion. She'd simply waved goodbye to her dad, raced inside, and discovered the news when all the other girls were already turning around and leaving.

Maybe a better daughter would've called her father right away and asked him to pick her up, but Chloe wasn't that good. As far as she was concerned, she had two hours of freedom, and there was only one person she wanted to see—Finn. She just hoped he didn't have the day off.

She spied Finn the moment she walked inside. He was wiping down one of the booths near the front.

When he saw her, he tossed down a towel and strode over. "Hiya. What are you doing here so late?"

"My class was canceled because my teacher got some weird stomach thing. So guess what? I have two free hours. Is it okay if I come in and watch you work?"

"That's what you want to do?"

"Yeah. I mean if it's okay. I'll buy a malt," Chloe added, just in case Mary was worried that she would take a booth without buying anything.

He grinned like she'd said something funny. "You can do that, but hold on, okay?"

She stood near the front while he talked to Mary. Moments later, he said, "Come on, let's go to the park."

"Really? You're allowed to leave?"

"*Jah*, for a little while I can. I haven't taken a break yet." Looking pleased, he added, "Mary told me I can take a half an hour." He reached for her bag. "She also said she'd put your bag behind the counter."

"That's so nice of her."

He grinned again. "That ain't no trouble. Now, come on. Let's go before a crowd comes in and Mary changes her mind. Want to go sit on our bench?"

"Of course."

Finn had taken her to the park for the first time last week. When she'd come in after school, the diner had been practically empty. Mary and Lane had told Finn that he could start taking his breaks when Chloe came—and had even suggested that the park would be a good place to visit. The park was large and had a giant jungle gym, swings, and a basketball court. There was also a walking trail with benches scattered throughout.

Chloe knew enough about Finn by now to understand that Mary and her husband tried to do as much as they could for their nephew. Finn had even confided that his father wouldn't allow him to eat supper when he got home from the diner at night, giving an absurd excuse about how Finn would mess up the kitchen.

She felt so sorry for him.

"Are you upset about missing your class tonight?" Finn asked.

"Not really. Practice has been really hard lately. It's kind of nice to have a break, if you want to know the truth."

"Are you worried about your dad finding out you didn't really have class tonight?"

She shrugged. "I'll just tell him that I didn't want to bother him, so I hung out at the diner. He won't care. I mean, not too much."

"Wow. I can't imagine that."

"I'm sorry that your father is so tough on you."

He shrugged. "It is how it is, right?"

She wished she could see him more often. See him when he wasn't working. "Hey, where do you live, Finn?" Maybe they could meet some place in between their houses on Saturday or something.

His expression shuttered. "You know where I live. It's a couple miles away, where most of the Amish live."

"That's not very helpful."

"That's all you need to know, though. Right?"

"Uh, no." She was starting to feel embarrassed about her idea of meeting him someplace. "Hey, Finn, if you're kind of far away, how do you get here? Does your aunt pick you up?"

"No. I've got a scooter." He paused, like he was waiting for her to tease him.

She wouldn't do that. "At least you have that, huh?"

He continued to stare straight ahead. "The scooter is fine. It gets me wherever I need it to."

"You're right. Except when it snows." She smiled.

"I reckon my feet will get me here when it snows."

Now she was even more embarrassed. She had two parents willing to cart her around while he didn't even have one. "I'm sorry you have to walk so much."

He kicked out a boot-covered foot. "My feet aren't special like yours. I couldn't stand on my tiptoes like you can no matter how hard I tried."

She rolled her eyes. "I'm thinking about getting my driver's license. I won't be able to get a car or anything, but maybe sometimes my mom will let me use hers. And then I could drive you home."

"You could . . . I suppose."

She laughed. "What do you mean? Would you not trust me?"

At last his expression lightened. "Since you haven't driven a foot yet, no, I don't."

"What? I'm offended."

"You're crazy. That's what you are," he teased.

She smiled. "I still want to see you more often. You know. More than just when I'm here getting ready to go to dance class. Can you get away on one of your days off?"

"I could try. Maybe . . . I don't know."

"Oh."

"Chloe, things at my house aren't real, um, happy. My father gets confused a lot. He gets angry too. He doesn't like me to leave even when it's for work."

"I'm sorry."

He nodded. "I am too. I wish my dad's brain was healthier or that he was nicer to me. That's why I, um, don't sound too eager for you to come to my house. It ain't a happy place."

"I'm glad you told me. I thought maybe you didn't like me as much as I liked you."

"I like you just as much. I'll try to figure something out."

"Is there any way we can talk on the phone at all? Do you have a phone?" Realizing he likely didn't, she shook her head. "Sorry. Forget I asked. I bet it's against the law for you to have one, huh?"

He chuckled. "It's against our rules, *jah*, but I'm technically in my *rumspringa*." And he was planning to leave anyway. "I'll try to get one."

"Never mind. I'm sorry. They're expensive."

"I'm working. I have money. I've been meaning to ask my aunt and uncle about getting one anyway. Or maybe one of the guys I met."

"Those ones who were sitting in that booth?"

"Yeah. One of them is former Amish. He might be able to figure out how I could get one."

"Finn, if you did have a phone, we could text each other."

He grinned. "We could. And talk on it too."

"I'd like that," she said softly.

"Me too. So, what will you do with your dad when he picks you up?"

"We usually go get something to eat. Sometimes he takes me home right after and other times I'll spend the night at his house—I've got a room there and all. I'll probably spend the night at his place."

"That's nice you get to stay at both of your parents' houses."

"I guess." She bit her lip. "I mean, I love my dad and I'm glad for the room and all, but he's been kind of weird lately." She paused, wondering how much to add, then figured that she might as well finish what she'd started. "You're not the only person with a weird dad, Finn. He left my mom for this woman

137

named Sandy, then broke up with her practically the minute he and Mom got divorced."

"Ouch."

"Oh, it gets worse. He was going on dates and stuff—at least he said he was until he heard that my mom met a guy."

"What's wrong with that?"

"Nothing, except my father is acting all surprised and kind of jealous. It's like now that someone else likes Mom, he likes her again too."

"For real?"

She nodded. "It's so awful. Now whenever we're together, Dad always asks me about Mom and Bo."

"The guy's name is Bo?"

"Yeah."

"Have you met him?"

"Not yet. Mom doesn't want me to meet him in case things don't get serious. But I think they already are."

"Wow."

"Yeah. My life is a soap opera."

"Sorry about that."

She shrugged. "It's nothing too bad, right? Oh, I almost forgot. Would you like my phone number? You know, in case you do get a phone?"

He grinned. "It's probably gonna be a while before I can text you."

"I know, but I can hope, right?"

"Write it down and I'll keep it." He paused, then added, "I could, um, always call you from the phone shanty down the street. Maybe."

"That would be great."

"Yeah? You, um, don't think it would be too weird?"

"I wouldn't give you my number if I didn't want you to

call, Finn," she said as she handed him a torn sheet of notebook paper with her name and number on it.

"Thanks," he said as he put it in his pocket.

• • •

An hour later, when the diner was pretty empty and his aunt had given him time to eat supper in the back, Finn pulled out Seth's card and called. Seth answered on the second ring.

"Yeah?"

"Seth, this is Finn. Um, you met me over at Lane's?"

"I remember. How are ya?"

"I'm okay. Um, I was wondering if you could tell me how to get a cell phone."

"You ready to get one, hmm?"

"Yeah."

"I can help ya with that. Where are you now?"

"I'm at the diner."

"I'll be over with one in about an hour."

"Wait, no. I'm going to pay for it. I just wondered if you knew how much one cost."

"Do you give your parents most of your pay?"

"Yeah, but not all."

Seth's voice softened. "I actually have some free time tonight and I'm right next to the supercenter. I'll pick one up for you and bring it by the diner and show you how to use it. And it'll be a gift."

Finn frowned. "I promise, I really didn't call to ask you to buy me a phone."

"I know. But I do know what it's like to need one, right? Accept it as a gift from someone who's been in your shoes."

"All right. Thanks."

"I'm glad you called. I'll be by within an hour. See you soon."

When they hung up, Finn realized that after so many months of feeling confused, things were finally starting to make sense. He still worried that he would completely mess everything in his life up, but there was a layer of hope starting to form over his fears.

CHAPTER 19

Another day, another hour listening to Grafton complain about his broken heart. At least this time Bo wasn't alone with the kid and all his problems. He'd called Lincoln in for an assist.

Lincoln had seemed amused by Bo calling for help and then even more entertained by the fact that Bo had been so serious about needing his presence. Five minutes in, though, Lincoln's amused concern gave way to impatience and then being just plain uncomfortable. Bo knew exactly how he was feeling. It wasn't that either of them didn't feel sorry for the guy, it was that his brokenheartedness was so over-the-top, it was almost painful to witness.

Especially since the kid wasn't listening to Lincoln's advice any better than he listened to Bo's or Mason's.

Before long, Lincoln cut off Grafton's excuses with a hand up. "I don't want to hear any more about Molly. You've got to calm yourself and give it a rest," he said. "Focus on something else."

Grafton stared at them both with puppy dog eyes. "I can't. It's impossible."

Bo inwardly groaned. Back in prison, there was a saying among some of the guys that the only thing that was impossible was to get out.

As expected, Lincoln didn't take kindly to it. His voice deepened. "Impossible's not a word you want in your vocabulary."

"She's not answering my calls."

"How many times have you called her?" Bo asked.

Grafton looked shamefaced. "A couple of times a day."

"How many is a couple?"

"I don't know. Twelve, maybe?"

Lincoln held out his hand. "Give me your phone."

"What? No."

"That ain't a good answer. You might not recall this, given that you had Molly on your mind and all—but when I met with you in the pen, I told you that there were rules to follow if you wanted to be in this program."

"I'm following them."

"Boy, you ain't working like you're expected to if you're calling some woman twelve or more times a day. I'm taking this until Friday at five."

"You can't do that."

"I reckon I can. Listen, it's Wednesday afternoon. You're only going without for forty-eight hours."

"But what if she calls back and I don't answer?"

"She ain't going to call you back, Grafton," Bo said. "She's not."

"But—"

Lincoln stopped him with a look. "This ain't up for discussion. I know it's hard, but I promise, you're gonna thank me for this."

Just as the kid looked like he was about to freak out, Bo's

phone rang. Sure he was going to ignore it, he barely spared the screen a glance—until he saw Joy's name pop up.

When it rang again, he picked it up. "Sorry, I've got to take this." Walking a few steps away, he clicked on. "Hey, Joy. What's going on?"

"Are you busy?"

"A little bit. Why? What's going on?"

"Well, it might be nothing . . . but I got a letter today."

Every muscle in his body tensed up. Hating how scared she sounded, he softened his voice. "What kind of letter?"

Bo could practically feel both Lincoln's and Grafton's attention shifting directly on him. He ignored it.

She started talking in a rush. "I don't know if it's anything, but it seems like it is. And it's unsigned. I think maybe I should contact the police? I don't know . . . what do you think?"

"Joy, honey, what did it say? Do you have it in front of you?"

"Yeah." Her voice quavered. "*You are still mine. I will never let you go.*"

Anger, followed by a dozen questions, filled his mind. He shoved them back, forcing himself to keep his voice calm and steady. "Where are you? Are you home?"

"Yes."

"Where's your daughter? Is Chloe there too?"

"No, she . . . she's with Tony."

"She coming back tonight or staying with him?"

"She's with him tonight."

So Joy was alone. "All right. I'm coming over, okay? I should be there in fifteen minutes."

"But maybe I should go straight to the police station?"

If the guy was sending letters to her door, there was every possibility that he was nearby watching for her reaction. "We'll talk about it when I get there. Are your doors locked?"

"Um, I think? I don't know."

"Walk around right now and check. I'm staying on the line."

"You're starting to scare me."

She was right. He was thinking about keeping her safe—not making her feel better. Tamping down his worry, he murmured, "I don't want to scare you, but go check, okay?"

"All right." She released a ragged sigh while he held his phone in a death grip. "The back door's locked." A few seconds later, he heard the deadbolt on the front door click into place. He closed his eyes, hating that she hadn't done that automatically. "The front door's locked now, too."

"You keep them locked, okay? I'll text you when I pull up."

"Hey, Bo? You know, you probably don't have to come right over." Her words were coming out fast, like she was embarrassed for calling him at all. "I'll be okay. I was just . . . just freaking out but I'm feeling a little better."

"I'm glad you called. I would've been upset if you hadn't. Now have a seat and try to relax. I'll be there soon."

"You really don't mind?"

That voice. So sweet. "I really don't mind at all."

"Okay. Thank you."

"Of course. Don't worry. I'm on my way."

When he disconnected, he dropped his head, hoping to release some of the tension that had been building in his neck while they'd been talking.

"What's going on?" Lincoln asked.

"Joy's been receiving threatening text messages and had a couple of phone calls with no one speaking on the line. Today she got a letter in the mail."

"So he knows where she lives," Grafton said.

"Yeah. I've got to get over there. She's freaked."

"Want some company?" Lincoln asked. "Grafton and me could look around while you check on Joy."

Part of him would like the backup. He wasn't afraid to find anyone, but he was afraid to overlook something and put her in further danger. He was probably being paranoid, but he reckoned that's what happened to anyone who'd served time. When you hang out with guys bragging about their bad deeds, you realize that more bad things happened under most people's radar than they ever imagined.

Looking at both men, he shook his head. "I appreciate it, but I think it's too soon. She's still learning to trust me."

Lincoln pressed a hand on his shoulder. "I think she already does. She called you."

Something shifted in his body and settled in. "Yeah. I better get on over there."

Grafton stepped forward, blocking his path. "Hey, Bo, I'm sorry about doing this again."

"No apologies needed, but if you've decided to move on, that's a good thing. Life's too short to dwell on a bad relationship."

"I know you probably think I'm an idiot, but if you need help with your girl, I'll be glad to watch her house or make phone calls or something."

"Thank you."

"Touch base later," Lincoln called out as Bo walked out the door.

Bo raised his hand, acknowledging that he heard.

When he walked through the main house, Seth called out to him. "Beauman, come here for a sec."

"I can't. Sorry," he said as he walked out the door.

Glad that Joy had allowed him to pick her up at her house before their date, Bo headed there practically on autopilot. It gave him a moment to not only give thanks that he had his phone nearby when she'd called, but to also wonder what was happening between them.

He didn't date a whole lot. Not because he hadn't had the opportunity, but because he was picky. Picky with who he wanted to spend time with and picky about how he wanted to spend it. Sleeping with women he barely knew didn't interest him.

And even though being physically close to Joy had crossed his mind, sex wasn't what they were about. He cared about her. She fascinated him. There was simply something about her that he wanted to know.

He hadn't even kissed her yet and he was feeling like she was the one for him. He shook his head. He didn't know what that was about.

All the lights were on in Joy's house when Bo pulled into the driveway. She was scared. He wished he'd brought her a bottle of wine or a pint of ice cream or flowers. Something that would've eased her mind a bit.

He pulled out his phone.

> I'm here. Walking to your
> front door.

She opened it the moment he arrived on her front step. "Hi."

Her hair was up in a messy bun and she wore black leggings and a baby-blue T-shirt. Her feet were bare. She looked so sweet—and scared to death. "Hey, sweetheart." Before he could stop himself, he pulled her into his arms.

She tensed for a second then wrapped her hands around his middle. Held him tight.

He closed his eyes, so glad she was seeking comfort from

him. Gently, he rubbed her back. "You okay?" he murmured. "I got here as soon as I could."

"Yes." Looking embarrassed, she pulled away. "I'm so glad you're here . . . but I think I'm overreacting."

"Joy. Honey, look at me." When her eyes met his, he reached for her hands. "I'm glad you called. I don't care if you're overreacting."

"You said you were doing something. What was it?"

He rolled his eyes, hoping to make her smile. "I was listening to a guy named Grafton cry and whine about a girl who broke his heart."

Her eyes widened. "Really? I . . . I didn't think guys did stuff like that."

"A lot don't. Grafton, all six-foot-one, two hundred pounds of him? He does it a lot."

"Poor guy."

"Yeah. But poor me too." He smiled. "Listening to a grown kid continually moan about a woman not being true gets old, quick. I hate the reason you called, but honestly, I was happy to have a reason to get out of there."

She smiled. "Glad to be of service."

He tugged on her hand. "Come show me this letter of yours."

As expected, the tension in the air rose. "It's over there, in the kitchen."

She pointed to the envelope on the counter, and he walked over and pulled out the paper. The words had been written in bold, black marker. It wasn't scribbled; there was something deliberate about the way the author had formed each letter. Whoever had written the note had taken his time on it.

He picked up the envelope and looked at the writing there. It was obvious that it was the same author, but the writing had been done in a ballpoint pen. There was nothing alarming about it, other than he thought it was odd to see writing done in all block letters.

"What do you think? Do you think I should've just thrown it out?"

He hated that she sounded worried, like he was going to disagree with her judgment or think she was overreacting. "I think you were right to be worried, sweetheart."

Her expression eased. To his surprise a small smile appeared on her lips before it vanished. "What just made you smile?"

Her face pinkened. "Sorry. It's just . . . well, I like it when you call me sweetheart."

"Is that all right?"

"Yes. It's just, um, unfamiliar. My ex wasn't into endearments."

"No?"

"No."

He grinned. "Good." When she frowned, he added, "Sorry, but I need all the help I can get to keep your interest, Joy."

She shook her head like she couldn't believe what he just said. "You're . . . you're something else, Bo Beauman."

"Right back at you. Now, we could go to the police station tonight, but it might take a while. They're going to ask you questions and then you'll probably have to file a report. I think you might as well wait until tomorrow."

"You sure that they won't think it was wrong of me to wait?"

"I'm sure. Besides, Lincoln called me when I was driving over. He's going to see if his buddy is available tomorrow. The guy's a detective and easy to talk to. If so, he's going to stop by, and that way you won't have to go to the police station."

"That's so nice of Lincoln."

"He was in the room when you called. I told him about what's been going on. He agrees that this"—he shook the paper in his hand—"is disconcerting, to say the least. His friend will help."

She nodded and took a small breath. "So I don't have to worry about that note any more tonight?"

"I don't think so. Put it out of your mind if you can."

She pursed her lips and nodded but didn't exactly look any more at ease.

There was no way he was going to leave her.

"So, since I'm here and you're alone, do you mind if I hang out for a while? Or would you rather I take you out? Want to grab something to eat?"

"You don't have anything else planned?"

"Nope."

"Well, um, would you like to stay a while? I could make some snacks. Do you like charcuterie boards?"

"You don't need to go to so much trouble. But I would like to stay for a while."

"I have beer. Do you want one?"

"How about a glass of water?"

She got him that, then poured herself a glass of white wine. "Do you mind?"

"Not at all. Come on. Let's go sit down and you can tell me about the rest of your day."

"It was pretty awful. You sure you don't want that beer?" she teased.

"If I change my mind, I'll let you know."

When she sat next to him with her feet curled under her, he kicked off his boots and simply listened to her talk.

And watched the way the ends of her hair curled around her shoulders.

And thought about how, in spite of the situation, he was glad to be seeing her again. He liked sitting on her couch with her, liked doing nothing, just talking. And he really liked that she'd called him when she'd needed him, and that he hadn't messed this up by being busy.

As far as he was concerned, he wanted to be at her beck and call.

CHAPTER 20

Joy's phone buzzed seconds before she heard a knock at the door. Both sounds were jarring enough to pull her upright in confusion. Sun was shining through the windows. It was morning and she'd fallen asleep on the couch.

She rubbed her eyes—and spied Bo sprawled out on the easy chair. "We fell asleep," she blurted.

He stretched his arms. "Yeah, we sure did." Obviously amused, he smiled at her.

She almost smiled back.

The knock sounded again, followed by the doorbell.

"I've got to get that. It's probably Chloe." Not bothering to look at her phone, she hurried to the door and was just about to turn the deadbolt when Bo spoke again.

"Don't open it without seeing who it is, right?"

"Hmm? Oh. Sure." Peering through the peephole she silently cursed. Chloe was there, looking like her normal self.

Unfortunately, Tony was standing by her side—and he looked fit to be tied.

"It's my ex and Chloe, Bo."

He was already on his feet. "Okay then."

Tony knocked on the door again. "Joy, come on. What's going on?"

He did not sound happy.

At last she turned the deadbolt and tried to pull out a real smile somewhere from deep inside herself. "Hi, you two. Chloe, what's going on?"

"She forgot a notebook," Tony said. "And her house key."

"It's important, Dad," Chloe said as she led the way inside. "Remember how I told you that it has all that stupid French vocabulary? I've got to have it for class today." She looked about to add something, then stared at Bo. "Hi," she said.

"Chloe, hurry up," Tony said as he walked through the door behind her.

Taking in her messy hair and Bo's sock-covered feet, Tony's eyebrows lifted. "What's going on?"

"I have company," Joy said.

Bo sauntered forward. She might have been half-asleep but she couldn't deny that he was a sight to behold, even after sleeping on a chair in a pair of jeans and a T-shirt. "I'm Sam Beauman, but everyone calls me Bo. Are you Tony?"

"Yes. Tony Howard."

"Good to meet you," Bo said, shaking Tony's hand as if they were at a cocktail party or PTA meeting. Looking down at Chloe, who seemed to be both sizing him up and trying not to be his instant friend, his voice gentled. "You must be Chloe."

"I am. I didn't know you were going to be here." She looked over at Joy. "Sorry, Mom."

Joy's cheeks were heating up. "It's okay. It's a long story."

"I came over to see your mother last night and we started watching a movie." He pointed to the two sets of blankets, one on the chair and one on the couch. "We fell asleep."

"You let him spend the night here, Joy?" Tony asked.

First, that was obvious, and second, it wasn't any of his business.

Joy noticed Tony looked affronted and shocked. Just like he hadn't first left because he'd found someone else and then filed for divorce because "what they had didn't work for him anymore." The possessive, almost comfortable way he was acting irritated her beyond belief.

"Don't get started, Tony. Chloe, go get your notebook or you're going to be late for school."

Their sweet girl's eyes looked from her to Tony and then over to Bo. After that, she turned, picked up her duffle bag that Joy hadn't noticed until that minute, and walked down the hall.

When the three of them were alone again, Tony folded his hands over his chest. Almost as if he was trying to compare himself to Bo.

It wasn't nice to think, but Joy felt like chuckling. Tony was a decent-looking guy, but Bo was just so much *more*. There was a reason that he was some company's go-to model for the outdoorsy stuff in their catalog.

"What's going on, Joy?" he asked. "How did the two of you meet?"

Just like Bo wasn't in the room.

Before she could answer, Bo murmured, "Does your ex interview all your boyfriends, sweetheart?"

Taken aback, she met his gaze. His expression was blank, but his light-blue eyes were bright with amusement. Oh, he knew exactly what he was doing.

"I'm not going to answer either of those questions right now." It was a cop-out, but she called for Chloe. "Get a move on, Chloe! You're going to be late."

Chloe reappeared with her notebook. "I've got it!"

"Grab your pack and come on. It's time to go."

"Okay." She looked at Joy. "Should I ride the bus home?"

"No, I'll pick you up today." She bent down and kissed her brow. "Have a good day. Love you."

"Love you too." Looking up at Bo, she smiled shyly. "Bye."

"Bye. Nice to meet you, Chloe." Bo said.

Her smile brightened. "You too."

"Let's go," Tony said. He headed to the door without another word.

After they walked out and Tony's car pulled out, Joy exhaled. "So that was my daughter and my ex-husband."

"And I'm guessing that this was the first time you've ever had a guy spend the night?"

There were so many things his question made her think about, she felt her cheeks heat. "You guessed right."

"Tell me if this is none of my business, but why is that? It's been four years."

"There are a lot of things I could say to explain but the simple truth is that I haven't dated anyone."

"No one since. . . ah, he left you? Really?"

She kind of loved how incredulous he sounded, even though it didn't make her feel too proud of herself. "It's a long story, but no. If you ever wonder why I sometimes act so awkward, it's because I'm out of practice."

He flashed a smile. "You're not out of anything."

She laughed. "If only that was true. But anyway, I'm sorry about this. I can't believe Tony acted like such a jerk."

"Sure you can."

"It was obvious we hadn't done anything. I mean other than sleeping. We have our clothes on."

He laughed. "Come on. First of all, lots of things can happen before sleeping on the couch. Secondly, if he knows you haven't been out there dating, he's probably thinking that you're still his."

That idea was repulsive. "I sure hope not."

He shrugged. "Then there's the part where I didn't make it too easy."

"I noticed you didn't apologize for calling me sweetheart in front of him."

"Why would I? We're all adults and it seems to me like he's coming and going far too easily. This might be where he used to live but it's not anymore."

She thought about that. Probably later, she'd really think on it and wonder if she'd subconsciously kept the door open for Tony just in case he had an epiphany and suddenly decided to come back.

"You're right."

Bo blinked. "That's it? You're not going to argue with me?"

"I'm not a big fan of arguing just for the sake of arguing. Would you like some coffee?"

"Yeah. Then we need to figure out what you want to do about that letter. Do you want to wait to hear from the detective or go to the station?"

She hadn't forgotten about the letter, but the drama with Tony had almost put it out of her mind. "Okay. Coffee first, then I think I want to go to the station. I know you trust Lincoln to get ahold of him, but I want to do something, you know? Not just wait here."

"Sounds good."

Realizing that she was now taking up even more of his time,

she murmured, "If you're busy today, I can do this on my own. I feel better today. Not as, um, emotionally raw."

"You're not going to go to a police station all alone if I can help it. I'm not too busy."

She smiled at him softly. "I'll make the coffee. The bathroom's down the hall, if you need it."

"Thanks. Oh, and Joy?"

She turned back to him. "Yes?"

"Your Chloe is a doll. Pretty as a picture. She looks just like you too."

Joy smiled as she walked into the kitchen.

CHAPTER 21

While Joy made coffee, Bo walked down the hall. The house's main bath was next to her bedroom. It was bigger than he'd thought it would be. There was an antique cast iron tub, a modern walk-in shower, two sinks, and two medicine cabinets. The floor was a glazed brick and the walls were painted a pale pink. It was a pretty place and filled with all things girly. Lotions and perfumes and a basket filled with hair ties.

It smelled like Joy. Feminine and classy. It was obvious she shared it with Chloe and that there wasn't a man around to tarnish the feminine vibe. Bo was glad about that. It would be a shame to mess up the sweet aesthetic.

He'd been in the room the night before but, because he'd been so tired at the time or because he'd been distracted and stewing on her letter—probably both—he hadn't noticed the sweet floral scent or the sheer girliness of it at all.

Now Bo was having a hard time not inspecting everything

more closely. He realized then that if they ever got to the stage when they were living together, he'd complain if she tried to make the little space more masculine. He wanted to see her hairbrushes and body lotion.

He wanted to see everything of hers that she kept from the outside world.

"You are halfway gone," he muttered to himself. He'd suspected as much when he'd felt his chest clench when she'd told him about her letter over the phone. That feeling had intensified when he'd held her in his arms.

Now, after seeing the way her ex was acting like she didn't even deserve a heads-up when he showed up out of the blue, and even acting like she owed him explanations for having a man spend the night? Well, that grated on Bo something fierce.

Yeah, he was more than just halfway gone. His feelings had reached a whole new level.

She'd told him where the spare toothbrushes were. After doing his business, he grabbed a toothbrush and a fresh washcloth and attempted to clean himself up a bit.

The scent of brewing coffee filled the hallway as he walked back to meet her. Needing the jolt of caffeine, he met her in the kitchen. Joy was leaning against the counter and sipping a cup like it was life-sustaining.

"I got out a cup for you. I put out milk and sugar too. I didn't remember what you took."

"Thanks." He filled a cup and put in a spoonful of sugar. "When do you want to go over to the police station?"

"Sooner than later." She looked down at herself. "I need to shower and get changed though."

"How long do you need?"

"An hour?"

He needed to do the same, which meant he needed to head

home. He contemplated logistics. He could meet her at the station, come back here to pick her up, or they could even meet somewhere halfway. None of the choices sounded like a perfect option—mainly because he didn't want to let her out of his sight.

But she was a grown woman and they had a long way to go before she was ready for him to be her man. "How about we meet at the police station? Then if things run long or you want to do something else you'll have your car."

She nodded. "That sounds good. You'll have yours too."

"I'm not thinking about me." That was true too. At the moment, he couldn't care less about the men he was supposed to meet with or the two houses he'd planned to inspect with Lincoln. "I'm happy to wait here while you shower, then take you to my place while I do the same."

She arched a brow. "Then head to the station together before you drop me back off here? No, I think it would be best for me to meet you there." After a pause, she added, her voice low, "Or, I could go to the station on my own. It's my problem, not yours."

No, that's not how it was going to go. Sometime in the last twelve hours, things between them had taken another turn. Joy would probably not care for the descriptor, so he kept it to himself, but her problems were absolutely his problems now.

Or, more to the point, he didn't want her to have any problems. He found himself caring so deeply about her happiness. There was a protective streak in him that wanted to take each of her burdens on so she would have nothing to worry about beyond her daughter and her work.

"There's no way you're going by yourself—unless you forbid me to come, I suppose. I'll meet you there."

Her eyes filled with relief. "Okay."

After taking a sip of coffee, he said, "Joy, are you going to tell Tony about the texts and the calls and the letter?"

"I'm not sure."

"Why wouldn't you want to tell him?"

"I'm afraid . . . no, I'm pretty sure that he's going to blame me if I do."

It took him a minute to control his reaction. "Say again?"

"He's never wanted me to do literacy training. He never understood my painting, either. He's always said my choices of jobs weren't safe."

"What does he want you to do? Sit at home?"

"No. I went to a couple of semesters of college. I had thought I wanted to do something in banking."

"Banking?"

She nodded. "I thought I could be a teller, then work my way up to something with more responsibility."

"Try as I might, I can't see you doing that."

"Me neither. I realized that while I like working with other people, I like it in limited amounts. The tutoring and painting give me that. The literacy volunteer work fills my heart."

"But Tony wanted you to go into banking?"

"Yeah. He thought it would be good for me to have more structure in my life." She wrinkled her nose. "He had other ideas too. Like maybe I could be an assistant manager of a boutique or something."

"An assistant manager." Because he hadn't thought she should be the actual manager. Every bit of what she was saying grated on him. "Joy."

"I know." She took another sip of coffee. "He could be really condescending. I realize that now." Looking away, she added, "Tony's told me more than once that the people I help learn to read can be dangerous. He'll say that this texting, letter-writing person is the direct result of my foolishness."

"I see." Bo blinked. His sisters would be having a heyday right about now. He'd never been one to be so guarded.

"What do you think?"

"About what? You telling him about this?" When she nodded, he weighed his words carefully. "This is how I see it. We'll talk to the cops and see what they say. If they give you some advice, I imagine you'll take it. Then see what happens. But you can't leave Chloe in the dark. She needs to be at least a little bit aware of what's going on, right?"

"Right."

"And if Chloe knows . . ."

"Then Tony is going to find out," she finished.

"Yeah. If that happens, I think it would be better if he heard it from you."

"Which brings it all back to him and me having a fun conversation."

"You don't have to do it on your own, Joy. I can be there if you want backup." He'd like to be there in case Tony decided to start twisting things around and putting the blame on Joy's shoulders.

She smiled at him. "As much as I like the idea of having your help, I don't think that would be the best choice."

"You could ask the cop we meet with to help you out."

"Really? Do you think that would be okay?"

"Of course. Especially if we meet with the cop friend of Lincoln's. Sergeant Kevin Heilman is a really good man."

She nodded. "I'm going to tell Chloe what's going on this afternoon, but I think I need a little bit to think about how to tell Tony."

"Sounds good." He finished his coffee and set it on the counter. "How about I meet you at the police station in ninety minutes?"

"That's perfect."

"I'll take off now."

She walked him to the front door. "Hey, Bo?"

"Hmm?"

"Thanks. And . . . could I give you another hug?"

In answer, he pulled her against him. This time a little more intimately than the night before. When she relaxed against him, he ran a hand down her hair. Pressed a kiss to her head.

And really wished he didn't have to let her go.

CHAPTER 22

It was only by chance that Finn was in his room when he received a text. It was noon and he'd been out in the barn for the last four hours. He'd gotten so filthy cleaning stalls, he'd run up to his room to take a shower and change.

When it buzzed again, he reached into its hiding place and ran his thumb across the screen. He really needed to stop forgetting to put it on silent.

Every time Finn's new phone buzzed, it practically gave him a heart attack. Thanking the Lord yet again that he didn't have to share it with his brothers, he pulled out his phone. He didn't have to wonder who was texting him. There were only two people who had his number. Seth—who'd not only bought the phone but had sat with him for fifteen minutes to show him how to use it—and Chloe.

His reason for getting the phone in the first place.

Just seeing her name on his phone's screen made him feel

good inside. Like not everything in his life was difficult. She was the exception. The reason that his future wasn't looking quite as scary as it once had.

Can you talk?

Sorry. I can't risk it.

Can you text at least?

Yeah. But aren't you at school?

I'm at lunch but I had to call you.
Finn, It's been the craziest day.

What's up?

First, when I woke up at my dad's I realized that I forgot my French notebook. He lectured me the whole time about being responsible. Then, when we got there—I met Bo!

> No way! What was he like?

> Finn! You've met him! He was at
> the diner with that other man.

It was the same Bo he'd met with Seth. Finn just about fell off his bed.

> Are you serious? Hold on. I'll
> call you.

After scanning the room and debating about where he could get the most privacy, he grabbed a book from the library to put on his lap and sat on the floor. If someone asked why they heard his voice, he could say he was practicing reading. It was a dumb excuse, but whatever.

Finally, he arranged some pillows around him to try to muffle his voice, and called.

"Finn?"

"Can you hear me?" He was whispering.

"Yep."

She was amused, and he didn't blame her. "I'm still getting used to talking on the cell phone." He was also getting pretty stupid. His father would be really, really mad at him if he discovered he was talking on a mobile phone to an English girl. "I don't have a ton of time, so tell me everything."

She giggled. "There's not a lot to tell. Supposedly he'd come over, they watched a movie on television and fell asleep in the living room."

"Uh-huh."

She giggled. "Yeah, I found that hard to believe too. But my mom was still in her same clothes and Bo looked all rumpled too. Mom was so embarrassed."

"How did your dad act?"

"You could totally tell he was freaking out."

"Wow. What did you do?"

"Nothing. I was sent to get my French notebook, which I kind of didn't even care about anymore."

Finn had to bite his bottom lip to keep from laughing. "I can see that. I would've just been staring at everyone."

"That's all I wanted to do. It was crazy. My dad kept staring at Bo like he couldn't believe he was with my mom. Then my dad started asking questions and acting like Mom had done something wrong. Which made both my mom and Bo mad."

"Whoa."

"Right?" She sighed. "I guess in a way I can't blame my dad too much. I always thought she'd date one day, but this Bo guy is a surprise. I mean, first I saw him talking to you—and second he's obviously younger than my mom, and really handsome. It was *so* awkward. This Bo guy kept darting looks at my mom, like he was debating whether to say stuff or not."

"No way."

"Luckily, we didn't stay long. Of course, Dad talked about Mom and Bo the whole time he drove me to school. He said all sorts of stupid stuff. Like she should be acting better."

"Because she fell asleep watching a movie?"

Chloe giggled. "I think so. I mean, I was shocked, too, but it's not like my dad has a lot to say, right?"

"Right."

"I wish you could have been there."

Finn grinned. "Me, too, though I probably wouldn't have been much help."

"You wouldn't have had to do anything. Just sit there with me while everyone went crazy. I could've made you popcorn."

He almost started laughing but caught himself just in time. "Are you upset about Bo seeing your mom?"

"Hmm. Not really," she said after a pause. "This Bo guy doesn't seem slimy or anything. What do you think?"

"I only met him once, but Seth and him are really good friends. Seth made sure to tell me that if I ever need something or have an emergency then I should call either one of them. He said that even Bo would drop everything to help me out."

"That's kind of how he acted when he was at my house. Not like he would do anything for me, but that he would do anything for my mom." She lowered her voice. "He acted like my mom is special. I kind of like that."

"That's good."

"I've got to go. I'll text you later, 'Kay?"

"Yeah. Bye."

When he hung up, he hurriedly put it on mute and hid it again in between his mattress and box spring. Then, after brushing his hair and gathering his dirty clothes, he walked back downstairs.

Rachel and Lucy were eating turkey sandwiches and his mother was at the sink. "Here you are," his *mamm* said. "I wondered when you were coming back down."

"Sorry, I um, was dirtier than I thought."

Rachel giggled. "I walked up to get you but your door was closed and locked."

"It's good it was locked, if you were just going to barge in without knocking."

Rachel gave him a long look. In that instance he knew that

she knew he'd been talking on the phone. After meeting her gaze, he said, "I'll put my laundry in the shoot and then fix a sandwich. I'm starved."

"I'll make you one, Finn. You just go sit down. You have to go to work soon anyway, right?"

"*Jah.*"

His mother's expression was warm and sweet when she placed a plate in front of him. On it was not one but two sandwiches, as well as a pile of macaroni salad. "Eat up, child," she whispered.

He knew his mother thought that he never got to eat at the diner. He wasn't going to tell her differently, since it would bring up a lot of other questions about her sister Mary.

Instead, he ate his food and watched as his sisters helped their mother with the dinner dishes, began preparations for supper, and then eventually left the kitchen to work on laundry.

Only when it was just him in the room did he dare relax enough to smile. Chloe seemed to really like him—maybe almost as much as he liked her. Plus, he now had a phone and could call and text her whenever he wanted. Things weren't good but they were a whole lot better.

CHAPTER 23

Joy's day turned out to be a little anticlimactic. Soon after Bo left her house, he'd called to say that the detective he'd told her about had reached out to him. The detective had told Bo that there would be no reason for Joy to go to the station before talking to him.

Bo gave Joy Detective Heilman's phone number so she could coordinate with him directly. When she called, he told her he was tied up with a court appearance, but he could be available late that afternoon. He was going to come around to her house at five or six.

Joy had been disappointed but had understood the reason to wait. Bo had worked with this detective before and he assured Joy that Heilman would not only take her concerns seriously but would treat her with respect. Waiting until she could speak with the detective would also help her not to have to tell her story first to whatever officer was willing to help and then repeating it again to Detective Heilman when he was available.

So, with nothing to do but wait, she'd spent most of the day painting, thinking about Bo, and debating how much to tell Chloe about what was going on. Chloe wasn't a little girl, but what was going on would probably scare her. Joy didn't want to frighten her daughter, but she also didn't want to keep so many secrets, knowing that it could be unsafe for Chloe as well.

In addition, she and Chloe had formed a really good bond in the four years since Tony's departure. In a lot of ways, she and her daughter were a team. Joy knew she owed it to Chloe to be open and honest.

Besides, Bo was in the picture now. Chloe likely had a ton of questions about him.

Deciding that the house didn't feel like the right place to have the discussion, she'd picked up some snacks, two bottles of water, and taken her to the park near their house. Chloe was comfortable there and the warm weather was ideal.

After parking, they carried the two sacks to one of the benches on the outskirts of the park.

"It's been a long time since we had a picnic out here, huh?" she asked when they sat down.

"A really long time." Chloe pulled out a bag of pretzels and nodded. "Not since I started dancing so much."

"I guess you're pretty curious about Bo, huh?"

To Joy's surprise, Chloe didn't look worried about Bo. Instead, she seemed kind of amused. "Kind of. Is he your boyfriend, Mom?"

"No. We're just friends."

Chloe raised her eyebrows. "He acted like he was your boyfriend."

"I guess he could be. I mean, maybe he will be. One day." She took a deep breath. "He and I get along well."

"It seemed like it."

She pressed her hands over her eyes. "I can't believe I fell asleep on the couch."

"I bet."

Well, now she was officially embarrassed. "I didn't plan for you and Bo to meet that way. Or for your dad to be in the mix. What a mess."

"He wasn't too happy about you having a guy there."

"I hope he didn't say anything to you."

Chloe popped another pretzel in her mouth as she shrugged. "Dad mainly just grumbled and looked like he wanted to complain, but he didn't."

"Well, he doesn't get to have a say in who my friends are."

"Does Bo sleep over whenever I'm not there?"

"What? Goodness, no. That was the first time and we both fell asleep on the couch while we were watching a movie." She took a deep breath. "I called Bo because I was scared last night. I received a strange letter in the mail, and I wasn't sure what to do. Bo came over to look at it and to help me decide what to do."

All the humor in Chloe's expression faded and her eyes widened. "What kind of letter was it?"

"I'm not sure. I think someone is trying to make me be afraid." She took a deep breath and plunged ahead. "I started getting weird hang ups and text messages a couple of weeks ago. Like a fool, I ignored them."

"You don't know who they were from?"

"Nope. I told Bo about them and he encouraged me to go to the police and file a report. But I didn't."

"Mom . . ."

"I know." She mentally kicked herself. Hearing herself describe how naive she'd been was embarrassing. "I should've known better. Anyway, a detective is coming over to the house later. That's another reason I wanted to talk to you right after school. I wanted you to know what has been going on before he shows up."

"Why do you think someone is doing all this?"

"I don't know."

Chloe frowned. "Dad says that some of the people you tutor aren't that great."

"Every single one of my students is very appreciative of me. They're usually embarrassed about not being able to read and desperate for help. I can't see any of them wanting to start sending me creepy notes."

Chloe folded her arms over her chest. "The note was creepy?" When Joy nodded, she added, "Can I see it?"

"I'd rather you didn't, but we'll see what the detective says. Do you have any questions?"

"Are you going to tell Dad about the notes too?"

"Eventually. I'm going to see what the police detective wants me to do. If he thinks Dad needs to know then I'll tell him."

"Is Bo coming over tonight too?"

She nodded slowly. "He is."

"Can I talk to him?"

"Of course, sweetie. He wants to get to know you."

"I want to get to know him too."

"That's your choice. Whatever makes you most comfortable." After taking a big drink of water, Joy finally relaxed a bit. "Now, how about you tell me about dance class last night and school today?"

"Well, it was canceled."

"What? What did you do?"

"Don't get mad, but I hung out at the diner and drank a vanilla malt."

"Chloe . . ."

"I know I should've called Dad but if I had been driving myself and went to the diner neither of you would've cared."

"I guess you have a point."

"I know I do. I needed a break anyway, Mom." She popped a pretzel in her mouth sipped some water, and then told Joy all about how Miss Diamanté always seemed to be in a bad mood, how the new ballet they were learning was hard but she might get a good part, and how her new toe shoes felt. Eventually, Chloe moved on to news about her dad's house and how Tony had made chicken soup, but it wasn't very good.

Joy sipped water and listened to story after story. She smiled and laughed and also tried her best to not let her imagination get the best of her. She couldn't dwell on what might happen or who might be putting them in danger. Not at that moment.

All she could do was remind herself to treasure the moment she had with her child. It was a given that they would have fewer and fewer opportunities to sit in the park on a Thursday afternoon. Chloe would one day be off at college and their time together would just be a memory.

When they got home, Chloe went to her room to change, and Joy walked to the mailbox to pick up the day's mail. There was another catalog, a water bill and another envelope with bold block letters printed on the front.

Bo had already warned her to not open any more letters so they could scan for prints. Hating the sight of it, she placed it in the center of the dining room table. She was chilled. Like she'd been out somewhere damp and cold and couldn't get the chill out of her bones.

"Mom?"

She looked up. "Yes, honey?"

"Do you still love Dad at all?"

"What brought this on?"

Her daughter shrugged. "No reason."

"There's some reason."

Worry filled her gaze. "Dad said that sometimes people change their minds. Like they're out of love and then in again."

Joy couldn't believe Tony had said all that to their daughter. "Maybe that does happen with some people, but it hasn't happened to us. It's not going to, either." Boy, she was going to give Tony a piece of her mind for spouting such nonsense and confusing Chloe. "We're too different."

"I know. But Dad said that he's been thinking that maybe you two should try to patch things up."

Tony was jealous, that was all there was to that. He was acting like a toddler: he didn't want a toy until someone else wanted it too. For whatever reason, that was how he thought about her.

Joy took a seat at the table. "Come here."

Chloe pulled out a chair across from her. "Yeah?"

"Listen. Remember when you were a little girl and your kindergarten teacher gave everyone a caterpillar to take home?"

She nodded. "We made homes for them in jars."

"You did. But then we had to listen to Miss Knepp and give it a real nice place to live. With lots of branches and leaves and such. Remember?"

"Yeah."

"Do you remember what happened to that little guy?"

"He made himself a cocoon."

"He did." Remembering Chloe's worry, she added, "You checked on him every morning and every evening before you went to bed. And then . . ."

"And then one day he was a butterfly." She smiled at the memory. "I was so shocked."

"You really were. And then we had to let him out in the backyard."

"And I started crying. I didn't want to let it go."

"But it was the right thing to do, right? Because no matter how hard we wanted him to be happy in that little container, he was different. He'd changed. That's what life is all about, Chloe. Sometimes people grow together, and their home is always good. But sometimes it's just not like that. Sometimes they grow apart instead."

"Like you and Dad."

"Yeah. Like me and Dad. And like you having your pretty room and not sleeping in a crib. I thought you were really cute in there, but it's not the right place for you anymore." She took a deep breath. "Just like in a couple of years you're going to go off to college and your room here isn't going to be the best place for you."

"I get it."

"Good."

"Are you mad at me for asking you about you and Dad?"

"I'm not pleased with your father for getting into my business, but I'm not mad at you. Not even a little bit. You can ask me anything." She smiled—and heard the doorbell ring. "I guess the detective is here. We better get up."

Even if it was uncomfortable, it was time to get everything out in the open. She'd put it off long enough.

CHAPTER 24

After double-checking who was at the door, she let in Bo and a nice-looking man with a worn tan and some deep wrinkles around his eyes. Like he smiled a lot and went out fishing every time he had a spare afternoon.

"Miss Howard? I'm Detective Kevin Heilman. It's nice to meet you in person."

She shook his hand. "I feel the same way. Thank you so much for coming over. I'm Joy and this is my daughter Chloe."

Chloe stayed by her side. "Hi."

"It's nice to meet you too."

After Bo and Chloe seemed to share a long look, Bo said, "Where would you like to talk about everything that's been going on, Joy?"

"At the dining room table. I left something there for you to see."

"This new?"

"Yes. It was in today's mail." She hated how her voice had suddenly taken on a tremor. Clearing her throat, she added, "Chloe, are you sure you want to stay here?"

"I'm positive."

"All right then." After getting glasses of water for everyone, Joy noticed that the detective had out a pen and paper and an iPad—and that the envelope hadn't been touched. That surprised her.

Bo stood up and gestured to the chair next to him. "Come have a seat, sweetheart."

Her stomach fluttered, though whether it was because she was uncomfortable with the whole situation or excited about Bo practically claiming her in front of the detective and Chloe, she didn't know for sure.

She sat next to him.

Detective Heilman leaned forward. "Joy, before we examine this letter, why don't you take me through what's been going on. Start with the first time you received a hang up or text. Which came first?"

"The hang ups."

"And when did they start taking place?"

"About two months ago."

"Were they from the same number?"

"I think so, but most of the time the number just said 'unknown.'"

"No one ever said anything?"

She shook her head.

"Are you sure?" When she tensed, Kevin's expression softened. "I realize I sound like I'm grilling you, but I'm not."

"I understand, and yes, I'm sure. Though, sometimes the person stayed on the line longer than others."

"When did you get the first text?"

"About two weeks after the calls, but they weren't very often. Not even once a week." She glanced at Chloe, but her daughter didn't look frightened.

"Did you save them on your phone?"

"No. I deleted them right away."

"You haven't saved any? Even when they became more frequent?"

"Not until last week. I got three last week."

"And then you received the letter on Wednesday."

She nodded. "And another one today." After double-checking that Chloe seemed to be hanging in there, she added, "I'm scared. I really don't know what to do anymore. That's why I called Bo for advice."

"She shouldn't be afraid to be in her own house, Kevin," Bo said.

"I agree." The detective wrote down a few more notes then got out a pair of latex gloves and a plastic bag. "Joy, I think it would be best if we looked at this letter next. After, we'll start making some lists."

"All right."

He put on gloves, pulled out a letter opener, and neatly sliced open the envelope. Feeling like everything was happening both too fast and too slowly, she inhaled sharply when he pulled out the sheet of paper.

"Easy," Bo murmured. "You're not alone."

She reached for his hand. He squeezed and kept a firm grip on it while Kevin read it, then held it up for them to read.

I SEE YOU. I SEE CHLOE TOO

It took a second for the words to register, then she was free-falling into her worst nightmare. A noise she hadn't known

177

she was capable of making was pulled from her body. Trying to control the tears, she started shaking. "Put that away."

"Mom?"

"I'm sorry."

"It's okay, girl," Bo murmured. "I'm not going to let anything happen to either of you."

Pulling her hand out of Bo's grip, she covered her mouth. Across from her, Detective Heilman carefully placed the letter back in the envelope then placed them both in a ziplock bag.

"I'll take this to the lab. Maybe someone over there will be able to lift prints from the letter."

Tears fell from her eyes as she nodded.

Bo stood up, walked to the kitchen, and got her a glass of water. He returned with the glass in one hand and a couple of tissues in the other. "You want to take a few minutes?"

"No. I'm okay." But she did blow her nose and take a big gulp of water.

The detective didn't seem annoyed at all by her distress. He wrote a few things on his iPad while she was attempting to regain her composure.

When she finally did, he stared directly at her. "Has this person mentioned your daughter before, Ms. Howard?"

"No." She couldn't even look at Chloe.

"Not by name?"

"Not ever. I didn't think he knew I had a daughter." She looked at Bo. "But you were right, weren't you? I was being so stupid. He probably has been watching me. Watching her." Feeling like every worst-case scenario was camping itself in her head at the same time, she stared at Chloe. "What if he attacks you? This is all my fault, right? I should've come to the police two months ago."

Tears filled Chloe's eyes. "Mom, what are we going to do?"

"Kevin, we need a minute," Bo said.

Looking from her to Bo, Kevin stood up. "Right. I'll go outside and make a call."

The moment he walked out the front door, Bo turned to Chloe. "Do you still want to stay in this room when the detective comes back? Obviously, this news is kind of hard to hear."

"I'm staying."

"Okay then." Before Joy knew what was happening, Bo reached for her and neatly pulled her into his arms. Thinking about Chloe seeing this, Joy tried to extricate herself from the embrace, but her heart wasn't in it. "Bo—"

"Hush, now. You ain't doing nothing wrong and Chloe isn't freaking out about me."

"I'm fine, Mom," Chloe called out. "Besides I think you really do need a hug."

"See?" Bo whispered. "Relax for a spell."

Everything inside of her wanted to argue a dozen reasons why she needed to move. And yell. And maybe even cry for a bit. But his hold felt too good. No, it felt too good to deny it. She relaxed her head against his chest.

"There you go," he murmured. "Now listen, okay?" He took a deep breath. "You aren't alone."

"But Bo, I'm—"

"You aren't, Joy. I know you've got a score of friends and you've got a good little family. So you can lean on them. But if you give me the privilege, I want you to give me a chance, yeah? Lean on me, too. Because, I promise, I am not going to let you fall."

"You sound so sure."

"I am sure. You and Chloe are in my life now. I want to be in yours too. Try and trust me, okay? Please."

The front door opened. The detective was joining them

again. Chloe was sitting nearby looking apprehensive and freaked out.

It was time she stopped being in denial and start dealing with everything. With Bo. With moving on from Tony. Start dealing with the texts and now these letters. She needed to even stop pretending that everyone in her life was wonderful, innocent, and good.

Obviously, that wasn't the case. She had a stalker. It was happening and she couldn't crawl under a rock and pretend that it wasn't. Not anymore.

After the detective sat back down, he pulled the notepad and pen toward him. "Joy, our next step is to try to figure out who might be doing this. I'm sure you've racked your brain—has anyone come to mind?"

"No."

"In that case, I think we should get together a list of possible people. And I know this is the hard part, but you need to think of everyone. Remember, they're sending notes and calling you anonymously. If they were being honest and truthful, they wouldn't be approaching you this way."

"Everyone has something to hide, Joy," Bo said.

She took a deep breath. "I understand."

"Okay, first of all, let's start with your ex-husband."

Warily, she looked at Chloe. Chloe folded her arms across her chest and stared right back. It was obvious that she wasn't going to go anywhere.

Trying to not think about what Chloe might say, Joy answered Detective Heilman at last. "I'm sure Tony doesn't have anything to do with this."

"How long have you been divorced?"

"Four years."

"Was it an amicable separation, and by that I mean are you

on speaking terms now? Do you ever see him?"

"It wasn't exactly amicable, but we do speak. We're cordial enough." Smiling at her daughter, Joy added, "We share custody of Chloe."

"Who filed?"

"He did."

The detective was still writing notes. "And the reason?"

She felt her cheeks heat as she felt Bo's intense gaze on her, too. "Um, Tony felt our marriage had run its course. He was seeing someone else and wanted out."

"I see." Detective Heilman looked up. "And since then . . . have you dated?"

"No."

"No one or just not seriously?"

"I haven't dated." She glanced at Bo. "I mean, I haven't dated anyone until recently."

Bo smiled at that.

"So, the two of you are close?" the detective continued, looking over at Bo.

"We're getting there, but we're just starting out." Bo's voice held a note of warning in it.

"All the calls started before I met him too," Joy added.

Kevin looked at the both of them. "Let's move on. I understand you sell paintings?"

"Yes. But I don't think any of those customers would write anything like the notes I've been receiving. I do most of my business through friends of friends. I don't say a lot to those people except when I drop off their paintings and they pay me."

"Can you give me a list of who you sold your paintings to in the last six months?"

"Yes, of course."

"Why don't you gather that together? We'll go a quick check to make sure no one jumps out."

"All right."

"Now I understand you also tutor?"

"Yes. I tutor and volunteer for ProLiteracy."

"Those folks you have far more interaction with, yes?"

Feeling like she was betraying them, she nodded.

"Do you have their names and contact information?" he asked, continuing to write.

"I don't think any of them are stalking me." Even though she could practically feel Bo's incredulous stare, she added, "They're good people. Plus, they're learning to read, right?" Jumping on that, she added, "Whoever is texting me and writing notes can read and write."

Detective Heilman put down the pen he was holding. "Joy, I'm not discounting anything you're saying. However, I think we'd agree that these notes aren't novels. No one needs to be able to read or write that well to compose the notes. Plus, it's been my experience that the majority of people who do things like this are known to the victim."

"You have to consider everyone," Bo said in a tone. "Not just men, either. Women are just as capable of doing this stuff as men are."

"Yeah, Mom," Chloe added. "People lie all the time."

"I realize that."

Kevin stared at her for a long moment, then seemed to come to a decision. "You know what? This is a lot to take in, especially since you've just gotten two letters in the last three days. How about you give me a list of five names? That will give us some place to start."

"And then, if you don't come up with anything?"

"Then, we'll dig a little bit harder."

"I still feel like I'm betraying good people whose only fault is that they never learned to read."

"I understand. But no one who is taking the time to call you, text you, and mail letters is going to stop on their own."

Joy held out her hand, took the pen, and wrote down five names. She felt like she was betraying all the people who had put their trust in her and she hated every minute of it.

While Bo looked on, she wondered if he was right—that she wasn't being realistic. That she was letting a soft heart interfere with logic. But if she did that, then surely she'd have to include him in her list of suspects too?

After all, he'd been in prison. She couldn't help but believe that was significant.

Her life was getting more and more complicated. So much so, she hardly knew where to turn to anymore.

A chill ran through her. Obviously, that was her stalker's intention. He was systematically making her world feel jarring and off-kilter.

No doubt he was currently feeling really pleased with himself.

CHAPTER 25

Joy had looked so shaken after Kevin left, Bo hadn't wanted to leave. He yearned to be something more to her than the guy she was just beginning to date. He wanted to be someone she could count on and depend on. He would've liked to coddle her that evening. Tell her to go take a long bubble bath in that cast iron tub while he made her and Chloe supper.

But that was too much, too soon.

So, after telling the detective goodbye, he'd chatted with Chloe for a few seconds. When her mom was in the kitchen he'd even mentioned Finn and said that he'd heard that the boy now had a phone. She'd smiled back, looking pleased that they had a little secret.

Ten minutes later, he'd hugged Joy goodbye, kissed her gently on the cheek, and then headed back to his house. He knew he needed to check in with the guys and probably even hang out at the house for a while, but he couldn't do it.

He was feeling a bit rattled too. He'd known a lot of men who'd committed crimes. He'd stood by Lincoln's side when Jennifer had been attacked. But everything felt different now. He cared about Joy, and he was annoyed as all get out that someone had decided to make her life hell.

That was why, after he'd gotten home and pulled out a beer, he'd sat down and called his mother. He might not be able to say everything he wanted to Joy, but there was someone who he could be completely honest with.

Besides, it had been over a week since he'd checked in with her. Feeling ashamed about that, Bo took another sip of beer, grabbed his cell phone, clicked on her name, and pressed Send.

She answered immediately. "Hello?"

"Hey, Momma."

"Samuel." She said his real name like always, like a breath of fresh air mixed in with warm-cookie goodness. "This is a nice surprise."

He glanced at the time and winced. It was half past six. "Sorry about the time. Are you in the middle of supper?"

"I am not." She sounded affronted. "I'll have you know that I ate an hour ago, just like always. I'm just sitting here on the front porch watching the sun as it thinks about going down."

"I'm jealous." He knew exactly where she was. Their old farmhouse had a beautiful front and side porch. It was wide and painted pale blue and filled with wicker furniture that seemed determined to withstand the test of time. For as long as he could remember, his mother would sip coffee there in the morning and spend her evenings there watching the sun set.

Back when he was a teenager, he'd been sure it was a waste of time. There wasn't much of a view from the front porch. Just an expanse of yard and the neighbor's house across the road.

"If you're jealous about watching the sun set, I believe you need to come home soon and visit for a spell."

"I'd like that."

"Do you have some time off?" Her voice was filled with hope.

That was the thing. Of course he did. Lincoln didn't hold with things like vacation days or timeclocks. Plus, Bo did so much of his job at off times—whenever the guys needed him— no one would ever blink twice if he said that he needed to take a week and visit his family.

So why hadn't he?

"I'd love to come see you, Momma."

"Except . . ."

He smiled. "Except that I'm kind of dealing with something right now."

"Ah. What is that?"

"I'm starting to see a woman."

His confession startled a laugh out of her. "Out of all the things I thought you were going to say, a woman was at the bottom of my list."

"Wonders never cease, right?"

"Indeed. Well, come on now. Tell me about her."

"All right. Her name is Joy. She's got long brown hair, brown eyes, and is as kind as all get out. She's also divorced and has a girl named Chloe."

"Does she, now?" Warmth filled her voice. "How old is that child?"

"Sixteen."

"Sixteen. Well, now. I'm sure she and you are getting along."

"We're just starting to get to know each other. Joy keeps a pretty close eye on her."

"I imagine that's smart."

Thinking about Joy's stalker, he nodded. "I reckon so. A woman can't be too careful."

"If I had to take a wild guess, I'd say Joy is taking baby steps in the relationship department because she's worried about her daughter getting too attached. Or herself."

"Yeah, maybe. I hadn't thought about that."

"That's because you're not a mother. Don't worry. Before you know it, you and Chloe will be chatting like y'all are good friends."

"I don't know about that, Mom. She's sixteen, not six."

"I don't think that's going to make a difference. Girls have always liked you. That was never your problem, was it?"

He frowned. "No, ma'am."

"So you don't want to leave Joy right now because you're making headway and getting to know her daughter?"

"I don't. But it isn't because of what you think. Someone is bothering Joy. Someone is sending her creepy notes."

"To her house?"

"Yeah. First she was getting texts, but it's gotten worse. Joy's worried sick and who can blame her?"

"Not me."

"I helped her talk to a detective today." Thinking about how upset Joy had been, he added, "I don't know if the detective is going to be able to help much, though. Joy didn't want to give him a lot of details about who could be messing with her. She seems reluctant to name people who she's close to."

"Trusting takes time, but I'd wager that distrusting does too."

He hadn't thought about it that way. "Momma, how come you're getting so smart?"

"Because I had to put up with you. And Eric, Carrie, and Janie." She chuckled. "Carrie wasn't easy on her best day."

No, she sure hadn't been. "Janie and I used to say that she

was born in a bad mood." Eric had always been a pill, too, but Momma rarely talked about Eric to Bo. Eric was sure that Bo was just one step up from pond scum. "So, uh, what have you been doing?"

"I've got my hands full with Vacation Bible School."

He'd attended that every year and knew it was almost as busy and chaotic as a three-ring circus. "You're not in charge of it again, are you?" Three years ago, she'd gotten sick from all the stress.

"No, but the fella who is seems to think that he's too busy to do much. He keeps telling me not to worry about things but I know for a fact he hasn't gotten anything organized. If he's not careful, we're going to have three hundred children wandering around unsupervised."

"Uh-oh. You need to give him what for."

"I'll keep that in mind. I've also been seeing someone myself. As a matter of fact."

He sat up so sharply that he almost spilled his coffee. "Who? Do I know him?"

"You do. It's Sean Davis."

It took a minute to place him. When he did, he was glad he'd put his cup down. The Davises lived in the house across from them. Lauren Davis had been his fifth-grade teacher. She'd died a couple years back. So he wasn't faulting Sean for dating. He wasn't even faulting his mother for dating. But the two of them? "I didn't think Sean was that old."

"Uhm."

"Sorry, Momma. I'm not saying that you are. But he's got to be quite a few years younger."

"He's forty-eight to my fifty-two, Sam. Neither of us would call ourselves old. I'm a little surprised to hear you say that."

He'd just been put firmly in his place. "I apologize."

"You don't have anything else to say now?"

He knew that fighting tone in his mother's voice like the back of his hand. "No, ma'am. I don't think that would be a good idea."

She chuckled. "Perhaps not. Relationships are tricky, aren't they? One moment everything's the same and then, bam, you start seeing a person differently. I used to think it was a matter of putting on rose-colored glasses, but maybe it's a matter of taking them off."

"Maybe so." He, of course, had been taken in by Joy from the moment he heard her voice. He thought she was gorgeous but he was pretty sure that he would have found her gorgeous no matter what her looks were. After all, he was living proof that good packaging didn't necessarily mean there was a good person inside.

"Sam, you know what? The highway runs in both directions. Would you like me to come up to see you? I'll see if Carrie or Janie want to come along. We'll stay just for the weekend. Not long. It's been a while. I could see your house. Maybe even say hello to this lady who's caught your heart."

"I'd love to see you, Momma."

"My goodness! You sound serious."

"You know I'd love to see you. It's just that with everything going on with Joy, I don't think I can get away. I don't want you driving up here on your own, though."

"Like I said, I bet one of the girls can spare me some time."

Here he was, making everyone move heaven and earth when he should be the one doing that. "Mom, you know what? I'll come to you. I'm sorry I—"

"Oh, no you don't. Don't you start overthinking things and worrying about what your sisters and Eric are going to say. They don't think near as harshly on you as you seem to think they do."

"Still—"

"Samuel, you came out here three times last year. It's my

189

turn. Now I'm going to figure something out and get back to you. And Son?"

"Yes?"

"You take a deep breath and take care of that woman and her girl."

"I will."

By the time they'd hung up, he'd gotten four emails and twice that many text messages. Skimming the texts, he saw they were all from his guys. Nothing urgent.

Realizing that it was heading toward eight, he rang Joy.

"Bo. Hi."

"How are you?"

"I don't know."

"You worried about everything?" Of course, the minute he asked, he wished he could've taken his question back. Of course she was worried. Some creeper was sending her texts and letters.

"Yes." She sighed. "Bo, I thought meeting with the detective was going to make me feel better. Instead, all I feel is more stressed out."

"Tell me why. Is it the cop or how I handled it?"

"None of that. It's that there's a good chance someone I know is making it their business to scare me out of my mind. I hate that."

"I do too. What do you need?"

"Nothing. I mean, you've done enough."

"I'm not asking, hoping you say you're fine. I'm asking because I hate the idea of you being scared and me not knowing."

"Bo, you're serious, aren't you?"

"Absolutely."

When she didn't answer right away, he got concerned. "Tell me what you're thinking."

"I'm not sure what we are."

He wasn't either. "I know. I'm not sure either." He knew what he wished they could be, but he'd learned long ago that wishes and dreams were for fools. "But don't you think that's okay? Maybe we can just keep going for a while."

She released a ragged sigh. "I can do that."

"Good. Now what are you doing tomorrow?"

"I'm tutoring in a little bit, then grocery shopping, getting Chloe, and doing dance class."

"Where are you tutoring at?"

"Sacred Grounds. I'm with Anthony. He's the man you first saw me with."

He remembered everything about that morning, from what she had been wearing, to the guy she'd been sitting with.

"You tutoring at nine again?"

"I am. Why?"

"No reason." Especially since he didn't think it would be a problem to get by there with Mason. Hearing the television on behind her, he murmured, "I'm going to let you go, but I'll see you sometime tomorrow. Have a good night now."

"You too." Her voice turned even softer. "Thanks for giving me a call tonight."

"Don't thank me for that. I called you for selfish reasons."

She chuckled. "I think I'm going to leave it at that. Bye."

Looking down, he noticed his beer bottle was empty and the sun was almost all the way down.

Deciding to stop worrying about everything, he took a hot shower and then sat in front of the television. Tried to focus on the movie on Netflix.

But all he kept thinking about was one day having Joy sitting in his living room by his side at the end of the day.

It sounded almost too good to ever come true.

CHAPTER 26

There was so much frustration and pain in Anthony's eyes, Joy felt like crying.

They were sitting at their usual table in the center of Sacred Grounds. Surrounding them was the usual line of people, the heavenly aroma of freshly ground coffee, and the low buzz of conversation mixed in with lilting instrumental arrangements pouring out of speakers. So it was the same as it always was, except that today everything seemed different. Anthony, who was usually her most positive and upbeat student, was in a funk.

"Come on, Anthony. I know you can do this," she coaxed. "You read the words last time we were together, remember?"

"I'm sorry, but I just can't," he said after attempting to read the five-word sentence another two times. He stared at the page another moment before looking away. "Every time I open my mouth, the words get stuck."

It had been a particularly hard session. Thankful that

Anthony wasn't her first student, she crossed her legs and tried another approach. There were a half-dozen ways to help an adult learn to read and she was determined to use every one of them until he was successful.

"Let's take it slower," she urged as she tapped the first word with a finger. "Now, what is this first sound?"

Anthony glared at it before closing his eyes. "Maybe we should stop doing this, Miss Joy. We've been meeting a long time now but instead of going forward, I'm going in the other direction. I suck."

If he'd been a little boy, she would have pulled him close and given him a hug. Instead he was a good four inches taller than her, weighed at least fifty pounds more, and looked like he'd rather be in a knife fight than hug a thirtysomething woman.

But appearances were deceiving. Anthony was so sweet. He'd had a hard life and far too many people walk in and out, who didn't believe in him. He'd told her once that he wished he didn't have to live alone and it had broken her heart.

She was not going to be one more person to do that.

"No," she said in her firmest tone. When he stared at her in surprise, she added, "I'm not giving up on you and you aren't either. I'm not going to let you."

"Joy, it ain't that I don't want to . . . It's just—"

"Nope. Uh-uh. You and I are not going to talk about anything but these five words right here." She tapped the page. "I know it's a stupid sentence but we're going to get through it." She lowered her voice. "Remember what those two *o*'s sound like together?"

"Oooh?"

"That's right. Plus, it starts with a what?"

"*B*."

"And it ends with what sound?"

Anthony dutifully made a *t* sound.

"Good. Come on now." When he still looked tense, she rubbed his arm. "Anthony, it's just us, right? I'm not going to criticize you or laugh." He'd shared how kids in his classes used to make fun of him—and even some of his teachers mocked him. She wished she could march into his past and give everyone a piece of her mind.

"B . . . oo . . . t," he whispered.

She smiled. "That's right. And you know the word *mom*. So come on now."

He blinked. For a second, something that looked like real anger lit his face. "You can sure get bossy, Joy. You're ordering me around."

"No, I'm trying to help you. Are you ready, Anthony?"

He nodded, seemed to brace himself, then very slowly repeated the word that had been giving him fits. "B . . . oooo . . . t." He blinked. "That's boot."

Joy was practically doing handsprings in her head. At long last, he'd gotten it! "You did it again. Yay!"

"You sound like a cheerleader."

She chuckled. "I guess I do. I'm so proud of you."

When he smiled, his expression transformed again. It was almost like she'd imagined that surge of anger she'd witnessed. "Me too."

"Now, are you feeling better?" When he nodded, she added, "Good. Let's read that whole sentence."

He stared hard at the words, seemed to mentally practice them, then said, "Mom put on a boot." He blinked like he was shocked. "Is that right?"

"Oh yes." Unable to help herself, she reached for his hand and squeezed it. He looked startled by her touch, but squeezed her hand back, blushing. "We've got the rest of this page to get through. Let's go."

It took another twenty minutes, but he did it. Anthony read the page. When he finished, he tilted back his head. "I'm sweating."

"I think I am, too. You're doing so good, Anthony. You're going to be in here sipping coffee and reading a book before you know it."

"I'd settle just for being able to read everything at the grocery store."

"I bet if you went to Kroger tonight you might be able to read more words than you realize."

He shrugged. "I wish I could, but I gotta go. I've got to get to work. These buildings don't clean themselves, you know." After glancing across the room, his voice flattened. "You've got company again."

"I do?" Apprehension slammed into her as she turned.

Seeing it was Bo, everything settled into place. She wasn't sure what was going on between the two of them, but she was sure that it was something good.

Bo was in a black T-shirt, jeans, and boots. His blond hair was a little mussed, like he'd been running his hands through it in a distracted way. He was also glaring at something on his phone. Two of his buddies were sitting next to him. All three of them were sipping coffee. How had she missed them coming in?

When one of the guys saw her looking their way, he elbowed Bo. He jerked his head up. Fastening those eyes directly on her.

Practically making the rest of the world disappear—or, at the very least, making her forget just about everything except her name. What could she do but smile at him?

He stood up.

"Is that your man?" Anthony said.

She blinked. How had she been so unaware that he was still there? "Kind of." When his expression seemed to darken, Joy added, "He's a good friend."

"Uh-huh."

She felt her cheeks heat. "Good luck with the rest of your day, Anthony." She was being a little abrupt but she wasn't comfortable with him getting so personal.

Anthony smiled, like everything was back in place in his head again. "Yes, ma'am." Shrugging his backpack on his shoulder, he quirked a brow. "So . . . next week?"

"I wouldn't miss it. You did great today. I really am so proud of you."

His gaze warmed like she'd given him the biggest compliment. "You always say that."

"It's the truth."

Anthony laughed as he walked out. Watching him walk with confidence, she whispered a small prayer of thanks. She was so proud of him.

"Morning, Joy."

Somehow Bo had walked to her side. She got to her feet. "Sorry, I didn't know you were here. I didn't even realize you and your friends were in the shop."

"I gathered that."

"Anthony and I . . . well, today was kind of a tough lesson. He had all my attention."

"Nothing to apologize for. Besides, getting to see that guy finally get those words down right?" He whistled low. "At first, I thought he was getting mad, but then he found success. It was a sight to see."

She wasn't sure what he meant by that but figured it didn't matter anyway. "Is everything okay?" Maybe the detective had given him some news?

"Everything's fine. We just happened to be nearby. They didn't complain when I suggested we stop in here for a few. Want to meet my friends?"

"Sure."

"Come on then."

Their table was just a couple of steps away. Since the coffee shop was half-empty, she didn't mind leaving her things on the table.

"Joy, this is Mason and Seth. Y'all this is Joy."

Both of the men stood up. Mason was the taller of the two. He had an easy smile and really white teeth. Seth looked to be the cleaner-cut of the pair. He was blond, blue-eyed, and seemed to take in everything about her within a couple of seconds.

"Hi," she said simply.

"Ma'am," Mason said.

Seth stuffed his hands in his pockets. "Joy, what you're doing is really great. I didn't mean to eavesdrop, but I swear when that guy read that sentence, I just about went over and hugged him."

She chuckled. "Me too. He's trying so hard and is so used to failing. His parents used to tell him he was stupid all the time. I hope I never meet them."

"Sorry, but I kind of hope you do," Mason teased.

"Why?"

"You'd give them what for, coming and going."

She laughed. "I'm hardly that. But I'll take the compliment. Thank you."

"You have a good day now," Mason said as he sat back down.

"I'll be right there," Bo told the guys as he walked her to her seat. "So, how are you doing? You good?" he murmured. "Did you get any sleep last night?"

"Not really. Every time I close my eyes, I keep thinking about every bad thing that could possibly happen."

"I know it's tempting, but that won't help you much. Now that you've got Kevin involved, things will start moving. Try and stay positive."

"I'll try, but it feels like all we're doing is waiting for another letter to arrive. Or something worse."

His lips formed a thin line. "What's going on the rest of your day?"

"I'm going to pick up Chloe from school, run her through a drive-thru, take her to dance, then help her with her homework when she's all done."

"What time will you be home next?"

"I don't know. Around four or so? I don't stay while Chloe's dancing."

"I'll make sure to have my phone nearby. Text me when you get your mail, okay?"

She was starting to feel like she was taking advantage of him. "There's no need for you to worry. If I have a letter, I'll call Kevin."

"I know you will, and I'm glad. But still, text me after you get your mail, okay?"

"Fine."

Bo continued to stare at her intently. "And if something feels off at home, you call me. I've got some stuff to do until about six, but if you need something, I'll send someone to come out and make sure you're all right."

"Are you serious?"

"Of course. I'm not going to joke about getting you help."

It was all too much. She was starting to feel like she didn't have anything to offer in return. "Bo, that isn't necessary—"

He stilled her protest with a firm but kind look. "Please? I promise, I can't get out of this appointment, but I don't want you being shy and not texting me that you need help. If you let me know, one of them will be over right away."

How could she refuse him now? "All right," she said softly.

"Thanks." He cupped her jaw with his hand and gently ran a thumb over her cheek before turning away.

She forced herself to sit down before the whole coffee shop watched her stare at him like a lovesick fool.

But when she heard a soft chuckle beside her, and noticed an elderly lady was watching her with bright eyes, Joy knew it was already too late.

Oh well. Pretending that Bo wasn't one of the best things that had ever walked into her life was proving to be impossible.

CHAPTER 27

"That's right, Bo," Winter murmured. "Yes. Put your arm just like that." The camera clicked. "Hmm. Okay, now look pensive."

Bo turned his head, stared at the white screen in front of him, and did his best to look *pensive*. The first time Winter had directed him to look that way half the room had burst out laughing. It turned out there was a whole lot of difference between looking pissed off and solemn and wary.

"Adele, fix that wrinkle on his shirt. Hmm. And, Davis, the light . . . yeah. Perfect." *Click, click, click.*

Bo remained motionless while the photographer looked through the latest shots.

"We're good. Wardrobe change." Winter looked at the computer printout of her notes. "Okay, we're moving on to the parka, modern jeans, black sweater combo," she called out.

"I need five," Bo said.

Winter glanced at her phone. "Take ten. I need to take a call anyway."

"Can I take that flannel, Bo?" Adele asked.

"Yeah, sure." He unbuttoned it and handed it over. "Let me get some water, use the john, and check my phone."

"Do you want something to eat?" Adele asked. "I can order you a sandwich."

They'd already put out a whole spread for him when he'd arrived two hours ago. "Thanks, but I'm good."

Adele smiled at him before walking back to wardrobe, which was essentially a huge room lined with two dozen mini clothing racks. Adele and Winter and probably some higher-ups had set up the outfits for the catalog and the order for him to wear them.

After using the facilities, he checked his phone, frowned when he saw a text from Joy, then exhaled when all she'd written was that she was home and there weren't any weird letters in her mailbox. Something deep inside of him seemed to settle into place at long last. She was all right. He texted her back, relayed that he was still in a meeting, and then tossed the phone onto the pile of his personal belongings.

When he walked into wardrobe, Adele was steaming a shirt.

"Where to next?" he asked.

"L. Want any help?"

He grinned. "Not yet." The first time he'd been hired to be the main model of Renegade's sportswear catalog, he'd been surprised when Adele had asked him to undress down to his underwear. He'd never been shy—and he'd lost any traces of modesty while in prison—so he hadn't been embarrassed to take off his clothes. However, being told by a young gal to strip had taken him aback.

But not as much as when she'd walked to his side and asked

if he needed help getting dressed. Once he'd realized she was serious, he'd said the first thing he could think of—not yet.

Which had become something of a running joke for the two of them.

Walking over to 'L,' he shucked off his clothes and put on the pair of cargo shorts and T-shirt. When the T-shirt practically felt like the seams were going to pull apart, he called out, "Hey Adele, something's up with this shirt."

"Hmm?" She walked over to his side, looking him over as she did so. "What's wrong?"

"Look at it. Don't you think it's too tight?"

She grinned. "No."

"Come on. Really?" He'd long ago given up having an opinion about the clothes they put him in, but this felt painted on.

She lowered her voice. "Don't freak out, but you're getting a bit of a following. Winter heard that people are ordering the catalog just to get more pictures of you."

"Yeah, right."

"Sorry, but it's true. Someone in marketing predicted that you're one of the reasons sales are up. So . . . one of the owners asked if we could stick you in a few more shirts that didn't hide too much."

"As in nothing?"

"Hey, I just work here. You could complain . . ."

"I'm not going to." He got paid too much for a couple of hours of standing around and looking "pensive" for that. "At least I have on clothes, right?"

She giggled. "Don't jinx it. Next thing you know, you'll only be wearing a pair of swim trunks or something."

He laughed as she walked around him, pulling on the fabric and smoothing out one of the pockets of his shorts. "Where are the shoes?"

"No shoes. Bare feet."

"Really?"

"We have a set with sand. We're getting fancy around here."

"Let's go!" Winter called out.

Adele sighed as she walked toward the set. "Come on, Bo. We don't want Winter to get in a snit."

Since Bo didn't disagree, he followed on her heels.

Sure enough, Winter situated him on a pile of sand, even going so far as to spray some water on his legs so some of the sand would stick to his skin. After a good ten minutes, he was posed and Winter was taking pictures again.

"Smile a little, Bo. No. Less. Like you've got a secret."

He toned it down, thinking that it wasn't a lie. He had a couple at the moment—not only was he not happy that he was going to have sand stuck to his legs all evening, but he had another secret about a certain woman with brown hair, kind brown eyes, and who likely couldn't care less about what he looked like.

"Davis, come spray some water on his arms. Bo, act like you're going to take the shirt off."

He frowned. "You know it's tight, right?" He was pretty sure he was going to look like a snake or something coming out of its skin if he tried to take off that shirt.

"You'll be fine." Winter smiled. "I promise, you look great."

"I'll help you out," Adele murmured. "I'll cut a slit in the back if you need."

He held up his hand and gave her a high five. "Thanks."

And so it continued. He pulled off the too-tight shirt while Winter took pictures. He changed clothes a dozen more times, and suffered through getting sprayed with water, oil, and sand.

Hair people restyled his hair and a makeup person put some concealer wherever there was a dark spot on his face. Another three hours later, he was finished. He wiped down his face and eventually put back on his regular clothes.

"Thanks, Bo," Winter said when he was about to leave. "Everything turned out great. I know everyone is going to be pleased."

"I appreciate you calling me."

"You say that every time."

"It's always true." None of them knew that every time he only kept a third of his $3,000 paycheck and sent the rest to his mother. This money helped her do all the extra things she'd never been able to do or get when she'd been raising four kids. Janie once told him about a time Ma had gone out and bought herself a new couch with a check he'd sent her. Another time, she went on a river cruise. Bo would put up with a lot of tight shirts and oil to be able to give her that.

"See you in six months," Adele called out.

He gave her a salute as he headed out to his truck. Then stopped short when he saw calls from both Mason and Joy. Punching in her number, he held it to his ear.

"Joy?"

"Hey, Bo."

"Everything good?"

"Yes. But, um, would you mind coming over here tonight? That is, if you don't have other plans?"

"I don't mind at all. Listen, honey . . . I just got done with something. Let me check in with Mason and then I'll call you back."

"Okay. Thanks."

Pulling out of the parking lot, he rang Mason.

"Hey. Are you free yet?"

"Yeah." No one besides Lincoln knew that he did this modeling gig on the side. "Why?"

"I think you need to come on over to the house. Grafton's

girl showed up, she's flirting with half the guys, and Grafton is about to lose it."

"You can't deal with it?" His legs were still covered with oil and bits of sand.

"I can give it a try, but he don't listen to anyone but you or Lincoln."

"Fine. I'll be there in twenty." Disconnecting, he thought about how he was going to let Joy know what was going on. Since there really wasn't any way to let her know—besides tell her the God's honest truth, he called her again.

"Bo?"

"Hey. Joy, sweetheart, I'm sorry but there's a problem with one of the guys. I've got to go calm him down."

"Oh." He could practically hear her inject a false note of happiness in her voice. "Well, um, thanks for letting me know."

"What's going on? Did you get another letter after all?"

"No."

"A phone call?"

"No. It . . . it was more of a feeling. I thought I saw someone outside. I'm sure it's nothing."

"I'll get there as soon as I can. Even if it's late, I'll be there."

"No. I don't want Chloe to worry. If you show up late at night, she's not going to be able to sleep for another week."

"I'd rather her see me there late instead of wondering where I am when her mother is freaking out. Give me an hour and then I'll call, okay? But if you see someone again, you call Sergeant Heilman and then call me. Nothing's more important than you."

"Thank you. I will."

When he hung up, he wondered how much longer he was going to try to do everything and be everything to everyone. It wasn't sustainable.

Worse, he reckoned it was a recipe for disaster.

CHAPTER 28

When Joy picked up Chloe, she noticed that her daughter couldn't seem to stop looking at her phone. That wasn't exactly a rarity, but Chloe didn't usually look at it so intently. "What's going on?" she asked at last. "Is Baylee in the middle of another drama?"

"No. I've been texting a guy—I told you about him. His name's Finn."

"I haven't heard his name before. Did you meet him in French class?"

"No. I met him at Lane's Diner."

Alarm bells went off inside of her. She pushed them back, reminding herself that just because Chloe met someone new outside of school it didn't mean that it was anything to worry about. "Really? What's he like?"

"He's Amish."

Joy couldn't have been happier to be driving. If they'd been facing each other, there was no way Chloe could have mistaken the look of sheer surprise that crossed her face. "I see."

Chloe laughed. "Oh, Mom. You should see yourself, trying to act like you aren't shocked."

"And here I thought I was doing so good."

"You aren't. Anyway, Finn is Mary and Lane's nephew. He started working there a few weeks back."

"And now you see him when you walk over there from school."

"Yeah. I always get a vanilla malt." She paused. "Sometimes Mary even lets him take his break with me, so we go to the park down the road."

"You didn't think to tell me any of this?"

"I'm telling you now, Mom. Besides, I'm drinking a vanilla malt and sitting on a park bench. We both know it's probably the tamest thing that's happening in the sophomore class."

Joy figured Chloe had a point. "How did he get a phone?"

"Some guy who used to be Amish got it for him."

"Isn't Finn worried about his parents finding out? Or are they okay with him having it?" She vaguely remembered the whole *rumspringa* thing. A lot of teenagers got cell phones during that time.

"He's really worried, but he says it's worth it."

"Because he gets to text you?"

"Yeah, and because he doesn't want to live at home much longer."

Joy felt like she had just jumped into the middle of some Lifetime drama. "Chloe, are you sure you want to be involved with him? This Finn sounds like he's got a lot going on."

"Like we don't? Besides, you and I both know that you don't always get a choice about living drama-free. Sometimes it just happens."

"You're right about that." Joy had never been so happy to

pull into the driveway. "Okay, let's get you organized for tomorrow, okay?"

"Yep."

Though Chloe was older now and could easily do everything on her own, she seemed to like their evening routine as much as Joy did. First came Chloe handing over her dirty clothes from both school and dance class. Then, if she had dance the next day, came repacking her bag with fresh tights, leotards, snacks, and sweats.

Then, while Chloe took a hot shower or bath—depending on the state of her feet—Joy made her daughter's lunch, set up the coffee maker, and looked at her own schedule for the next day. When Chloe came out in pajamas or sweats, Joy sat with her while Chloe ate a snack. The whole thing only took about an hour.

They'd started the routine soon after Kevin had left, when Joy had been feeling betrayed and Chloe had been confused. The predictable schedule had served two purposes. First, it had given them both something to do besides compare their lives to how things used to be. It had also helped fill up the evening so neither of them had too much time to mope.

Now, though, it was a good opportunity for them to connect. Joy was thankful for it too. One day Chloe would be driving. When that happened, Joy knew their time together would be even less.

Joy had just sat down with a cup of hot peppermint tea when Chloe looked up from her bowl of cereal. "Hey, Mom?"

"Yes?"

"How often do you see Bo?"

"It depends. I saw him today when I got done tutoring over at Sacred Grounds. We talked for a while then both went to do our own things. He might stop by later, if it's not too late. If he does, he probably won't stay long."

"When else do you see him?"

"Not as much as you think. I was honest when I said that he and I are just starting to see each other."

"You know, you can go on dates and stuff. You don't have to stay home every night."

"Thanks." She smiled. "So anything else?"

"No."

"Are you sure about that?"

Chloe pushed her bowl to one side. "I guess I'm just trying to figure out how serious you two are. Dad said that he didn't think that Bo was the kind of man you should be seeing."

It took a second, but Joy forced her expression to remain noncommittal. "When did he tell you that?"

"On Saturday night. He asked me if Bo had been over much."

"That isn't any of his business."

Her eyes widened. "Are you mad at me? Was I not supposed to say anything?"

"Honey, you can talk to him about anything you want. Your father is the one who shouldn't be asking you questions about my private life. He knows better."

"Oh. Well, I guess it doesn't matter anyway."

"I'm not following you. What doesn't matter?"

"Dad said you'd probably only ever want to be married to him."

Joy sputtered. "To your dad?"

"Yeah. Do you think that's true?"

"I hope not. I don't know what the future holds. We'll have to see what happens. But just between you and me, I kind of hope that isn't the case. Dad found Sandy, right?"

Some of the light left her eyes. "Right. Of course, she was awful so it's good they broke up."

"Honey, you know as well as I do that relationships are really hard. Sometimes everything goes really well, and sometimes it doesn't. That doesn't mean that people don't love each other anymore."

"Yeah."

"One thing I know for certain is that both Dad and I love you a lot. No matter what."

"I love you too, Mom." Standing up, she said, "I'm going to go watch TV."

"Alright, honey."

Only after Chloe went to her room did Joy give into her irritation. That was vintage Tony, without a doubt. He didn't want her, but he didn't think anyone else should have her either.

She strode to the living room and picked up her phone, determined to send Tony a text. Just to show him that he couldn't get away with talking about her with their daughter.

She slid her thumb across the screen, realized she had two messages, and froze.

Feeling as if she was in slow motion, she clicked on the message icon. And saw one from Bo and one from an unknown number. Before she lost her nerve, she clicked on it.

> Don't run away. Don't hide
> from me.

A cold sweat poured off of her as she read the words. Read them again. Her fingers hovered over the screen, ready to delete the offending message. Ready to pretend that she hadn't received it, that she hadn't noticed it.

But, just like a bad ink stain on a white shirt, the evidence wasn't going to go away. She could attempt to bleach it out of her mind, but it would always be there. Faded, maybe not as strong in her mind, but always there.

Quickly, she clicked on Bo's name and read his text.

> Still feel badly about not being
> able to come over earlier. You
> doing all right?

As a matter of fact, no, she was not. But what was she going to tell him? That her ex-husband, who had told her that she wasn't enough for him four years ago, was starting to act like maybe she was worth his time after all?

It wasn't like she and Bo had a close relationship, anyway. Oh, there was some chemistry between them, but she wasn't even sure if he really liked her or if his feelings had gotten confused with a need to protect her from a mystery stalker.

Finally texting him back, she typed:

> I'm fine. You?

> Yeah. Guessing you got Chloe
> home from dance? You
> haven't seen anyone else
> lurking, have you?

A tiny chill ran through her. He'd remembered. And, even more than that, he'd taken the time to ask about her.

> I haven't seen anyone else. I
> bet I just imagined it anyway.

Still no messages, right?

I just got one, but it's okay. I'll
call Kevin about it tomorrow.

Immediately, her phone rang. "Girl. What's this about?"

"Hi to you too."

"Don't give me that. When did you get another message?"

"I just saw it. Chloe just got settled for the night so I checked
my phone. I had two. One from you and one from him." She
frowned. "Or her. Or whoever it was."

"What did it say?"

"I don't remember exactly." Of course that was a lie.

"What's going on? Are you mad at me? I promise, I really
had to go by the house. This guy who just got out is kind of a
handful. He's driving everyone crazy."

"Bo, of course I'm not mad at you."

"Then why didn't you call me as soon as you saw it?" His
Kentucky accent was thicker. He seemed upset—almost like
he was hurt.

"I'm starting to feel like I'm too much trouble." With a fake
laugh, she added, "Maybe I'm like that guy who just got out of
prison. I'm driving you crazy with my drama." And where this
was coming from, she didn't know.

He didn't say anything for a long second. "Look, it's only
eight thirty. You good with me coming over?"

"Bo, there's no need."

"Joy, are you good with me coming over tonight? I could
be there in twenty minutes."

"You're not giving up, are you?"

"I'm not a quitter. And you didn't tell me yes or no."

"Bo, I'm . . . I'm not in a good place tonight. It doesn't have anything to do with you or even the stalker. I just think I ought to go to bed."

"Can you give me a reason?"

"I just did."

"Joy, can you give me a real reason?"

Before she could decide whether or not to answer, the words started pouring out. "My ex-husband is being a jerk. I'm so mad right now I'm afraid I'm going to scare you off." She closed her eyes. Could she sound any more needy and/or ridiculous?

His voice softened. "I'm not scared. I'll see you soon, okay?"

"Bo, I just told you—"

He kept his voice low and measured. "Joy, I hate to break it to you, but I'm not just good at my job, at calling cops and counseling felons. I'm also real good at listening to pretty women complain about their ex-husbands."

The surge of jealousy that hit took her off guard. Was she just another needy woman he was looking after? She didn't think that anyone would take on her problems when there were so many other women out there who didn't have an ex-husband or a stalker . . . Or maybe he had a crazy hero complex. She knew women who loved crushing on men who were unattainable. Maybe this was his odd version of that. "Sounds like you have a lot of experience in that area."

Ouch. She'd somehow just managed to sound both insecure and jealous at the same time.

His response was immediate. "As a matter of fact, I don't. Thank the good Lord. What I'm trying to say is talking about a jerk of an ex sounds like a nice break from all the awful and scary stuff that's been happening lately, right? Talking about exes is normal stuff."

She opened her mouth to protest but closed it right away. Why was she trying to push Bo away? He was gorgeous, capable, and kind to her and her daughter. He'd taken her concerns about the notes seriously and had even helped to make sure she talked to a detective with a good reputation. In addition, he had been doing everything he possibly could—short of renting out a billboard in the middle of town—to demonstrate how he felt about her. She certainly didn't need that either.

The simple truth was that she wanted to be around him. She wanted to see him.

"See you soon."

"There you go."

He hung up before she had the opportunity to ask if he was talking to her or to himself.

CHAPTER 29

When his brother Eric called as he was driving, Bo had come close to letting it go to voicemail. He loved his brother, but he always felt bad when he talked to him. He knew Eric didn't respect him and had some strong feelings about the mistakes Bo had made in his life. Bo couldn't deny that Eric had every right to feel the way he did—but that didn't mean he felt he needed to listen to his opinions every chance he got.

"Eric," he said as a greeting. "How are you?"

"I'm all right. What about you?"

"Good."

"Did I call at a bad time?"

"I'm on my way over to see someone but I have a couple of minutes."

"You got another idiot to straighten out?"

The insinuation chafed him but he pushed it away. This was

nothing new and no good would come out of correcting him. "No. It's something personal. I recently started seeing a woman."

"Oh yeah? What's her story?"

"Nothing that she would appreciate me sharing before you've met her."

"Wait. She's that kind of gal?"

His brother's condescending tone was starting to get pretty old. "What's going on?"

"I called to see if you were going to be home anytime soon. Are you planning to come for Easter?"

That was at the end of the month. "I should be. Why?"

"Beth asked."

Beth was Eric's oldest daughter. She was sixteen. "You can tell her I'll be there if I can. I'm planning on it."

"Okay. Good."

Something was going on with him. "Why?"

"I don't know. She hasn't told Rebecca or Mom. But she was anxious to see you."

"Do you want me to call her? I could reach out to her tomorrow. Text her in the afternoon when she's done with class."

"Do you mind, Bo? She adores you."

The hesitancy in his brother's voice caught him off guard. "Of course not. You know I don't mind helping out family."

"Thanks."

"No reason to thank me. I love Beth. I love all your kids."

"So what's this woman like?"

Usually he would never tell Eric anything but something inside of him was saying that it was time to do a bit of sharing, too. "She's divorced. Has a teenaged daughter. Sweet."

"Where did you meet her?"

"At a coffee shop."

"Whoa."

"What? Are you surprised I drink coffee or that I speak to people there?"

"I guess I deserved that."

"Eric, I've made a lot of piss-poor choices in my life but I'm not what you think I am."

"What is that supposed to mean?"

"That half the time I feel like you think I'm hanging out at biker bars doing Jell-O shots or something."

"Would you blame me?"

And, there it was. "Yeah. I would. I can't change my past, Eric, but you choosing to not accept my present gets old."

Eric didn't say anything for a few seconds. "You're right. I've been kind of a jerk."

There was no "kind of" in it at all, but he figured that he had to take what he could get. "I'll see you on Easter and I'll call Beth tomorrow."

"Why don't you bring this woman home for Easter? Everyone would love to meet her."

"I don't think she's ready for that."

"Why? Does she have a past too?"

And there it was again. One day Bo hoped Eric would come clean about why he was so against everything that Bo was. When he did, Bo knew he'd be anxious to hear all those reasons. Today wasn't that day, though. "See you Easter Sunday." He hung up.

Luckily, he was parked outside of Joy's house. He took a deep breath and rolled his shoulders. He didn't want to bring his crap into her life. It was just too bad that his crap happened to involve his brother.

She opened the door seconds before he knocked. "I was looking for you."

"I'm glad we're not waking Chloe up."

"She would be thrilled to see you though."

He smiled. "Ditto." Scanning her face, he saw something in her eyes that made him want to look a little more closely. "You look like you could use a hug. Want one?"

She nodded just seconds before stepping into his outstretched arms.

Joy pressed against him, half molding her body to his. He gently wrapped his arms around her and pulled her even closer. She was five or six inches shorter than him and so soft. He'd dated several women who worked out as much as he did and while he appreciated the work and dedication to create the bodies that they had, he much preferred her soft curves. He ran a hand up and down her back. Brushed a kiss on the top of her head.

"Bo, I can't believe how you make me feel. It's like you enter the room and lift my mood."

"Good. I like you telling me that."

She pulled away. "Would you like something to drink? I have some beer." She wrinkled her nose. "And a bottle of pinot noir."

"What's that look for?"

"I wish that I had something else that you might like. Something better instead of beer or red wine."

"I like both, but I like water too. How about that?"

"I'm on it."

"While you do that, how about you let me see that text."

"Bo, you don't need to . . ."

"Sorry, but I do." When she called out her password, he smiled, picked up her phone, and scanned through her texts. Until he came up on the latest one. "Have you sent it to Kevin yet?"

"Not yet. I'm going to do it tomorrow."

He had to trust her. Had to let her take care of it. "All right."

"Thanks for not arguing with me."

"I don't want to argue with you, sweetheart. Now tell me what's going on with your ex."

"Can we talk about you first? What's on your mind?"

"Other than a kid who's still giving me fits because he can't get over his girl cheating on him, I'm thinking about my brother Eric. He wants me to reach out to his daughter tomorrow."

"How old is she?"

"Sixteen."

"Why does he want you to talk to her?"

"I'm not sure. Me and Eric don't exactly get along well."

"Why?"

"Ah, because he's an executive in a Fortune 500 company and I'm his felon older brother. I haven't given him a lot to be proud of."

"Bo." She looked horrified. "Don't say things like that."

"I can't help it. No reason to not say it anyway. It's true."

"You're a lot more than the worst part of your life."

He liked the way she said that. "I hope so. It's still hard, though. It's like Eric can't help but be sure he knows exactly who I am. No matter how hard I try to tell him differently, to show him that I've changed, he doesn't want to accept that he could be wrong."

"Everything you are saying is exactly how Tony seems to think about me."

There was pain in her eyes. Pain and maybe regret too. Like whatever this Tony thought, it might be true. He hated that. Hated that some clown could make her feel like she was less than.

"What does Tony think?" It was hard to control his voice, so he didn't sound all possessive and pissed off.

Her eyes flared. It was obvious that she was taken aback by his tone. "Only that he was the best I could ever hope to get."

Something shifted inside of Bo. He fought off the smile that was hovering on his lips. He might not ever be Eric's level of best, but he was far from the worst. Better than a guy who could walk away from a sweet wife like Joy and a little girl who needed him.

This was something he could work with. Leaning closer, he shook his head. "Sorry, but your ex-husband is an idiot. More importantly, he's wrong." He lowered his voice. "He's so wrong. You can do a whole lot better than him."

A tiny smile appeared on her lips. "You sound so certain."

"That's because I am."

And then finally, at long last . . . after way too long to wait— he leaned closer, into her space, smelled the scented lotion on her skin. Unable to stop himself, he pressed his lips on the pulse in her neck.

Feeling the pulse point, imagining that it was speeding up because she was just as breathless as he was becoming, made him groan. He gently nipped.

"Oh!" She jerked back. Startled. Her eyes were wide.

Carefully, he ran his hand along the nape of her neck. Felt the silky strands of her hair brush against his knuckles. Met her eyes. Paused just long enough to let her know that she was in charge. She could pull away if that was what she wanted.

He really hoped that wasn't what she wanted.

Instead of moving back, Joy leaned closer. He felt her tremble. Her eyes went to half-mast as her lips parted slightly.

That was all the invitation he needed. So he kissed her. He kept it soft, gentle. She tasted just as sweet as her skin. Sweeter than he'd imagined. Better than his dreams.

Joy gripped his shoulders.

Running a hand along her spine, he claimed her lips again, deepening the kiss. Tasting her. Wanting her. Letting her know, as well as he could, that he was never going to let her go.

CHAPTER 30

"I can't believe I had to hear about this guy from Mom," Alice complained. "Why didn't you pick up the phone and call me too?"

Joy was having lunch with her younger sister who was also their family's force of nature. Alice—also known as Alice-Sells-Real-Estate to pretty much everyone in Cincinnati who was either trying to buy or sell a house—was incredible. She was rich, successful, and had married a down-to-earth guy named Joel who'd been a happy house-husband for most of their married life. They had three kids, a Labrador named Cindy, and were both beautiful.

She was also a lot to deal with if Joy wasn't up for the hurricane that she was. Which was why she hadn't told Alice anything.

Of course, she hadn't told Rand anything either. Chloe had told her grandparents about Bo two nights ago—much to Joy's shock and dismay.

"I didn't tell you about Bo because I didn't want to have

this exact conversation. I also didn't want you wasting your day driving all the way to Chillicothe."

"I'm not wasting my day. I wanted to come see you."

"I'm just saying that you're really busy. There was no need for you to make a special trip."

"Sure there was." Looking a little hurt, Alice added, "I care about you. Chloe too. We all do, Joy." She leaned a little closer. "Now tell me about this guy."

"I care about you too. But that doesn't mean I want to discuss Bo."

"How come? I heard he's hot."

"Because—wait, did you just say that Chloe called him hot? She didn't say that . . . did she?"

Alice chuckled. "No. Joel did some recon."

"How?"

"Joel's sister Courtney is a cop." She waved a hand like it was common knowledge. "She can do things like that."

So now multiple family members knew about Bo. "At least Chloe didn't show you a picture of him." Of course, the minute she'd said that, Joy started to get worried. Her sister could be crazy—and didn't have a whole lot of boundaries—where Joy was concerned. "Or did she?"

"I haven't seen a picture yet. But was Courtney right?" Eyes practically twinkling, she added, "Does he really look like a young Brad Pitt?"

Joy couldn't lie about that. "Oh, yeah. He's gorgeous, like double-take gorgeous."

"I want to see. Pull out your phone. Do you have a picture of him?"

"A picture, like I took a selfie of the two of us one afternoon?"

Alice was acting like that was perfectly possible. "Yes. So . . . do you?"

"No."

"Joy. Really?"

"Come on. I wasn't about to embarrass myself or him by doing that. And no, I'm not going to take his picture next time I see him." It was hard enough wrapping her head around the fact that she was dating a younger guy who inspired second glances wherever he went.

"You are such a spoilsport. And you need to be sneaky, like say that you want to do a selfie with him or something. Guys are used to that."

Even imagining such a conversation made her wince. "He's not going to want to do that." The next words came out before she could stop herself. "I can't believe he likes me."

"He does, hmm?" Alice smiled. "Did he ask you to go steady?"

That was a joke in reference to their parents, who were sure that such questions still came out of teenagers' mouths. "No. but . . ." Oh, who was she kidding? She had to tell someone! "He kissed me two nights ago."

Alice's eyes lit up. "I knew it. I told Joel that there had to be something between you—otherwise you wouldn't have let Chloe meet him."

She didn't want to involve her sister in her stalker situation, but Joy didn't want her thinking that she was so ga-ga over Bo that she had forgotten all sense of decorum. "He's helping me out with some things. I've been receiving some weird texts and notes."

Immediately, Alice's teasing expression turned serious. "What? Who are they from? And how can this Bo guy help you?"

"It's a long story, I don't know, and he has been listening to me and he got a cop involved."

Alice pulled out her phone. "You have a perfectly good

223

sister-in-law who's a cop. She should be involved too." She looked down and swiped the screen.

"No. I don't want Courtney involved."

"Why?"

"Because Courtney is technically your sister-in-law, not mine. Plus . . . I just don't. I can handle this on my own."

"You're not making any sense."

"Look, I'm tired of being needy. I don't think this is anything to worry about. It's getting taken care of."

"Not really, since you've now got a new guy and a cop involved."

"Please don't tell Joel or Courtney. Or Mom and Dad."

"Or Rand?" Alice added sarcastically. "If you want to keep this stalking thing a secret, you're going to have to give me something more, Joy. Right now, I'm not feeling very reassured."

"Fine." She reached out and clutched her sister's hand. "How do you think I feel? You and Rand are successful. You and Joel have got a great marriage and great kids."

"You know Chloe is great."

"Of course she is. She's amazing. I'm just saying that compared to you guys, I'm a screw-up."

"Where is this coming from? You're great, Joy. You do a lot of good in the world. You tutor and volunteer and help people. You paint beautiful pictures. You're doing such a good job with Chloe. She's adorable."

"I never finished college."

"Yeah, because your jerk of a husband acted like he couldn't survive if you didn't quit school and marry him." She scowled. "And then he showed his true colors."

"I don't want to rehash Tony. All I'm saying is that you, Rand, Mom, and Dad have all dropped everything in order to help me more than once. More than twice."

"That's what family is for."

"Alice, you already help pay for Chloe's dance lessons." That was her big embarrassment. Chloe's lessons were expensive and Tony's solution when Joy had told him that he was going to need to help more with the tuition was for Chloe to simply stop dancing.

Less than a week after Joy had complained to Alice about Tony being a jerk, the dance academy had written Joy a note to tell her that Chloe's dance lessons were paid in full. Alice still helped Joy with the tuition.

"Joy, Joel and I wanted to do it and we haven't missed the money at all. You know I make plenty selling houses."

"That's what I'm talking about. And don't even get me started on Rand, because he let Chloe and me live with him for two months."

"You needed him, and he would've been upset if you hadn't taken him up on the offer. Tony the jerk was acting stupid, acting like he could cheat on you and take your house at the same time." She grinned. "I still think one of my proudest moments was telling him to move out because you were moving back in."

Joy giggled. "I had almost forgotten about that. Anyway, you know what I'm saying. If things were reversed, you'd feel awkward and guilty too and don't even act like you wouldn't. You would."

"Maybe," she allowed.

"You would. I know it. Just give me a chance to figure things out with Bo and this, um, stalker. If they get worse, then I'll let you know."

"What about Mom and Dad? Are you going to tell them?"

"No way."

"Come on. Be reasonable."

"Alice, you don't have the easiest job in the world. Or the

safest, right? What would you think if everyone jumped in and gave you advice every time it looked like you couldn't handle something?"

"But I can."

"I want to one day be able to say the same thing. One day I want to say I can handle something—and know that you think I can, too. Give me two weeks. Please?"

Her sister looked like she wanted to argue, but in the end she nodded. "Okay, fine. I don't like it though."

"I realize that."

"And, ah, Joy?"

"Yes?"

"You're probably not going to believe this, but none of us sit around keeping score. You're our sister and we love you. End of story."

The words, said in her sister's matter-of-fact way, made Joy's eyes tear up. "Just when I'm about to tell you to mind your own business, you say something like this."

"It's not like anything. We love you. And we love the person you are, Joy. Not the person we want you to be. There's a difference there, you know?"

Swallowing the lump in her throat, she nodded. "I know. I love you too."

CHAPTER 31

Lincoln rarely asked Bo to come to his office for a meeting, so this afternoon's summons was not only unusual, but it also felt a little like being called into the principal's office.

Bo was even more surprised when he saw Seth already waiting. "What's going on? Any idea?"

"Nope. I was hoping you would know," Seth said. "I'd just gotten home when I got the boss's text."

"Too bad you had to turn back around." Seth lived in a pretty three-bedroom house on the edge of the Amish community. It was a good forty-minute drive from his house to T-DOT.

Seth shrugged. "It wasn't a big deal. Now I'm just trying to figure out who might be in Lincoln's office right now. All the guys who report to me have seemed to be doing okay." The wrinkle between his light blond eyebrows deepened. "At least, I thought they were."

"Am I late?" Mason asked as he strode closer. As usual, he

sounded a little panicked. "Adrian needed gas and the stupid place only took cash. It took forever to get in and out."

"You're not late," Seth said.

Bo looked around. "Where's Adrian?"

"He's going over some paperwork for a couple of grants he and Lincoln applied for. I reckon he's in the kitchen grabbing something to eat too."

Seth frowned. "I forgot Elizabeth was working in the kitchen today. I'm hungry. I hope she didn't make enchiladas." Seth loved almost everything the woman cooked, but he was not a fan of enchiladas.

"Text Adrian to ask her to make you a plate," Bo said.

"On it."

While Seth texted Adrian, Bo stuffed his hands in his pockets and tried not to look concerned. The three of them not only were Lincoln Bennett's closest friends, but all had positions in the organization directly under their boss. Bo worked with the newest guys assimilating out of the pen. Seth was in charge of the core business, flipping houses in the county. He supervised teams of ex-cons, teaching them how to do simple plumbing, refinishing, and carpentry.

Mason, who was younger and often was the most outspoken, had recently moved into being Lincoln's bodyguard-slash-enforcer for the ex-cons. It had been Bo's position for years before Mason took it over.

Everyone in Madisonville knew that Lincoln was in tight with both the warden and the guards. If he was willing to vouch for someone's job and housing for the next year, there was a better chance that a guy would be released early.

Just as importantly, it was a well-known fact that Lincoln ran a tight ship. If a guy messed up, Lincoln was quick to pull him out of the program—since the integrity of T-DOT mattered.

No one in the prison, law enforcement, or the companies who supported them were going to give T-DOT the time of day if the ex-cons were allowed to run wild.

Consequently, there were a lot of bitter men both in and out of prison, either who had never been chosen for the program or had been tossed out. Resentment and the need to get back at the guy for perceived transgressions was high on their lists. Mason not only ran interference between the men and the boss, but also saw to it that Lincoln was never completely alone.

Not only did Lincoln rarely travel anywhere by himself, someone was always parked outside Lincoln and his wife's house, making sure they were safe. Lincoln had used to balk at the measures—until Jennifer had come along. Now that they had a baby, too, Lincoln took it all in stride.

"Hey, did something happen?" Mason asked. "Did somebody go after Lincoln and I didn't hear about it? Charlie was on duty last night." He pulled out his phone, brushing his thumb over the screen.

"If something did, I haven't heard. Calm down, buddy," Bo said. "It's a given that if something bad was on his mind he would've called."

"Yeah. You're right."

Seth drew in a breath, obviously about to add his two cents, when Lincoln's door opened. Their boss looked at the three of them, almost seeming surprised that they were standing there waiting on him.

"Did you knock?" he asked.

"No," Seth answered. "I thought you were in a meeting."

"Oh. Yeah. I guess I was . . ." Lincoln's voice drifted off. "Sorry I kept you guys waiting out here in the hall, though."

Bo exchanged glances with the other two guys. If he hadn't been worried, he was now. Lincoln was a lot of things but forgetful and absent-minded wasn't one of them. "You want to talk now, Boss? Or do you want us to wait a spell?"

"Now's fine. Come on in." He turned and walked to his desk. Sat down behind it and motioned to the empty chairs. "Have a seat. Oh, and Mason, close the door, yeah?"

After closing the door, Mason leaned against it. Whether he was hoping to get out of there fastest or wanted to be the first to approach anyone who knocked on the door, Bo wasn't sure.

Bo and Seth sat down on the two chairs next to Lincoln's desk while Lincoln reached into his pocket. They all remained quiet while Lincoln looked at something on his phone.

After a few more seconds passed, Lincoln said, "So, there's some crap going on. First, I heard from Evan Hayes, the new warden over in Madisonville. There was a fight two days ago involving Sammy." His scowl deepened. "I'm sure you guys remember him."

"Oh, yeah," Bo muttered. Sammy had been every new inmate's worst nightmare in the pen. He was every cliché, nightmare, and rumor about an inmate personified. Once a guy put him in his place, he left him alone, though. Bo had given Sammy a bloody nose when Sammy had made the mistake of thinking that Bo was okay with being grabbed. The only person he knew of who hadn't had a go-around with Sammy was Lincoln. The story was that Lincoln was so big and looked so hard when he entered, even Sammy had thought twice about giving him grief.

"He was hard to forget," Mason said. "Don't understand the concern about the fight, though. Half the population in that prison has had words with the guy."

Seth chuckled. "Love how you say words instead of punches."

"You know what I mean." Looking restless, Mason shifted on his feet. "What's going on? Most of the guards practically looked the other way when someone was fighting off Sammy."

"Yeah, well, this fight was a little different. It was between Sammy and Colt."

Bo frowned. Colt had been paroled and gone into their program almost a year ago. Bo had worked with him, but they had ultimately kicked him out of T-DOT when he'd failed to show up at work—and Bo had seen him mistreat a woman.

He'd read Colt the riot act—both about his laziness and about his disrespecting women. As he'd expected, his lecture hadn't gone over well. Colt had flipped out and actually tried to hit him. Pinning him to the wall, Bo had ordered the man to leave.

A lot of guys coming out of prison weren't exactly gentlemen, but Colt's actions were on a whole other level. Bo had never had a moment's regret about his decision, though he'd had a bitter taste in his mouth about the guy moving into their program in the first place. He'd contacted Colt's parole officer and given him a heads-up too.

Less than a month after being turned out, Colt had been in the local jail with charges filed against him for attempted rape. "I thought for sure Colt would've gotten sent someplace else besides Madisonville."

"Me too. I was hoping he'd get sent down to the maximum over in Lebanon, but he didn't." Lincoln's blue eyes turned even more stormy. "Anyway, Colt and Sammy got in a fight, a lot of words were said, and somehow Sammy was declared the winner. He's also scheduled to be released on Friday."

Mason cursed under his breath.

"I'm guessing some of those words were about you?"

Lincoln shrugged. "Some. He talked about all of us. From what I heard, he not only has a beef with me, but with Bo and you, Mason."

"Bring it on," Mason grumbled.

"Settle down, Mason. What I'm trying to convey is that the kid has some issues, and they aren't good. Rumor has it that he's going to try to make a name for himself."

Bo tensed. "We need to up your security, Boss."

"Yeah, maybe," Lincoln allowed.

Bo turned to Mason. He nodded, showing Bo that he was already thinking about who to put on security over at Lincoln's house.

Seth, on the other hand, was still looking at Lincoln intently. "Is that it, Boss?"

Lincoln took a deep breath. "No. Jennifer's pregnant again. She's feeling a little tired, so I'm going to take her away for a couple of days. Her mother's going to watch Hunt."

Mason grinned. "Congratulations."

"Thanks."

"Where you going away to?" Seth asked.

"Just to a cabin in Hocking Hills. Neither of us want to be too far away, we just want a break. We're going to sleep, walk, make s'mores . . ." Lincoln grinned. "Whatever she wants."

There was a time when Bo would've sworn that a word like s'mores would have never passed his boss's lips. Now, though? It felt right. "Sounds perfect. I'm happy for you."

Seth's lips twitched. "And idyllic."

Lincoln grinned. "Right? I never thought I'd be so excited to hole up in a cabin in the middle of nowhere but it's sounding pretty good." Turning serious, he added, "One of the reasons we're going to that cabin is because cell phone reception is next to nothing. That means I'm going to be out of range when Sammy gets sprung. You three are going to be in charge."

Already thinking about logistics, Bo asked, "How do you want us to handle everything?"

Lincoln waved a hand. "If Jennifer or Hunt were going to

be at the house, I'd give you directions. But with them out of the picture, I'm gonna let you guys figure it out. I'll do what I can to help, but I'm asking you for this favor. Jennifer needs a break, and I don't want to let her down."

"Understood," said Mason. "But, ah, Boss, I think I should assign a pair of guys to the trip."

"No."

"If y'all are on your own and there ain't no reception . . . you're going to need some help."

"I hear you, but Jennifer's not going to relax if she knows two guys are sleeping in an SUV while we're in the cabin."

Mason rolled his eyes. "That girl. I've told her a dozen times that guard duty ain't no big deal."

"I tell her that too. But to be honest, I'm okay with she and I having a little bit of privacy. Plus, I was serious about Sammy being a worry." He frowned. "Warden Hayes said one of the guards overheard Colt giving Sammy an earful about T-DOT—especially you, Bo."

"Okay, moving on, let's go through how everyone else is doing. Bo, you start. Everyone good?"

He nodded. "I've got a couple who aren't going to be real pleased about Sunny getting out but no one who's going to jump ship to his side."

"Fair enough. Seth?"

Seth pressed his hands on his knees as he obviously took some time to consider every guy in the program. "Everyone's good, except for Jacks."

"What about him?"

"Something's off. He's squirrely. He's been showing up at work, but I had to talk to him the other day about getting off his phone. It took him a minute."

"Want me to talk to him?" Mason asked.

"*Nee*," Seth said.

Bo drew back. Seth had grown up Amish but rarely spoke Pennsylvania Dutch unless he was rattled.

Lincoln was staring at him intently too. "You bring Jacks in this afternoon. I'll talk to him."

Seth shook his head. "That ain't necessary, Boss."

"I know, but I made the choice to bring him into the program, even though one of the guards had tried to talk me out of it. I won't get in his face. I just want to remind him that I haven't forgotten about him."

"He'll realize that real quick," Bo joked.

Turning to Mason, Lincoln said, "I'm afraid you're going to have your hands full. Not only are we gonna have to keep close tabs on everybody, we're also going to have to step up the watch around here."

Mason nodded, as if everything their boss was saying wasn't going to be a huge amount of work.

Thinking quickly, Bo said, "Maybe Charlie should get more involved. He's been wanting more responsibility."

"Like that idea," Lincoln said. "Charlie's smart and built like a tank. No one is going to argue with him."

"You might want to give your new girl a heads up, Bo," Mason added.

It took Bo a second to realize that Mason had asked him about Joy. He turned to him in surprise. "I think that's giving Sammy too much credit. Joy and I aren't even an official couple."

A muscle twinged in his jaw before Lincoln nodded. "Even if that's true, this Sammy could be a problem. Figuring out who you've been spending time with won't be hard for him to do. And messing with her would be an easy way to make you hurt."

Lincoln had a point. "I'll think about that." Imagining a

person like Sammy messing with Joy made his heart practically stop.

And even though he thought that the possibility of anyone targeting Joy was small, there was still a chance. It wasn't like any of them knew what Sammy was capable of outside of prison.

Feeling Seth's concerned gaze on him, Bo swallowed. "I believe in T-DOT. It sure saved me. But sometimes I wonder if what we do is worth the risks."

"It is," Lincoln said without a hint of doubt in his tone. "We help one man at a time. That one man is enough."

Bo felt his cheeks heat. "Sorry. You're right. I'm just . . . just rattled, I guess."

"That's why there's all of us," Seth said. "This stuff is hard. You need someone to have your back."

"Yeah."

Lincoln studied him. "Bo, let us know if you want to talk about the letters and phone calls Joy has been getting. Even if it doesn't have anything to do with ex-cons, we can still give you some ideas about what to do."

"You can't do everything alone," Seth added. "It's impossible."

Though everything inside of him was wanting to protest, to say that he could take care of his own, he didn't want pride to interfere with common sense. "Thank you. I'll let y'all know."

"Don't forget that, Bo," Lincoln murmured. "Take it from me—don't do stupid stuff when you don't have to."

"I hear you loud and clear, Boss." Of course, he also knew that when things got bad, there weren't always a lot of good options.

CHAPTER 32

Joy was beginning to wish she was anywhere else but in the middle of Sacred Grounds. Everything about the day's visit felt off. They were playing the music too loud. The usual barista wasn't there, the lines were longer than usual, and the man behind the counter had messed up her usual mocha latte. In addition, more than a handful of people had glared at her because she'd been taking up a table for so long.

But the worst part of the situation by a long shot was her student's attitude. She didn't know what was wrong with Anthony, but he seemed angry, impatient, and agitated. It was like his usual self had taken a hike and this imposter was in his place.

Joy knew from experience that some sessions were like that. Everyone involved was human, which meant that sometimes they didn't get enough sleep, or were worried about kids or work or family problems. Usually, when it was obvious that struggling over words wasn't going to help either of them, she would end the session early. Unfortunately, she was afraid that if she did that today, it would make things worse.

Joy settled for watching the clock and praying that the time would move a little faster.

"Let's give it another try, okay?" She pointed to the workbook. "The car . . ."

Anthony took a deep breath and put one finger next to hers on the page. "The car was r . . . re . . ."

"Come on, Anthony. I know you know this." She had no idea what was going on with him, but he was acting weird. He knew colors, and it was pretty obvious, anyway.

He inhaled sharply and glared at her. As if it were her fault he was struggling.

She drew back as a twinge of unease filled her.

"R . . . red."

"Good. Now, let's go on to the next line." When he didn't begin right away, she leaned back in her chair. "Are you ready?"

He scowled. "Give me a minute, will you?"

Taken aback, Joy mentally counted to five and reminded herself that he was an adult and doing this on his own time. She needed to give him some grace. Unable to help herself, she glanced at the time on her phone.

He scowled. "Why are you looking at your phone again?"

"I was checking the time."

"Why?"

Joy's patience was officially gone. He wasn't a child, and she was feeling a little taken advantage of. She did volunteer work because she wanted to help adults learn to read. However, she wasn't a therapist. She didn't appreciate him being a jerk while she sat by his side. "Why do you think?" she snapped. "I wanted to know what time it was."

"How come you're so anxious? Do you want to leave?" He made a big show of scanning the area. "Is he waiting on you somewhere that I can't see?"

She blinked. "Of course not."

"How come?" he continued, his voice rising. "Why isn't your man here, Joy? Why isn't that guy sitting here like he always is? How come Bo isn't here, watching me?"

A pair of college-age girls who were sitting at a nearby table glanced up in alarm. "Anthony, lower your voice. Furthermore, what Bo does is none of your business."

He flinched. "Joy, I thought we were friends."

"I thought we were too, but you're being really mean today." Frustrated and confused, Joy decided that she'd had enough for one session. "You know what? I'm just going to leave." She opened her tote bag and started to gather her things. "Text me if you still want to meet next week."

"If I say yes, will you even be here?"

"Of course I will. We've been meeting for months." She was starting to get pretty worried about him. "Anthony, what is going on? Did something happen at home or at work?" She tried to remember what he'd recently been talking about but was drawing a blank.

His expression shuttered. "Yeah."

"Do you want to talk about it?"

He shook his head. "No." He breathed deeply. "You know what? You're right. We should call it quits today." He started putting his things in his backpack. "Let's go. I'll walk you out."

"There's no need. I can see myself out."

"You don't even think enough of me to do that? Bo always walks you out. I've seen him. You like it too. I've seen you smile when he offers his arm. Do you really hate me so much?"

"Of course I don't hate you." Another flicker of unease filled her. There was something by his statement that really bothered her. It was more than just the creepiness of it. No, there was something else that she couldn't seem to put her finger on.

Though she was tempted to tell him to just leave, he was acting so angry she was afraid he'd make a scene. Quickly, she put away her teacher's guide and reading glasses. Her phone buzzed, signaling an incoming text. She noticed it was from Bo just as she tossed it in her purse.

Anthony was on his feet, looming over her now. She stood up and tried to smile. "I'm finally ready."

He nodded, his expression completely blank.

Walking by his side, she walked to the door, vaguely aware of another couple grabbing their seats. Though the management had never complained about her taking up a table for so long, maybe it would be a good thing to start going somewhere else. Somewhere less crowded.

When they got out, the warm sun felt good on her skin. She'd done it. She'd gotten through this awful session. "I hope you have a good rest of your day," she started to smile.

But then his hand wrapped around her forearm.

Staring down at it, she tugged. But instead of releasing her, his fingers tightened.

And then pulled on her arm.

She stumbled. "Anthony, what—" Only then did she realize he was holding a knife and it was pressed against her side. Shocked, she tried to step away.

"Don't, Joy. Don't say a word." Looking down at the hunting knife in his other hand, Anthony breathed in deeply. "I've been practicing. I know how to hurt you now. Come with me."

There was no way. "Release me. You—" The rest of her words were cut off by searing pain. He'd cut her. He'd cut her badly.

Her brain turned into a fog as what was happening slowly registered.

Just as he pulled her down a set of brick steps under Sacred Grounds that she'd never noticed before. Pulled her through a door that at first glance looked like boarded-up plywood.

Just as she screamed.

She felt the sting of a blade on her back as the cold, hard bricks of the walkway slapped her head.

All she could think was that Anthony sure wasn't who she thought he was—and that she really wished she'd answered Bo's text before she'd left.

CHAPTER 33

Chloe didn't know where her mother was. Every Sunday night, they went through their calendars and wrote down everywhere they knew each of them was going to be that week. It took a while, and Chloe would be lying if she said it was her favorite activity. But, on the flip side, they'd both agreed to stick to the schedule as well as they could. That meant Chloe knew what days to walk to the diner, when her dad was going to pick her up, and when her mom was. Or when she was supposed to either ride the bus or get a ride home with a friend.

She also knew when and where her mom tutored, and when she was going out to deliver paintings.

All that meant that Chloe had been expecting her mom to pick her up from school. When she was still standing there fifteen minutes later than usual, she knew something was up.

Especially since her mom wasn't answering her phone and she always answered her phone.

So, she was stuck and she didn't have her ballet bag. It was probably in her mother's car, wherever that was.

After trying to call her mom a third time, Chloe knew something was wrong. She tried her dad, but only got an away message. He was out of the office for the day.

Starting to get worried, she called Finn. To her surprise, he answered right away.

"Hey. What's going on?"

After briefly explaining the situation, she said, "I'm not sure what to do now. I guess I could call one of my friends but what do I do then? I'm supposed to go to dance at four."

"Well, why don't you walk over here?" he asked after thinking about it for a minute. "Your mom can always drop off your bag here. And if you don't get ahold of her, at least you can tell your teacher."

Just the thought of seeing Miss Diamanté without being perfectly dressed in her leotard and tights made her feel like throwing up. "Maybe."

"How about this, then? Come here, I'll get you a malt, then we'll call Bo."

She kept forgetting that he knew Bo too. "You don't think he'll get mad if I call about my mom?"

"Nope. Maybe he even knows where she is." He paused. "Um, do you think they could be together?"

She frowned. She knew what Finn was insinuating—that maybe Bo and her mom were together and lost track of time. She supposed that could happen . . . if it was some other woman besides her mom. "No. My mother lives and dies by our Sunday evening calendar. She doesn't forget to get me from school. Ever."

"Okay, then. Well, um, do you want me to see if I can meet you halfway?"

She grinned. This was why she liked Finn so much. He

always put her first. No other boy in high school would offer to leave work just to walk her someplace. "I'm good. It's not far. I'll see you soon."

Hanging up, she started down the familiar route. It felt funny, though. Most everyone who left the high school on foot was long gone. She felt conspicuous and awkward. Once again, she doubted her decision to devote so much attention to ballet. If she'd gotten a job she might already be halfway to saving up for a car. Or at least, she wouldn't be living in fear of a sixty-year-old dance instructor who acted like the world was going to end if she didn't have her hair up in a perfect bun at five minutes to four.

By the time she got to Lane's, she was feeling pretty wrung out. Her parents had really spoiled her. She'd always been able to count on them. Now, when neither of them were available, she didn't know what to do.

"Do you want to sit over at the drink counter or in a booth?" Finn asked.

"I don't care. Maybe a booth?" she asked. "I'm kind of freaking out."

His eyes filled with sympathy. "Come on, then. You sit down and then we'll figure out what to do. Hey, do you want your usual vanilla malt? I could go ask Lane to make it real quick."

"That would be great . . . but could we call Bo first?"

"Sure." Pulling out his phone, he said, "Do you want me to call or do you just want to use my phone and I'll go away?" He frowned. "I don't know what most folks would do. Is that weird?"

"I want you to call and sit here with me."

He slid in the booth across from her and grinned before clicking on Bo's name. "Ready?"

She nodded. "Yeah." Watching Finn press Send, Chloe prayed that Bo would pick up. If he didn't answer either, she was going to go crazy with worry.

"Hiya Bo. It's Finn. Oh. *Jah*, I guess you would know it was me." He paused. "Um, actually, I've got Chloe here. She wants to talk to you. It's important." After another second, he handed the phone to her.

Putting the cell phone up to her ear, she said, "Hi Bo. I'm so glad you answered."

"Me, too. Girl, are you okay? What's going on?"

His voice was a little rough but sounded kind too. "Um, have you talked to my mom today?"

"I did this morning."

"But not since?"

"No, but I don't usually call her in the middle of the day. I texted her a while ago, but she didn't respond." Sounding more concerned, he added, "Is everything okay?"

"Mom was supposed to pick me up from school and didn't. She didn't answer when I called, either."

"Do you think she lost track of time or something?"

"My mom doesn't lose track of time. Or if she does, she lets me know that she's going to be late." Trying to get Bo to understand, she rushed on. "Mom has my dance bag in her car too. If she couldn't have picked me up, she would've dropped it off at school or something. Mom doesn't forget things like that." Chloe took a deep breath. She was starting to panic. "I'm kind of worried."

"I'm glad you called, girl. That was the right thing to do. Now, where are you now? You aren't home alone, are you?"

"My dad's out of town, so I walked to the diner from school. Finn said I should call you." Feeling even more anxious, her voice hitched. "Bo, what if she got in a car accident?"

"If she did, we'll find out and then we'll deal with it, right?"

"Yes." She closed her eyes. "I'm sorry. I guess I'm freaking out for no reason."

"No, you did the right thing and Finn did good for calling me. There's no reason to worry by yourself when you've got people who can help out, too." His voice softened. "Now, it's likely nothing has happened to your momma, but we care about her, so we want to be sure, right?"

"I don't know."

"Okay, even I've seen that fancy, complicated calendar your momma's got going on. Do you remember what she was planning to do today?"

"No. Maybe tutor?"

"Hmm. Okay, you sit tight at that diner. Or do you want to go to dance class? I can find you there if you'd rather be there."

"No way. I'm not going anywhere."

"Sounds good. I'm going to swing by your house to see if your mother's car's there. Is there a hide-a-key around or something?"

"Yep. It's under the grill."

"If I don't see her, I'm going to go to that calendar and see where she was today and try and see if I can find her. I'll call you if I find out anything and you do the same. Okay?"

"Yes."

"Let's see. No matter what, I'll come over to get you within the hour. I'm not going to leave you to sit in that diner all night."

"Thanks."

"Hey, Chloe, I know it's hard, but try not to worry. We don't know that anything's the matter, right?"

She drew a deep breath. "Right."

"There you go," he murmured. "All right. Put me back on with Finn."

She handed the phone to him. "Bo wants to talk to you."

Finn put his cell to his ear, answered a couple of questions with *yes* or *no*, then hung up. "He said that I'm supposed to get you something decent to eat and he'll pay for your meal when he gets here."

His statement was so matter-of-fact, she giggled. "That's it?"

He smiled. "I'm starting to realize that Bo not only is nicer than he first comes across but he's also real good at giving orders." Lowering his voice, he added, "He also asked me to look after you."

"I don't need you to do that . . . but you don't mind?"

"I don't mind."

For the first time since she realized her mother was missing, Chloe felt like she could breathe easier. "I'm so glad you're working here, Finn. I don't know what I'd do if we hadn't met."

He smiled at her softly. "I'm really glad too, Chloe."

She just about melted, his words were so sweet.

CHAPTER 34

Seth, who'd been sitting next to Bo when Finn called, had insisted on going with him to Joy's house.

"If she's there, I'll say hi and wait while you figure out what's going on," he explained. "If she's not, I can help you look."

Bo couldn't fault Seth's logic, so he'd agreed with the plan without complaint. Besides, he had a feeling that something was wrong. A lot of parents lost track of time or let their phone batteries die—or a dozen other small things could happen that prevented them from immediately connecting with their kids.

Joy wasn't one of those parents.

From the first time he'd met Joy, he'd sensed that everything about her was cautious and thorough. She was careful with her heart, with her space, and with her daughter. No way was she just going to not show up if Chloe was expecting her.

Just as importantly, Chloe didn't seem to be a girl who got

upset or worried about her mother easily. She wouldn't have gotten Finn to call Bo unless she was really worried.

She was really worried.

When they were halfway to Joy's house, Seth said, "Whatever you're thinking, you need to put it away. You don't know anything right now."

"I hear you."

"Are you sure? Because you're looking like you're about to go off half-cocked."

"I'm not. I just don't like loose ends or things that don't add up."

"Life is filled with those things. You know it as well as I do. Just because something doesn't make sense, that doesn't mean everything has gone to pot. It just means you've got a hurdle or something to get over."

As Bo pulled into Joy's driveway, he raised an eyebrow. "Is that some more of your Amish wisdom?"

"*Nee*. I reckon it's more common sense than anything else," he said as he got out of the truck. "If I learned anything with Lincoln two years ago, it's that love can make a man go off half-cocked. I'm trying to save you a little bit of heartache."

"Thanks, though I'm not sure I'm in love."

"You might not want to admit it, but it's there." Seth grinned. "Which is, for sure and for certain, something I learned back in the day."

"Do you think you'll ever go back?" Bo asked as he scanned the area.

"Nope. Even if I wanted, I couldn't. They kicked me out." He strode over to one of the windows of the garage. "No car in here."

"That's what I was afraid of." He walked through the small metal fence to the concrete patio pad by the back door.

Wondering, exactly what Chloe could've meant by "under" the grill, he crouched down to look beneath it. "Chloe said there's a key hidden somewhere down here." Running a hand along the cement, he murmured, "Any ideas?"

Seth got down on a knee. Then, to Bo's surprise, looked up. "Here ya go." He yanked down a key attached to a magnet. "It's a clever spot. Foolish as all get out, but clever."

Bo slipped it in the door and turned it easily. "First thing I'm going to tell Joy when I see her is to stop hiding keys outside her door."

As he feared, the house looked as it might if someone expected to come back before too long to straighten up. A cereal bowl sat in the sink, along with a coffee cup and a spoon. A box of cereal and a loaf of bread was on the counter. Shoes were in the middle of the living room.

"I'm going to take a look around, Bo," Seth said.

"Good idea." He didn't want to invade Joy's privacy, but they knew too much about crimes to not check out her house.

While Seth did his tour, Bo located the calendar on the wall. Sure enough, Chloe had dance and there was a notation that Joy would pick her up. The only other note was that Joy was tutoring that morning at Sacred Grounds. Blessing her organized, detail-oriented mind, he read the name of her student. Anthony.

He closed his eyes, picturing the man in his head.

"Everything looks like you'd expect, I reckon," Seth announced. "The master bed is made, the girl's ain't. Nothing looks rifled through or disturbed though. If something happened to her, it didn't happen here."

"I think it happened at the coffee shop. At Sacred Grounds."

After locking back the door and returning the key—on the off chance that one of the women would need it—they hopped back in the truck and drove the short distance to the coffee shop.

It was now close to five and Sacred Grounds was closed. He and Seth looked in the windows, but nothing looked out of place.

Until Seth clasped the back of his shoulder. "Ain't that Joy's car?" He pointed to a back parking lot.

Feeling like he was walking through mud, Bo stared at the vehicle. Heart pounding, he approached and looked inside. It hadn't been broken into. It simply looked abandoned.

Joy had come to Sacred Grounds for her 9:00 a.m. appointment with Anthony and never made it back to her car.

"I think we've got a problem," he murmured as he strode back to his truck. "Is Lincoln gone yet?"

"I'll call him and see. You gonna call Chloe?"

He nodded, though he felt like he already had a lead weight around his neck. He dreaded even the thought of upsetting that girl. It was the right thing to do, though.

"I will. I'll call Kevin too. Something happened, Seth." Besides, if Chloe could reach out to Finn and both of them could summon the nerve to call him, he knew he could find the strength to call her and deliver the bad news. It broke his heart, though. He suddenly wished he lived just a block away from his momma. One phone call would send her over to Chloe like a torpedo. Though she wouldn't be able to make everything better, his mother would soothe and comfort the girl.

In the distance, they heard a faint crash. Both men looked around, actively attempting to find the source of the noise. The area seemed completely empty, though.

"Must have been a cat or something," Seth muttered.

"Yeah," Bo replied.

Neither of them believed it.

CHAPTER 35

Joy wasn't sure how long she'd been in Anthony's small room in the basement of Sacred Grounds. Her brain was a little fuzzy and her back and side hurt from knife wounds. Her entire body felt weak and sluggish. And she was freezing, lying on his underground brick floor for who knows how long.

She was alone.

As seconds passed and her throbbing head cleared, she slowly became aware of her surroundings. It was a dark place, with only two narrow windows near the ceiling letting in a bare sliver of natural light. Instead, a single light bulb illuminated the space. It cast a strange glow in the room, giving everything a faint yellow cast.

It seemed that Anthony lived in an efficiency apartment. The single room was likely not any more than three or four hundred square feet. An unmade twin-size bed sat in one corner. An old, gray metal card table holding a computer stood next to one wall; and a chair in front of a small television on a crate sat near the opposite one. In the back corner was a small kitchenette—nothing more than a hot plate and a dorm-room-sized refrigerator. Just behind her was a door, likely leading to the bathroom.

It really was a cold, depressing space. Not because of the size and the location but because there was nothing personal, nothing homey or comforting in it. Honestly, it looked like Anthony had set himself up in someone's unfinished basement.

And then she saw all the photos.

Dozens of pictures of herself were taped to the wall just to her left. Photos of her alone, with Chloe. In her car. Walking. With other clients. When Joy noticed that her hair was highlighted in one of the photos, she gasped. She'd gotten highlights two years ago in a misguided attempt to freshen up her look. All that had happened, of course, was that she had blond streaks slowly growing out over the next two years. She'd only recently gotten the last of them trimmed out.

Those photos told a story all on their own. Anthony had been stalking her for years.

She shivered again, this time not from the cold as much as the knowledge that she'd been oblivious to him all that time. She'd been living, dreaming, driving, helping him . . . all while he'd watched and documented. It was frightening how oblivious she'd been—that he'd fooled her so well.

She needed to get out of here.

Gathering her strength, she scooted across the concrete floor. Her back and sides protested the efforts; the bit of warmth she suddenly felt illustrated that her wounds were bleeding again.

She ignored the pain as best she could, intent only on getting closer to the edge of the twin bed—she needed something to help her up, and that bed looked to be the most stable thing in the room.

After several excruciating minutes, Joy gripped the corner of the mattress, pulled, and was able to sit upright on the second attempt. Sweat ran down her back as she sighed in relief. All she had to do was use the mattress to get to her feet, and then get to the door.

Then, somehow, she was going to get out of there. She was just going to need to pray harder.

The door opened behind her. "You woke up."

Still kneeling next to the bed, she jerked to face him. Anthony's face was calm and impassive. He was eyeing her with a look of concern. "You are really hurt. And you're bleeding bad, Joy. Do you hurt?"

"Yes."

"Poor Joy." Regret, laced with something that looked a lot like satisfaction, shone in his eyes.

Desperate, her mind raced. Joy had no experience or knowledge dealing with being kidnapped and beaten, but then again, who really did? Anthony was obviously confused and evil. "I need to leave, Anthony. I can't stay here."

A line formed between his eyes. "Yes, you can. This is where you will live now."

"No. I have my daughter. She needs me."

Looking obstinate, he shook his head. "I've seen Chloe. I've watched her too. She's old."

"No, she's just a girl."

He shook his head again. "No. She has your husband. She doesn't need a mother."

"She does need me. I need her."

"No. You need to stay here." His voice became firmer. "You are here now."

Her mind spun. A dozen excuses and protests came to mind,

a dozen things to try to convince him to let her go. None of them seemed like they would make much of a difference, but she had to try. She had no choice.

"Anthony, please. I . . . I'm bleeding. And I'm hurting." She frowned, hoping she looked as awful as she felt. "It's not safe for me to be here. I could get an infection or bleed too much. I need to go to the doctor."

"I will fix you." He held up a gray-looking towel. "I'm going to wipe up your clothes."

No way did she want him coming near her again. No way did she want him touching her, not with his hands or with that grungy towel. Thinking quickly, she added, "If you wipe the blood with the towel, then your towel will get dirty and red. You don't want that, do you?"

Looking confused again, Anthony stared at the towel in his hands.

"Will you let me go to the bathroom at least? Then I can wash up."

When he hesitated, Joy pressed on. "If we're going to live together, you're going to have to let me go to the bathroom to get clean, right? I mean, that's what friends do."

"Right."

"Then let me get clean now before I get sick."

He licked his bottom lip. "You don't get to stay in there very long. I'm going to time you."

"I don't want to. Only long enough to get clean and go to the bathroom. That's not too much to ask, is it?"

Anthony stared at her. Perhaps it was only two or three seconds, but it felt like an eternity. "No. No, it is not," he whispered.

She felt like she could finally breathe again. Hopefully there would be a window in the bathroom. Even if it was too small to slip through, at least she'd be able to yell for help.

But first she had to get to her feet.

She shifted enough to face the mattress. Then, gripping handfuls of the sheet and blanket with both hands, she pulled herself up inch by inch. The muscles on her right side, where he'd cut her, screamed in protest. Her head pounded. When she was standing at last, the pain was so intense she was nauseous and dizzy.

But she had done it.

A burst of pride filled her. She hoped it was enough to propel her to the bathroom. All she could do was take one step at a time.

Anthony moved to the side and watched her move. The sweet, kind expression she'd been so accustomed to seeing on his face was nowhere to be found. Instead, he looked upset and irritated. His breathing seemed to become more labored and anxious with every step she took.

When Joy reached the bathroom door at last, she thanked the Lord for being with her. She was pretty sure she would've never made it those four feet on her own.

She walked inside the bathroom and closed the door. It was already illuminated. She turned, hoping for a window to appear, but there wasn't one to be found. Only a small shower with a torn curtain, a cracked mirror, a toilet, and a sink.

Tears filled her eyes as she realized that escaping was going to be even harder than she'd thought. Then, thinking of Chloe, she pulled herself together and turned on the sink.

Somehow, someway, she was going to get herself out of Anthony's creepy room. She was going to pray, hope that somehow Chloe had alerted Bo or the police that she was missing. That someone would discover her car parked outside Sacred Grounds late at night.

People were going to be looking for her and she wasn't going to give up. She put her hands under the cold stream of water at last. Splashed some on her face.

"Joy, are you clean now?"

"No," she called out. "I need more time."

She figured that said it all.

CHAPTER 36

It had been less than two hours since Chloe and Finn called Bo, but it felt like an eternity. He stood now next to an unmarked police car with Mason, Lincoln, and Seth in the parking lot next to Sacred Grounds.

Without telling Bo, Seth had called Lincoln and relayed everything that had happened. In turn, Lincoln had spoken to Jennifer, and they'd both elected to postpone their trip to the Hocking Hills another day or two. Jennifer's mother had been delighted to have extra time with Hunt.

Bo might have felt guilty about ruining his boss's vacation if he hadn't been so scared. Unfortunately, he knew exactly what *could* be happening to her. One didn't spend as much time as he did around convicts without hearing stories.

After speaking with Tony—who was, unfortunately, in California but getting on the first flight out—Bo had driven to Lane's Diner to speak to Chloe in person.

Bo didn't know if he would ever get completely over how terrible he'd felt when he told her the news; watching the hope fade from her eyes to be replaced by fear was nothing he ever wanted to experience again. After helping her speak to her grandmother and aunt, he'd left, knowing that Finn, Lane, and Mary would be watching over her before her relatives picked her up, which relieved his mind. Chloe's grandma was going to take her to her house until Joy was located. No one wanted Chloe to go home—just in case whoever took Joy decided to pay her house a visit.

Now that he'd done his best for Joy's daughter, all Bo cared about was finding her momma. He was no detective, though, and beyond a sixth sense broadcasting that she was nearby, he had no idea where to look first.

Luckily, Detective Heilman did have some ideas. After speaking with Bo and seeing her vehicle, Kevin asked for more officers to join them. They'd jimmied the car's locks, hoping for more clues about who she might have been seeing that morning. Kevin had even asked another officer to go to Joy's house and take a picture of Joy's calendar.

Lincoln had been on the phone too. He'd started calling in favors with some of the less-law-abiding citizens in the area. It was a long shot, but they all knew that all sorts of unexpected things could have happened to Joy. Any information could help.

After Tara, the owner of Sacred Grounds, had been notified of what was happening, she'd started to work the phones too. She didn't have any security cameras, but she did reach out to the employees who'd been there earlier. They, in turn, were asked to call, text, or email anyone they knew who might have been in the coffee shop when Joy had been there.

Everyone agreed that someone had to have seen something. A lot of people were used to seeing Joy tutor at one of the tables.

In addition, while Joy might not stand out, Anthony did. He was a big man, always kind of scruffy, and he often got emotional.

With all of that going on, Bo had allowed himself to feel hopeful. He might know a lot of terrible things that could have befallen Joy. Just as importantly, he also was aware of how many things could've gone wrong with whoever abducted her. Best-laid plans often went awry. With someone like Anthony, who didn't seem to have a tight lid on his temper, something had to have gone wrong if he was involved.

Unfortunately, as the clock ticked and darkness descended, Bo's optimism faltered. There was no doubt about it—he was scared. Scared out of his mind.

"Hey," Lincoln said. "Come on back to the house with me."

"I can't."

"Buddy, I get that you want to be where her car is, but there's next to no chance that she's nearby. Whoever took her likely carted her off in his vehicle. You know I'm right."

"Sorry, but I . . . I just can't. I need to feel like I'm doing something."

"You can pray just as easily back at the house as you can here."

Bo scowled at him. "I don't want to pray. I need to *do* something."

"Look, I know how you're feeling. I like being in charge and I like getting things done. But you've done all you can. You need to leave the bulk of this in the cops' hands. You need to let them do their jobs."

"I feel like she's nearby. I can't describe it. I just know she is."

Lincoln's expression turned bleak. "Sam, sorry, but that's unlikely. You *want* her to be here. I know you do, but wishes are for children and fools." His voice lowered. "You know that too."

Anger boiled inside of Bo. Both from Lincoln's words as

well as the knowledge that his friend was probably right. "Just give me another five minutes, okay?"

Lincoln had just nodded when Kevin waved them both over. "Come on. Heilman wants us."

Kevin Heilman was speaking to Tara as well as a young couple who looked like they were in high school.

"What's going on?" Bo asked.

Kevin motioned to the kids. "As you know, Tara called the employees, who reached out to everyone they knew who might have been there this morning. This couple was. Bo, Lincoln, this is Amanda and Dane."

"Hi," Amanda said.

"Would you two tell these guys what you just told us?"

"We saw that woman you are looking for arguing with a big, mean-looking guy out on the sidewalk," Amanda said.

"We were sitting in my car, getting ready to pull out," Dane added.

"The lady was trying to get away from the guy but he had her elbow."

"Then it looked like he was prodding her on her side."

"And then?" Bo asked.

Amanda pointed down the sidewalk. "Then we saw them go that way."

Bo looked at the sidewalk, suddenly noticing that two officers were kneeling on the ground with flashlights. "Detective!" one called out.

"One minute," Kevin replied. Turning to Tara, he said, "Any idea what is down that way?"

She shook her head. "Nothing, really. There used to be an antique mall, but it closed down. Nothing's that way except . . ." She gasped. "Oh, there's an apartment down there. A guy's been living down there for a few years, I think."

"Who?" Lincoln barked.

Tara blinked. "I . . . I think it's the guy Joy was with."

"Detective," the cop called out again. "We need you now. This is definitely blood!"

Kevin Heilman pulled out his radio and started spitting out codes as fast as he could speak. When Bo tried to pass them, he thrust out an arm. "Not yet."

Bo shook his head. "You don't understand."

"I do. But we've got to be smart." When Bo started to argue, Kevin looked at Lincoln. "Get a handle on him. Now."

Lincoln's hand gripped his arm. "He's right. Take a deep breath and think, Bo."

Seconds later, Seth and Mason flanked his sides. "We're close," Mason said. "If you ain't praying, then you better start now."

At last, Bo closed his eyes and prayed. But all he could seem to do was pray that he wasn't too late.

CHAPTER 37

It was dark out now. Which meant she'd been locked in Anthony's room for almost twelve hours. Joy was no doctor, but even she realized that she wasn't going to survive much longer if she didn't get to the hospital. In her more lucid moments, she'd begun to understand that it wouldn't be a foregone conclusion to anyone that Anthony had abducted her. Until that morning, he'd always been sweet and easygoing. Plus, he had always acted like he had a really, really hard time reading, let alone writing. She would never have believed that he'd just been pretending to be illiterate this whole time.

He wasn't too bright, but he was sneaky and devious. He'd sure fooled her, and obviously, since he'd been living under the coffee shop for several years, he'd fooled his landlords, and even the managers of Sacred Grounds. Everyone thought he was a very sweet, down-on-his-luck man. No one was going to suspect him.

Not even if they discovered her car there.

Regret filled her. Regret that she hadn't spent more time with Chloe. That she hadn't told her mom how much she appreciated her—even when they didn't see eye to eye.

That she and Tony hadn't parted ways years earlier. That she hadn't found a way to come to terms with the fact that, even though he was a good man and a good father, he hadn't been a great husband to her.

There were so many regrets and wishes, she had a feeling that even God himself was wishing she'd simply act instead of continuing to catalog all her mistakes.

No, that was wrong. She imagined the Lord himself was smiling because He knew that she'd appreciated one person who'd come into her life very much. She was so grateful for Bo.

He wasn't perfect, but he was perfect for her. He didn't want her to be beautiful or talented or even younger. Instead, Bo only wanted her to be herself. For some reason, he thought she was enough, just the way she was.

Joy wished she'd felt that way more often in her life.

Lying on the floor again, she closed her eyes and tried to count her blessings. The Lord had gifted her with Bo and she was grateful, even if they'd only gotten to know each other for a short while.

Even if they'd never done anything but talk and share a single kiss.

That brought her up short. What was she really doing? Cataloging her regrets like she was giving up?

There was no way she was okay with that happening. She was going to get out of this stupid basement apartment. She'd rather get killed escaping than spend one more minute of her life drowning in self-doubts and regrets.

Pushing aside her pounding head, her weakness, and the

way the wounds on her side and back felt like they were going to split open again, she forced herself to only think ahead.

And somehow managed to get to her feet.

Anthony was sitting behind his computer, his eyes fastened on the screen, like the real world was located on a twenty-inch monitor instead of in front of him. She couldn't believe how he'd pulled the wool over her eyes. It turned out that he could read just fine. He'd fooled her and the folks at ProLiteracy something awful.

Joy took advantage of his distraction and walked toward the door.

She'd almost reached the doorknob when he surged to his feet. "What are you doing?"

"I'm leaving." She turned the handle. To her amazement, it rotated easily. She opened the door wider. "Help!"

"No!" He rushed to her side, jerked her back. Hard.

She slammed against the door, but her hand on the frame saved her from being pulled completely inside again. Praying that someone was nearby, she screamed at the top of her lungs.

"No!" Anthony yelled. He grabbed at her shirt.

She felt it rip as he threw her to the ground. When picked her up and threw her again, a sharp pain sliced through her lungs. When he grabbed her again, she screamed. "Help me! Someone, please!"

"Joy? Joy!"

"Yes!" she screamed again, just as Anthony yanked at her arm.

She landed on her knees. Pain lashed through her. Vaguely, she wondered if Anthony had just broken her kneecap.

When Anthony pulled on her, she resisted, flinging herself on the steps. Not even caring that her lips and nose were on the hard, dirty cement. All she could taste was the blood on her tongue and the fresh air.

Then, to her amazement, they weren't alone. People shouted, entering the room like a swarm of bees. Joy tried to cry out, but it was hard. Anthony's arms felt like a vice around her midsection.

"No," Anthony shouted in her ear—just before someone pulled him away.

At last, she could breathe.

More voices surrounded her. It sounded like every one of them was calling out orders.

Except for one. "Easy, now."

She knew that voice. She closed her eyes and leaned into it. Two hands lightly ran up and down her body, whether they were assessing damage or attempting to soothe, she didn't know. All she was aware of was that they weren't hurting her.

"I've got you," the familiar voice whispered.

That familiar, so southern, so masculine, so *everything* voice was there. He was there.

"Bo." Even with her weary ears, she could tell that her voice was faint.

"Yes, you brave, brave girl. It's me. I'm here. I'm here and I'm not going to let you go."

Joy opened her mouth. She knew she should tell him something. No, tell him that she loved him. But it hurt too much to talk.

He reached down and lightly pressed his lips to her temple. "I love you too."

At last, she relaxed.

CHAPTER 38

Bo had never been the type of man to believe in platitudes. He'd liked hearing the truth, even when it was unvarnished and painful.

Sweet, meaningless phrases always reminded him of the nurse at the clinic that his momma had taken him, Carrie, Janie, and Eric to when they were growing up. That nurse always proclaimed that booster shots weren't going to hurt when everyone knew that they would. She'd jab him with a needle, smile, and put some stupid cartoon Band-Aid on top. That's when she'd say he wouldn't be sore for too long.

But that had been a lie too. His arm had always been sore for days.

So that was his earliest memory of hearing people spout things that everyone knew weren't true. It hadn't been the only time he'd heard those things, however. Maybe he'd been gullible or just plain bad, but for a while, he'd even started to believe those obvious lies—lies like thinking no one would know when he'd done stupid stuff.

Or that grades didn't really matter.

Or that avenging a gal was the right thing to do.

Or that being in prison for just a couple of years wasn't going to be too bad.

Or when his momma had gathered them all together to say that their Daddy was going to be all right—but he'd died just a month later of throat cancer.

Bo swallowed the lump in his throat. He'd been upset about that one for years. Like it was his mother's fault for wanting to believe that a miracle would happen when the love of her life was dying and she had four kids to support.

So yeah, he'd never been real good with words that felt like nothing more than useless phrases . . . until this moment.

Now, he was clinging to every single word of comfort he could get his hands on.

Which was why he kept telling himself the same three things over and over again.

Joy is safe. She isn't going to die. I haven't completely failed her.

Those same three sentiments had rung through his head as he'd watched the EMTs carefully load Joy into the ambulance.

And when the cops had shaken his hand and said that they would be in touch—and that they'd be praying for his girlfriend's recovery.

He'd even spouted some new variations of platitudes out loud when he'd called Chloe and her grandmother to relay the news, and when Tony had called from his car on the way out of the airport.

He'd also been telling himself those same three things for the last three hours in the hospital's waiting area. Various people had come out and given them all updates. Joy had needed several rounds of tests, then had been taken into surgery when it was evident that one of her broken ribs had splintered and a piece of bone had punctured a lung.

So it wasn't that Bo didn't believe that Joy had survived and was going to eventually be all right. It was that he couldn't seem to wrap his head around what he'd seen in that crappy room. That it had been freezing, she'd been on the floor, and that there were pictures of her everywhere.

That room had been essentially right under his nose for the last twenty-four hours. She'd been hurt badly. Abused and tortured. All by someone he'd never even considered to be a threat. He didn't know if Joy was ever going to forgive him. Against all his better judgment, he'd believed Anthony's sweet, guileless words. He'd taken them at face value.

How could he have been so stupid?

Lincoln walked to his side. "You've been standing here by yourself long enough. Come sit down and talk to me."

He was standing in a small alcove leading to a pair of doors. It didn't seem like they led to anywhere particularly important because hardly any medical personnel went through them. Lincoln had just come over to stand by his side.

"I don't know if there's much to talk about right now."

Lincoln's blue eyes narrowed. "There's everything to talk about. Come on, now."

He brought Bo over to a pair of empty chairs surrounded by at least a dozen of their friends. Seth, Charlie, Adrian, Chance . . . the familiar faces went on and on. Though many of them had also sat in the waiting room when Lincoln's Jennifer had been attacked, this was different. They'd all known Jennifer—and they'd all had a soft spot for her.

Hardly any of the guys had even seen Joy.

"I can't believe everyone's here," he murmured.

"That there is your problem, Samuel," Lincoln said. "Somehow, you've forgotten that you're one of us."

"I haven't forgotten that. Of course I haven't."

"If that's true, then you should've known that if one of the girlfriends of one of our friends gets abducted and taken to the hospital for emergency surgery, then we're going to show up."

Put that way, Bo realized that Lincoln was far from wrong. Of course he would be there for any one of the guys. Why would he expect so much less of everyone else?

"Sorry," he muttered.

Obviously exasperated, Lincoln shook his head. "I'm not looking for an apology. I'm looking for a way into your head."

"There's no need for that. I'm fine."

"Sorry, but you're not. And you shouldn't be." Lincoln's voice hardened. "Bo, your girlfriend was abducted by her stalker. She was found bleeding on a cement floor."

Tears filled Bo's eyes as the last bit of control he'd been clinging to slowly evaporated.

Unable to stop the tears, he looked away. "All right, fine. I am not fine. I'm a wreck." He swiped a hand across his cheek. "I'm currently freaking out and half dying inside because I came this close to losing her and it's all my fault." He held up two fingers, barely an inch apart. "I failed her."

Seth took the chair on the other side of him. "It wasn't your fault that Joy was abducted by that guy," Seth said. "He was sneaky and had his heart set on snatching her for years. He fooled everyone into thinking he was just some poor soul who needed a helping hand. If anything, it's because of you that we were all there."

"I told everyone that you refused to leave," Lincoln explained. "If we'd all left, it would've taken even longer to get to Joy."

Uncomfortable with their praise, he said, "I don't know how

I'm going to face Joy again. And what about her girl? I'm sure she hates me." Raising his head at last, Bo looked up at two of his best friends. "I didn't keep her safe."

Seth grinned. "She don't hate you. I know this for a fact."

"What? She told you?"

"No, but she told Finn and Finn texted me." Seth held up his phone with a grin. "I've got an 'in' into the teenage mind."

Lincoln chuckled. "Just when I think I've got you figured out, you prove me wrong, Seth."

Seth grinned. "If that's the case, you aren't the first one. But seriously, she told Finn that you saved her mom. She's grateful to you."

"I should've done more. I should've been smarter."

"All you can be is yourself and try your best. The rest is up to God," Lincoln said. "You can't change fate and you can't change His will."

Swallowing hard, Bo nodded.

Lincoln placed a heavy, reassuring hand on his shoulder. "Chloe and her dad were visiting with the cops and a social worker but now they're here. You need to go see that girl, Bo."

He wanted to, but he didn't want to put his needs before hers. "Are you sure?"

"If you want a relationship with Joy and Chloe, her ex-husband is in the picture. Might as well deal with it, yeah?"

"Yeah." Before he gave himself another excuse to back out, he got to his feet and started across the room. He could practically feel all of his buddies watch him. But instead of feeling awkward, it felt reassuring. They had his back.

Both Tony and Chloe were staring at him too. Tony looked ravaged. Not a trace of the confidence that had been so present in his eyes when they'd first met still lingered. He got to his feet.

"I'll never be able to thank you enough," Tony said as he clasped Bo's hand. "I owe you."

"We were all looking for her. You don't owe me anything." Thinking of Lincoln's words, Bo added, "I hope we can all get along. I love Joy."

"It's obvious that you do," Tony said. "These last couple of hours have taught me a lot. I . . . I've been selfish where she's concerned, but no more."

"I feel the same way." Bo turned to Chloe then. She had her legs up on the chair and her arms wrapped around her knees. Her eyes were swollen from crying, but she was also gazing at him intently.

He crouched down in front of her. "Chloe, honey. You okay?"

Instead of answering, she launched herself into his arms. "I . . . I was so afraid," she said.

He caught her easily, wrapping his arms around her body and holding her tight. "I know. I was afraid too."

"Everyone says that that man was really mean to her. And that she was really cold." Tears dampened his shirt. He rubbed her back. After glancing at Tony, who gave him a nod, Bo stood up with Chloe in his arms. Without thinking, he carried her over to a chair in a corner and sat down with her on his lap. She was in a tight ball. Unbidden, he realized that she was positioned the way Janie used to be when she'd yell "Cannonball!" so Bo would toss her in the lake.

"You're just a little thing, Chloe."

She hiccupped. "What?"

"I was just thinking back to when one of my little sisters used to love for me to toss her in the air so she'd land in the lake. I was just thinking that you're like her. Tiny but strong."

A hint of a smile formed on her face. "I like that idea."

"Me too."

Chloe moved to the seat next to him but continued to gaze at him intently. "Do you think Mom is going to be all right?"

"I do. She's strong. But she's also got you and me and your dad and everyone else to be strong for her when she isn't. We can help her out when she needs it."

"Grandma said she's going to stay with us as long as Mom needs. That way she can take care of her."

"That's good. You're momma's going to need all of us being strong so she won't have to be."

Chloe nodded. After a second, she said, "Hey, Bo?"

"Hmm?"

"You . . . you're not going to go away, are you? I mean, you meant what you said to my dad?"

"About me loving your mom? Yes. I love her and I'm not going to let her go." Finally feeling like the weight of guilt that he'd placed upon his shoulders was easing, he straightened and kicked his legs out in front of him. "Truth be told, one day, I'm going to figure out a way to weasel into your lives so well you forget what it was like to not have me there."

She smiled. "Good."

When the doctor came out, he looked around the room, seemed to find him, Chloe, and Tony, and walked directly to their sides. "You're Joy Howard's family, yes?" When they all nodded and got to their feet, the doctor smiled. "She's out of surgery. We sewed up her wounds and repaired the damage that the bone shard did to her lung. The good news is that it was better than we feared. She's going to need to stay here a couple of days, but I expect her to make a full recovery." He smiled at Chloe. "She'll be ready to go home in no time. A nurse is going to come out in a half hour or so to tell you when she can see family. Take care, now."

"Thank you," Tony said.

Bo nodded. "Yes, thank you."

Chloe smiled at the doctor until he turned away. Then, she turned, scanned the area, and practically danced across the room. "Finn! Guess what!"

Watching her go, Bo couldn't help but smile as Finn stood awkwardly by Mason's side . . . just before he opened his arms and held her close.

Watching the two teenagers hug, Tony frowned. "Who is that?"

"That, buddy, is our future."

He sighed. "I guess it was too much to hope that Chloe would wait until she was twenty-one to have a boyfriend."

"I'm afraid so. He's a good kid, though. She could do worse."

"Does Joy know him?"

"I don't think so."

Tony grinned. "Hearing that Chloe's got herself a boyfriend might just be the thing Joy needs to make a full recovery."

Bo chuckled. "I'll be sure to ask how Chloe's boyfriend is going to fit in her fancy kitchen calendar."

CHAPTER 39

Finn had been having his own personal crisis while everyone else was out looking for Chloe's mom. From the minute she'd called him from the school parking lot, Finn had stopped debating about whether to leave home or not. Chloe had needed him—and he'd needed someone to lean on.

That was when everything had become so crystal clear. Aunt Mary and Uncle Lane were the people in his life who he could depend upon. Not his father with his weak grip on reality or his mother who was never going to take anyone's side but her husband's.

If he had gone home and shared anything about Chloe or her missing mom, the only thing that would've happened would be that his phone would've been taken away. Right before he'd been made to quit his job. And then he would've been forbidden to leave their farm.

To his surprise, Finn wasn't even all that bitter about it. One day, he surely would be. All he'd felt in the moment was relief. He could finally stop sneaking around and lying. He could finally stop being someone he wasn't.

After filling in Mary about Chloe, he'd told her about his decision.

"Don't take this lightly, Finn," she'd cautioned. "Your parents aren't going to take this well."

"I know. I wouldn't expect any different." He'd gathered his courage. "Is there any way I could live with you and Uncle Lane until I save enough money to get a place of my own?"

She'd stared at him hard. Then shook her head. "*Nee.*"

He'd been shocked. "All right. I . . . I'll ask Seth if he has an idea."

Mary chuckled under her breath. "Oh, Finn, you silly boy. Of course you can move in with us. I'd be happy to have you. Lane is going to be pleased too. My 'no' was because there's no way you're going to just move in with us for a couple of months until you find some cheap place of your own. If you want to move in with us, then you're going to need to stay awhile."

"Do you mean it?"

"I'm positive about it." She'd opened her arms and pulled him in for a hug.

Later, after Chloe's grandmother had come to get her, he and Lane had gone to his house. There, he'd said his piece and gone into his room and gotten his things.

His parents—as expected—had been stoic and furious. His siblings had been confused and upset. As best he could, he hugged each of them, told them that he loved them and that they could always find him at the diner.

And then he and Lane left. He'd cried the whole time back to their house.

Four hours later, he'd gotten another call from Chloe and

woken up his aunt and uncle to let them know the news. All Mary had said was that he better get dressed so they could go to the hospital.

And now he was standing in the middle of a very crowded waiting room with Chloe in his arms. "I don't know how you got here," she murmured.

"It's a long story. All that matters is that I'm here now."

She searched his face. "Are you okay?"

He was floored that she could think about him at that moment. But maybe that was why he'd liked her from the minute she'd run into him at the diner. Chloe was different than most girls. She was sweeter, kinder, prettier, and more talented than anyone he'd ever met.

Every time he was around her, he wanted to be better too. He wanted to have goals like she did and have big dreams. He wasn't sure what his future was going to be like, but he was pretty sure he at least had a future now.

He was very thankful for that.

●●●

"You can go on back now, Bo," Kate, Chloe's grandmother, said. "Joy's asking for you."

Bo had been hovering near the door, waiting his turn. When the nurse had come out into the waiting room, she'd announced that Joy could only have two or three visitors. Kate had asked Bo if he wouldn't mind waiting to see Joy until after Chloe and she had had their turns.

While he'd waited, he'd shaken Tony's hand and promised to stay in touch. Tony had already arranged with Kate to take Chloe to his house the next day so Joy's mom could nurse Joy for the first day or two after she got home from the hospital.

After Tony left, Bo had hugged Seth and Lincoln, shook hands with about six other guys, and promised to check in the next day. Then, he'd sat down, picked up a bottle of water someone had left him, and downed half of it. At long last, his body and head seemed to adjust to his new reality. Joy had been found, she was in recovery, and was going to be okay. She also loved him. He'd also told both her ex-husband and her daughter that he loved Joy.

He could hardly believe it. After a lifetime of looking for a future, he'd finally found it while standing in line at a coffee shop. The Lord certainly had a sense of humor.

"Bo?" a kind-looking nurse in a pair of pink scrubs called out.

He stood up. "That's me."

She smiled at him. "Joy's been asking for you."

Bo swallowed a lump in his throat as he followed the nurse through a pair of metal doors and down a hallway.

"We've already got her room ready. If you'd like, you could chat with her for a moment, then walk by her side while we wheel her from recovery to her room. What do you say?"

"I say that sounds like a real good idea," he murmured.

She grinned as she pulled back a curtain, revealing Joy, two machines, and a whole lot of tubes and blankets. "I'll be back in five minutes."

Bo was barely aware of the nurse leaving. All he could see were Joy's pretty brown eyes gazing at him.

"Hey," he said as he walked closer. Leaning down, he pressed a kiss on her brow. It looked to be one of the few places on her face that wasn't bruised or cut.

"Hey." She swallowed. "I . . . I heard that you saved me."

"What? That's not what I heard, girly. I heard you were well on your way to saving yourself." He brushed his lips against her brow again. "All I got to do was do a last-minute assist."

She giggled before wincing. "That sounds like you."

Unable to stop touching her, he carefully brushed a strand of hair off her brow. "What does?" he asked gently.

"Never taking credit. Never wanting to be in the spotlight."

"I don't know if that's the case or not. But, ah, maybe I don't need to be," he whispered.

She frowned. "Why?"

"I've got you, Joy Howard. Being with you is all I want. Honestly, it's more than enough."

Joy smiled just as the curtain pulled back.

"Bo, are you ready to see Joy's new digs for the next couple of days?"

"Absolutely," he replied. He stepped out of the way as an orderly and another nurse appeared. All of them checking the various monitors and hooking and unhooking things so they could wheel Joy down the hall.

Then, while the medical personnel chatted with each other, Bo walked beside Joy. Smiling whenever she glanced his way.

Nothing more needed to be said.

Joy had survived, Chloe had trusted him enough to reach out, and he and Joy loved each other. Everything was going to be okay.

EPILOGUE

ONE YEAR LATER

It was a quarter past two. Ignoring the women congregating in the kitchen—and his wife's knowing look—Bo strode toward the stairs. Taking a moment, he listened for the telltale sprinting of a seventeen-year-old girl.

Crickets.

Obviously, it was time to get involved. Lifting his chin, he called up the stairs. "Girl, if you don't get a move on, you're gonna be late!"

He heard a thump . . . and then her door open. "I won't be late, Bo!"

"Your dictator dance teacher is gonna get mad if you waltz in after three. You know she will."

"Hold on. I'm looking for my keys!"

Hearing the first bit of panic in her voice, Bo settled in. At least now he had something to do instead of fret about the time. Never in his wildest dreams would he have believed that he'd ever worry about getting on a wiry, old-lady ballerina's bad side. He did though. She scared the crap out of him.

More importantly, he'd never imagined that he would do just about anything to make a teenage girl happy. Even if it meant watching the clock so she didn't have to.

Or finding her car keys yet again.

He walked toward the front door, to the table that used to be spotless before his girls moved in.

Nope, not a key to be found. He knelt down to sort through the pile of shoes Chloe tossed at the bottom of his coat closet. Just last week, he'd found her keys under a pair of tan flats.

Picking up her Uggs, her old Nikes, and some kind of expensive flip-flops, he felt around on the hardwood. No keys there, either.

Chloe appeared on the landing, full-blown panic on her face. "Bo, could you help me find my keys?"

"Already on it. Come on down."

Half dragging her dance bag—which looked as if it weighed as much as she did, she hurried down the stairs. Her hair was slicked up into a bun and she had on a full face of makeup. She was ready for her big performance.

Almost.

"What am I gonna do? Miss Diamanté is going to kill me if I'm late!"

"She's not going to yet." He grabbed hold of her bag. "Come on, sugar. Let's look in the kitchen and the laundry room."

"That's it! I tossed the keys on the washing machine last night when Mom told me to take care of the laundry." She winced. "Bo, how come I always lose those keys?"

"I don't know. You never lose sight of your phone, that's for sure. Come on. Come get those keys and tell your mother goodbye."

She paused. "Do I have to? Maybe I could text Mom from the car."

"Nope."

"Bo, all those ladies are going to want to talk."

"Trust me, I'll get you out of here on time." He lowered his voice. "Now, you go give your momma a hug. She'll be sad if you don't and I don't want her sad."

She hurried into the kitchen where Joy, Joy's sister Alice, his two sisters Carrie and Janie, and both his momma and Joy's all were. Joy also happened to be holding a set of keys.

"Here you go, honey. Fresh from the washing machine."

"Oh my gosh, Mom. Thank you!" Chloe hugged her tight.

"Of course. Now go break a leg, Cinderella."

"We'll see you in the theater!" Alice called out.

"Okay. Thanks." Looking panicked again, Chloe looked around. "Bo?"

"Right here, girl. Come on, I'll walk you out."

She ran out the back door. It slammed shut just as he approached.

All six women laughed.

"She's giving you a run for your money, Son," his mother called out.

"Don't I know it." He walked into the garage, stepped over yet another pair of forgotten shoes, and strode out to the driveway. Chloe was carefully unlocking a six-year-old Chevy like it was a Porsche.

He walked to the Chevy's back seat and tossed her bag inside. Still standing next to the car, his stepdaughter smiled up at him. "I guess I'm ready now."

"Let's double-check. Now, do you have your purse and your license?"

"Yes." She smiled.

"Money?"

"I don't need any." At his look, she nodded. "I have the twenty you told me to hide in my wallet."

"Good. Your phone?"

She held up her purse. "It's in here."

"All right then. Since I already saw you have half your closet in there, I guess you're ready to go dance the lead tonight." He winked. "Get ready, your momma's likely going to take a hundred pictures."

"She always does."

He winked again. "Drive careful now." Wagging a finger, he added, "Don't you speed. If you're late, Miss D can just have a conniption fit without you."

"I won't speed."

He stepped back. "Off you go then."

She didn't move. "Hey, Bo?"

He turned back around. "Yeah?"

"You're going to be there too, right?"

Swallowing the lump in his throat, he murmured, "Do you really think I'm going to miss seeing my best girl be Cinderella?"

Her smile broadened. "Thanks for helping me with the keys and Mom . . . and everything. I'm really glad I have you, Bo."

He was really glad about that, too. Afraid he was going to get emotional, he tapped her door. "Get on, girl. It's time."

He leaned against the garage door's frame as he watched Chloe get in, buckle her seat belt, then put the car in reverse. In no time, she'd backed out of the drive and headed down his street. And then she was gone.

He stood there a moment, thinking about how much he adored that girl. He wasn't her father—Tony did a good job with that—but Bo knew that he'd become an integral part of Chloe's life. Just as she'd become an important part of his.

He was already dreading her going off to college.

"Bo, are you all right?"

He turned to find Joy standing inside the garage. "I didn't hear you come out. How long have you been there?"

She walked out to his side. She had on a cotton dress that skimmed her calves, pretty sandals, and a prettier smile. "Long enough to hear Chloe make sure you were going to be sitting in the audience," she teased. "Long enough to realize that you're a little choked up."

"I swear, that girl has wrapped herself around my heart."

"She feels the same way about you."

"I'm glad."

Realizing that they were finally alone for the first time all day, he pulled Joy close. "How long do you think we have before someone comes outside to check on us?"

She raised an eyebrow. "Five minutes. Maybe ten?"

"That's long enough." He bent down and kissed her. When she relaxed against him, he ran a hand down her back and deepened the kiss.

After too short a time, she pulled back with a laugh. "What was that for?"

"I just don't want to forget."

She frowned slightly. "Forget what?"

"This," he said, waving a hand at the messy garage, the full house, his wife in his arms, his shuttling Chloe out of the house. "I don't want to ever forget moments like this, Joy."

Her expression softening, Joy leaned close and kissed him again. Then looked up at him and smiled. "You won't. Besides, if you do . . . I know exactly how to make you feel better."

"And what is that?"

"We'll just have to make more moments that are just as good."

Bo smiled. He liked the sound of that. He liked it a whole lot.

ACKNOWLEDGMENTS

As I finish up the last work on this novel, I'm reminded once again of how many people help make a book a reality. First, I'm so grateful to God. He's taken me on such a journey with these books! I'm grateful for His gifts and for the words He gives me. I'm also very grateful to my husband Tom, who is always so encouraging and supportive. He not only often helps me plot, he also listens to me chat about characters like they're my new best friends . . . and never even reminds me that they're all made up.

I'm also very grateful to Lynne who is my first reader. Lynne not only gets my manuscripts in decent shape for my editors, she also gives me honest feedback. Thank you, Lynne!

I'm once again so appreciative of the Blackstone team. Thank you to Vikki Warner for supporting this series, and to Ember Hood for both her edits and suggestions for improvement. Ember, I think we've worked on eight books together now! Thank you for everything you've done for me.

I'd also like to give a huge shout-out to my publicist Jeane Wynne. Jeane, thank you for encouraging pretty much everyone you know to read *Edgewater Road*. Your belief in this book and the series means more to me than you'll ever know.

Finally, I want to thank the many readers who took a chance on this series, wrote to tell me that they were pleasantly surprised . . . and then wrote again to tell me that they were anxious to read Bo's story. I hope you will be pleased with *Sycamore Circle*.